GOOD VIRGIN GONE BAD

BAD BOYS OF REDWOOD ACADEMY

EMILIA ROSE

Visit my website at emiliarose.com
Cover Designer: The Book Brander
Editor: Jovana Shirley, Unforeseen Editing, www.unforeseenediting.com

CHAPTER ONE

ASTRID

MAYBE I WAS A LITTLE BUZZED, okay?

I stumbled into A'dré's living room and through the grinding bodies, moving my hips to the music and finally feeling myself. All day long at Redwood, I kept up this good-girl persona, the nerdy virgin who'd never break a rule.

But fuck that tonight.

My beer sloshed over the edge of my red Solo cup, and I scanned the room for my friend Ruby. Between the number of drinks I'd downed and this not being a party hosted in Redwood, I didn't recognize most people here.

Strands of bright pink hair twirled around on the outskirts of the dance floor. I pushed past a couple of people, shoving their shoulders so I could get through, and finally found Ruby, all up on some senior from our rival school.

Lips curled into a smile, she turned around so she could grind her ass against his front, grabbed my wrist, and pulled me forward. I swayed my hips to the beat and intertwined my fingers with hers.

She shouted over the music, her words drowned in the sound.

"What?" I yelled back.

She pulled me closer so her lips were near my ear. "That guy you like and his friends from Redwood are here," she said into my ear, then pulled away and nodded toward a couple of couches.

"What guy?" I asked, glancing over my shoulder.

The Crew sat on the couches with beers and weed, bullshitting with each other while Calix was gazing in our direction. At me. More specifically, my hips moving to the beat. When I raised my cup to my lips again, he lifted his eyes to mine.

If I had been sober, my cheeks would've flushed red, and I would've hidden behind my hair.

But drunk Astrid did not give a single fuck.

I continued to dance and smiled at him, wanting him to come over.

Calix had been in more fights than I could count, and I had had a crush on him for four years now, but I refused to even look in his direction in school. I didn't want him to know how much of a freak I really was—at least when I was sober.

What was worse about this whole entire thing was ... Calix was my best friend's brother. And Diya would absolutely hate me if she found out that I'd had a thing for him since I had gone over to her house the summer before ninth grade.

Calix drew his tongue across his lower lip and dropped his gaze again, sipping on his glass. Annoyed that he just wanted to stare, I turned back around toward Ruby and danced to the music, downing my drink.

She giggled. "Oh, you're so going to regret this tomorrow morning."

Someone seized my hips from behind. For a moment, I thought it was Calix, but it was a tall, big-handed dude, *not* from Redwood. He had to be at least twenty years old, and he was at a high-school party, but I didn't care.

I wanted someone to touch me.

Throwing my ass back, I leaned forward with my hands on my

knees and bucked my hips up and down, the same way I would if I were riding his dick. He ground himself into me against the back of my skirt.

When his hand started traveling up my thigh and inching closer to my skirt, someone yanked him away from me. From over my shoulder, I watched as Calix slammed his fist into the guy's face and sent him back through the crowd, his beer still in his hand.

Fuck, was that all I had to do?

Once the twenty-year-old left, Calix moved closer to me. Standing at least six foot something with tattoos covering his left arm, he grabbed my elbow and leaned down to talk into my ear. "What're you doing here, Astrid?"

"You know my name?" I asked, twirling around and placing my hand on his shoulder.

He dropped his hands to my hips and curled his fingers into my ass. "Don't play with me like that. What. Are. You. Doing. Here?"

"I. Am. Having. A. Good. Time," I stuttered, another giggle escaping my mouth. I found myself wrapping my arms around his shoulders and pulling him toward me, pressing his body against mine. "Now, show me one."

"Show you one?" he asked with a low chuckle that—*God*—did something terrible to me. Then he took my waist and led me out of the crowd. "I'll show you one, if that's what you really want."

With the alcohol finally setting in—okay, maybe it had a while ago—I closed my eyes and felt him graze against my backside. When I reopened them, he was guiding me to The Crew, who all sat around the back couches, drinking and smoking.

My cheeks flushed. *Is this a good idea? Probably not.* But I didn't care.

He sat back down in his spot and pulled me into his lap. I inhaled sharply, my pussy clenching, and let him grind himself against my ass from behind. The others watched me—one of Redwood's good girls—sit on their friend's lap.

I let him press himself against me, grind against my pussy.

Fuck. It feels too good.

"Turn around for me," he ordered, holding my hair back. "Straddle my waist."

"Here?" I asked as I glanced around the group. "Right … here?"

"Don't worry about it, Hellcat," he murmured into my ear. "Nobody's gonna see."

I blame the alcohol for this.

After I straddled his waist, I rested my pussy against his bulge and clenched. His cock felt so big, huge, massive against my wet panties. I grabbed on to his shoulders and rubbed my clit against his jeans, aching to relieve myself.

Being drunk and horny was a bad combo for a good girl.

A *really* bad combo.

Calix reached between us and undid his button, then his zipper. I swallowed hard and gazed down at his hard cock pressed against his briefs. Pre-cum stained the fabric near his swollen head. I curled my fingers around the waistband.

Fuck. *Fuck!*

God, this was the hottest damn thing I had seen.

I wanted him. All of him.

Unable to stop myself, I slid down the front of his briefs to reveal his head and sucked in a sharp breath.

My gaze snapped up to his.

He stared back at me, eyes hazy with lust and lips parted slightly. "Keep going."

I continued to pull down his briefs until his entire cock sprang out of them and smacked against the front of my skirt. He wrapped his hand around the base and gently took my chin in his other hand.

"Lift your skirt for me."

Pussy clenching, I glanced over my shoulder at the others at the party. Once I was certain that nobody was paying attention to us—other than The Crew—I pulled my skirt up enough for Calix to see my lacy black thong.

God, this was so wrong. He was my best friend's brother, for fuck's sake!

He dropped his hand from my chin to the front of my panties and swiped his thumb across my clit. I whimpered and clutched my skirt harder, bunching it up in my hands.

"Calix," I whispered, "there are so many people."

"Do you want me to stop?" he asked, drawing the edge of his nail across my panties.

I swallowed hard and shook my head. "No."

No, I didn't want him to ever stop. But I should've. I should've stopped this before it started. I should've never picked up a drink tonight. Because tonight wasn't just any other night.

Tonight was the night this good virgin turned bad.

CHAPTER TWO

ASTRID

"I'M GOING to pull your panties to the side," Calix said. "I wanna see that little pink pussy."

Nodding, I gazed between us as he stroked his cock in his other hand, faster when he swooped his index finger around my thong and pulled it to the side. A low grunt escaped his mouth, and he slipped two fingers between my pussy lips to rub my clit.

After releasing my grip on my skirt, I grabbed his shoulders. "Calix ..."

"I didn't tell you to drop your skirt," he said. "Lift it for me and watch."

Not wanting him to stop, I lifted my skirt again and sank down onto him a few inches. I wanted him to be inside me, but I knew that we couldn't do anything here. We were in the middle of the party. It'd be way too obvious.

"You're aching for my cock, aren't you?" he hummed, removing his fingers from my clit and tugging me closer to him so he could rub the head of his cock against my pussy instead. He rubbed it back and forth, across my clit, his pre-cum decorating my lips.

"Calix," I moaned.

"How does it feel, Hellcat?" he asked.

I furrowed my brow and stared at him, pussy quivering. "Please, don't stop."

He drew the head of his cock to my entrance. "You want more?"

"Yes, but …" I looked around again. "Someone will … someone will see."

Again, he grabbed my chin with his free hand. "Look at me. I promise nobody will see. It's just me and you, right here. Don't worry about the others. The Crew will take care of them for us, if anyone dares to glance over here. Okay?"

Fuck, my pussy is pulsing.

"Okay," I whispered. "But I'm a …"

"A virgin," he finished. "I know."

After sucking in a sharp breath, I clutched my skirt harder, "I don't want it to hurt. You're so big, and I've only stuffed my fingers inside me before. You're going to … to stretch me out."

"Baby," he cooed, head against my entrance, "it's not going to hurt for long." He pushed a centimeter into me and grunted. "God, you're so fucking tight." He slipped another inch inside me, putting pressure in all the wrong places.

"Calix," I whined.

Suddenly, someone wrapped their arm around my torso and placed their large fingers against my clit. I sucked in a sharp breath, tightened around Calix, and glanced over my shoulder at Frasier.

Frasier was another one of Redwood's billionaire players and Crew member, who flirted with everyone.

"Fuck," Calix grunted, pushing another inch into me. "Your pussy just got so wet, Hellcat."

I tightened even more. Frasier moved closer to me, pressing his bulge against my back and wrapping his other hand around my upper body to grasp one of my breasts. Only two sets of hands, and I was already about to lose it.

How would I feel if *all* five of them touched me at once?

"God," I moaned, legs trembling.

"That's it, baby," Frasier murmured. "You've almost taken all of him."

"Am I doing good?" I asked.

Calix grunted, shoving the last inch into me and grasping my hips. "So fucking good."

My walls wrapped around every inch of his dick, clinging to it as tightly as they could. I dropped my skirt because I couldn't hold on to it anymore and took his shoulders instead, my fingernails digging into his thick muscles.

Frasier moved both hands to my breasts and pinched my nipples through my shirt. I moaned and tightened even harder, the heat growing between my legs.

God, this feels way too freaking good.

"Please," I whispered. "Give me more."

"The good little slut is begging for it now," Arch said from the other couch.

Arch—*fucking Arch*—was my stepbrother since last year. He got into trouble with his father, bad-mouthed everyone, and probably should've been suspended five times over now, but he was still here.

"Please," I found myself saying again, begging and pleading more, loving the feeling of being called a slut. I wanted Arch to call me that over and over, degrade me even further.

All this time I spent at Redwood, being a good girl …

Nobody knew about this side of me.

Calix slowly pulled out of me, then pushed himself back in. I threw my head back, pussy tightening so much around him. He had only just started, and I was already halfway to the best orgasm of my life.

"Call me a slut again," I whimpered. "Please."

Arch smirked and stood, taking a fistful of my hair and forcing me to stare up at him. "You're a fucking slut, Astrid. Getting fucked in the middle of a party in front of four other guys, begging me to call you filthy names. Open your mouth and stick out your tongue."

Panting as Calix began thrusting in and out of me quicker, I stuck out my tongue and stared up at him. He clutched my throat in his free hand and spit into my mouth. My eyes widened slightly, and I squeezed Calix's dick harder than I had before.

"More," I begged, sticking out my tongue again. "Do it—"

He spit into my mouth again, then smacked it. "A dirty fucking whore."

"Fuuuuck," Calix grunted. "Your fucking pussy …"

Rush, the grumpy racing fanatic, and Cairo, one of my friends from Physics, sat on the opposite couch. Rush's hand was down his pants, and Cairo's gaze was intently on mine, as if he wanted to come over here, too, but there wasn't much room on this couch.

Frasier pinched my nipples again and tipped me right over the edge. I threw my head back and moaned, pleasure rushing through me.

"That's it, baby," Frasier praised as I bucked my hips back and forth on Calix's cock. "Ride out that orgasm."

After stilling inside me, Calix seized my hips and grunted, "Fuck, Hellcat." He took my chin in his hand and forced me to stare at him. "You're a good virgin gone bad tonight."

CHAPTER THREE

ASTRID

WITH MY HEAD POUNDING, I slowly sat up and blinked my eyes to adjust to the harsh sunlight flooding through the windows.

Where am I? What happened? How much did I drink last night?

I faintly remembered …

Oh my God.

I stared around the empty room, littered with red cups, weed, broken glass, and … Rush, who was sprawled out on the couch beside me, shirtless, his usually grumpy face soft from sleep.

My eyes widened. *Oh my fucking God.*

I reached between my legs. I didn't have underwear on anymore. Or a shirt.

No. Fuck no.

It really didn't happen last night. I didn't lose my virginity to The Crew, did I?

Mouth drying, I shot up to my feet and pulled down my skirt to cover my bare pussy. *Where the hell is my underwear?!* I flipped up the pillows beside me and tiptoed around the broken glass, searching for any piece of clothing I could wear that wasn't *this.*

When I finally found Rush's shirt under the couch, I tugged it over my head and used my hair elastic to tie it in the back so it wasn't swallowing me whole. This looked decent. Right? I mean, nobody at school knew it was his shirt except me … right?

School …

I found my phone on a side table. *Shit, I'm late for school!*

"Need a ride?" someone said from behind me.

After leaping into the air, I twirled around and faced Frasier and his playboy smirk. Dressed in an old-money white polo shirt, he leaned against the doorframe with one hand stuffed into his khaki pants.

"I'm fine," I said, peering at Rush, still fast asleep on the couch.

He had turned onto his side, and I spotted the large scars down his back, which looked like they were from some kinda knife fight.

"You sure you wanna be that good girl who misses class after a Thursday night party?" Frasier asked, twirling his keys around his finger and clicking his tongue. "I don't think that'll go over well with your good-girl persona."

"It's not a persona," I said, crossing my arms. "Thank you very much."

"Seemed like a persona when you climbed on top of Calix last night and rode his dick."

My cheeks burned with embarrassment. "I … I did not ride his dick."

"For everyone to see too."

Mouth drying, I snapped my gaze up to his. "Nobody saw, except you guys … right?"

His smirk widened. "I dunno. Maybe. You gonna let me drive you to school?"

I narrowed my eyes. "If I don't, are you going to tell everyone?"

"Come on. I'm not a dickhead, like your stepbrother." He moved closer to me, standing at least a foot taller with the most attractive scent of cologne that I had ever smelled. "Anything that happens between us, baby, you know I'll keep it between us."

Warmth gathered between my legs. *Anything that happens, huh? Does he mean …*

"Okay, but not because I like you," I said, checking my phone and realizing that if we didn't leave, like, right now, I would be in deep, deep, deep shit! "Only because if I walk, then I won't even make it back before the end of the day."

Grinning, he nodded toward the door. I glanced around the party to make sure that I didn't forget any of my belongings and followed him out of the front door. My heart pounded inside my chest.

What has gotten into me lately? Did I really sleep with Calix last night?!

Part of me still couldn't believe it. And now I was getting into the playboy's car after he promised whatever happened between us stayed between us?

Fuck, this isn't going to end well. It never did when a good girl fell for the bad boys.

After sliding into the passenger seat of his Bugatti, I clicked on my seat belt and sucked in a low breath. We'd head right to school, and I would force him to let me out a couple of blocks before the parking lot so nobody saw me getting out of his car.

It was a foolproof plan.

If anyone saw, I knew what kind of rumors would swirl around Redwood. It had happened last semester with Vera and Blaise, one of Redwood's bad boys. Never mind how many times Jace Harbor, our football star, and his stepsister came to school together!

I didn't want to be associated at *all* with The Crew.

They were bad news, and what had happened last night would never happen again.

Never, never, never again.

To my surprise, Frasier didn't say much on our way out of this town and back into Redwood, except for when he took a turn that

I hadn't expected and began driving down a back road that definitely didn't lead to school.

"Just a quick stop," he murmured. "I haven't had breakfast yet."

"Frasier, this is the middle of nowhere," I said. "There is no breakfast place anywhere."

He pulled over to the side of the road and parked the car. "I know. I know, baby. I want a taste of ..." He pushed his fingers underneath my skirt and right into my wet pussy. I grasped his wrist and tensed up, his two big fingers driving me crazy already. "This pussy."

My eyes widened slightly, the pressure building up in my core. "Wh-what?!"

"Nobody has to know," Frasier murmured into my ear, his fingers stuffed deep inside me. "Calix told me how wet you were for him last night, and I want my fill of you. I'm too jealous, too greedy. I *need* my fill of you too."

CHAPTER FOUR

ASTRID

FRASIER DIDN'T EVEN GIVE me a chance to speak. He continued murmuring dirty things into my ear, his fingers pumping in and out of me quickly. If I were in my right mind, I'd think of how much of a dick he was for not letting me get a word in, but … but, God, it was so, so hot.

"You're so pretty, baby. So wet for me. Tell me how good my fingers feel inside you."

"Frasier …" I whimpered, glancing at a car passing us. It wasn't like we were hidden—at all—just parked on the side of the road. "I think—"

"Forget about anyone else," he murmured, drawing his nose against mine. "Tell me."

Another whimper left my mouth as he built me closer and closer to an orgasm. I clutched his wrist and arched my back against the seat, digging my head into the headrest. I pressed my lips together to stop myself from screaming out in pleasure.

"Tell me, tell me," he murmured. "I wanna hear it."

"You feel so good!" I cried, legs shaking. "Please don't stop."

He pumped his fingers faster, deeper. I stared over at him, my jaw slack.

"I know," he murmured. "I know. I know. I know. Let it all out for me."

Pleasure coursed through my body, and my legs trembled wildly. I cried out, my body jerking against the seat. He doubled down and pressed his mouth against mine, eating up all my moans.

Once I finally came down from the orgasm, he pulled his fingers out of my cunt and stuffed them into his mouth, sucking off all my juices. A low groan left his mouth. "You taste so fucking good."

I pulled my thighs together. "Frasier … we should probably get to—"

Frasier seized my hips and sat me on his lap, burying his face into the crook of my neck.

"Frasier—"

"I'll be quick, baby," he said, pulling his cock out of his khakis and positioning himself at my entrance. "I promise, I'll get you to school on time. I can't let you go without hearing more of those sexy moans while your pussy is gripping my big … fat"—he thrust into me—"cock."

My eyes rolled back into my head, and my head lolled back from the insane pleasure coursing through me.

Drunk sex was great.

Sober sex? Oh my fucking God! When I wasn't impaired and could make logical decisions and … and …

With his hands sliding up and down the sides of my body, he pounded up into me at a quick pace. I gripped on to his shoulders, my tits bouncing in Rush's shirt. Frasier placed his mouth against the shirt, finding my nipple and biting down on it.

He helped me move up and down on his cock, staring up at me with his mouth still latched on to my nipple. And when he stopped thrusting upward, I continued moving on him, letting him fill me completely, then pulling him out.

"Oh my God, baby," I cried. "Oh my God!"

"Don't stop," he murmured, tugging up on my shirt to see my tits. "Keep going. You're doing so good. So, so, so good for me."

I sank my nails into his shoulders and whimpered, "You like the way these big titties bounce in your face?"

As soon as the words left my mouth, I wanted to take them all back. They sounded so awkward, coming from me, especially *sober* Astrid!

"Fuck," he grunted, sucking one of my breasts into his mouth and dipping his hand between my thighs to rub my clit. "I love the way these titties bounce in my face, baby. Keep going. Keep going for me. Keep bouncing. They're so fucking sexy. You're so sexy, baby. Look at you. Bouncing like a good little slut for me ..."

He continued and continued murmuring dirty words against my body, and I couldn't handle it anymore. His fingers moved faster against my clit, and I lifted myself off him as an orgasm ripped through my body.

"Holy—"

Frasier grabbed my hips and forced me back down onto him, his mouth on my ear. "Stay deep as you come. I wanna feel this pretty pussy milking my cock." He captured my earlobe between his teeth and growled, "I want my cum so deep inside you that it gets you pregnant."

I clawed at his shoulders, crying and squirming and unable to stop myself from moaning.

"Frasier!" I cried, my legs trembling so uncontrollably that I couldn't lift myself back off him even if I tried. My head was hazy with all the dirty words he mumbled against me. "It's too much pressure."

"You can take it," he said, sucking my bottom lip between his teeth. "My girl can fucking take it."

The orgasm didn't stop rolling through every bit of my body. I clutched on to him tighter as he seized my hips, ready to make me come *again*. He wasn't giving up. No, he was going to make me come so hard for a third time!

"I'm going to dump every last drop into your fucking pussy," he growled into my mouth. "And you're going to take it. You're going to beg for it. Beg for *me*. Tell me that you want me to get you pregnant. Call yourself a dirty slut, a whore, *my* whore."

"I'm a dirty slut," I cried, tits moving against his chest. I couldn't control the words that left my mouth; they just continued to spill out over and over and over. "Your whore! Please, fill my pussy. Make The Crew jealous. Get me pregnant, Frasier!"

One thrust. A second thrust.

And suddenly, he was buried deep inside me, lifting his hips off the driver's seat and forcing my hips as close to him as he could get them, grunting and groaning into my mouth, telling me how much of a good girl I was, how I was taking it so well.

Pleasure exploded through my body, and I curled my toes. "Fuck!"

He pumped into my cunt a few more times, much slower, a low grunt drawn out from his mouth. When he finally stilled, he grabbed my chin and forced me to look into those sinful eyes of his, to stare at the playboy of Redwood.

He probably said all those filthy words to other girls he fucked in his car like this, but I couldn't seem to care because it wasn't even seven in the morning and I had already come three times.

"Are you always this horny in the morning?" he murmured. "Because if you are, then I'll pick you up every morning, baby. You'll be my little secret plaything."

CHAPTER FIVE

ASTRID

WALKING INTO REDWOOD'S CAFETERIA, with my hands around the plastic tray of crappy food, I immediately started toward my usual table, busy with my friends chatting. My heart pounded inside my chest, and I couldn't help glancing toward The Crew, perched in the far corner.

Each and every one of them were looking right at me. Me!

Oh fuck. They haven't told anyone, have they? My mouth dried. *Surely, they haven't.*

If they had, all of Redwood would have known by now. But honestly, maybe … maybe this was … all some sort of misunderstanding: Maybe they were supposed to find another girl last night.

Why did they find me? Was I that easy?

Yes. The answer was, yes, I really was that easy.

I swallowed literally no spit in my mouth and averted my gaze from them. What was I going to say to everyone? Diya, my bestie, had to already know what had happened. Ruby would've told her that I'd hooked up with her brother, wouldn't she?

No, friends didn't do that to friends, right?

After setting down the tray, I slowly sat in my seat and looked around at the other girls who were chatting with each other. Diya looked up at me with a smile on her face, her brown eyes brighter than usual.

"I heard you were late today," Diya said.

"Oh, yeah?" I started my grandiose lie that I had made up after I fucked Frasier in his car this morning. "I accidentally slept in."

I side-eyed Ruby, wondering if she was going to say anything, but she had the biggest dark circles underneath her eyes, and I wasn't sure if she even remembered last night. Hickeys covered her neck, and her pink hair was thrown up into a messy bun.

"So, how was the party last night?" Diya asked, opening her carton of milk.

"The party?" I repeated back, my mouth dry.

She giggled. "Yes, the party. You know, the one you went to with Ruby?"

"Oh, that one." I scratched my neck. "Yeah … that one."

Diya arched a brown brow. "Okay, why are you acting so weird?"

"Oh, am I?" I giggled nervously.

Fuck, what can I tell her? I lost my virginity to her brother? No. No, no, no, no, no, no, no. How can I do that to her? She is one of my best friends. I promised myself, even though I had a crush on him, that I would never sleep with him, even when we were out of high school.

It'd only cause drama, and now I had to explain something to her.

I opened my Diet Coke and sipped. "Oh … yeah, nothing really eventful happened."

Way to act suspicious, Astrid!

She narrowed her eyes at me. "Why are you acting like that?"

Someone shouted from across the cafeteria, and I snapped my gaze up to The Crew. Frasier was leaning back against the brick wall, huge arms crossed over his chest and the biggest grin on his face. And that stupid little Calix sat right beside him, mirroring his smirk.

Fuck!!!

"No reason!" I exclaimed, standing. "Listen, I have to go to the bathroom."

Before Diya could say another word or ask me another question, I shot up from my seat at the cafeteria table and hurried out the door and straight to the bathroom.

What could I say to her? I needed to come up with an excuse.

It was obvious that I was hiding something, and I really didn't want him to tell her before I did. I didn't want her to think I'd betrayed her by sleeping with her brother. She had told me so many times how much she hated him, and for me to fuck him …

My heart was racing, and my mind was all over the place. God, what had I gotten myself into? Not only had I slept with my best friend's brother, but I had also let my stepbrother watch. And one of my good friends too? What had gotten into me?

I pumped my legs as fast as I could without running, not wanting to get in trouble with our new principal—Principal Stoll. He was stricter than Principal Vaughn had been and always found reasons to punish students.

Of course, I'd acted that way because of the alcohol last night.

I tugged on a strand of my hair and chewed on the inside of my cheek. I would never in my right mind have done something like that without alcohol.

Maybe it was spiked? Maybe I was actually drugged last night!

As I passed the boys' bathroom, trying to make a break for the girls' room to get my shit together, someone snatched me by the upper arm and yanked me into the empty room. I yelped, but he smacked a large, callous hand over my mouth.

Suddenly, I was thrust up against the door, and an angry Rush stared down at me.

"Take it off," he growled at me.

"What?" I asked, brow furrowed. "What are you—"

"You stole my fucking shirt," he said, grabbing me by the

collar and tugging me closer. He stared down at me through dark eyes.

Rush was always grumpy, but I had never seen him like this.

"I am … I'm sorry. I didn't have any other clothes to put on."

"I don't give a fuck. I want it back. Now."

I stared up at him, nostrils flaring. "Or what?" The question came out before I had a chance to stop it. I didn't know where the hell all this confidence had been coming from lately, but when I was alone around The Crew, it seemed to flow from me.

"Or what?" he snarled back, as if he didn't believe I had talked back to him. "If you don't fucking take my shirt off right now, I'm gonna rip it off of you."

"I don't have anything else to wear."

"Not my fucking problem. Take it off now."

After a few moments of debating whether I should or not, I decided against it. Because he really, really wouldn't let me walk around half naked at Redwood Academy. How was he gonna rip the shirt off anyway? He wasn't that strong, and this was good quality.

"No," I said, twirling on my heel.

I grabbed the door handle, about to pull it open, when his hand snapped against the wooden door and forced it closed.

"Do you really wanna play games with me, Hellcat? Because I can play games."

CHAPTER SIX

ASTRID

ONE MOMENT, Rush had his hand on the door, and the next, both of his hands were on my collar, ripping the shirt straight down the middle. I yelped and covered my exposed tits.

How is he so strong?!

"Rush!" I exclaimed. "What are you doing?!"

"I told you to take off the shirt, and you decided to be a little fucking brat about it."

"So, you ruined the shirt for both of us?!" I exclaimed. "Are you crazy?!"

Someone waggled the door handle behind me, and my eyes widened even more. If anyone came in, then they would see me almost naked in the middle of the boys' restroom with Rush Parker, the grumpy ass who didn't talk to anyone.

"Let me in," a familiar voice said behind the door.

Rush grabbed me by the elbow, ripping my arm away from my tits and pulling me away from the door. I stumbled into the wall and stared in horror as Arch stepped into the bathroom to see me completely exposed, dropping his backpack onto the floor.

Arch clicked his tongue at me and stared at me through his

brows, his chin tilted down. "Finally get to see Hellcat's nice tits," he murmured, stalking toward me while I flattened out against the wall, trapped between Rush and Arch. "What happened to your shirt?"

"*My* shirt," Rush growled.

I glared up at Rush, then turned my attention to my step-brother. "None of your—"

Arch wrapped a hand around my throat, pinned me to the wall, and smacked one of my tits with his rough hand. "Don't be a brat with us, Astrid. We own you after last night. Don't want anyone to find out you're fucking around with The Crew, do you?"

"I'm not fucking around with you," I snarled at him.

"You fucked Calix in front of us all at the party, then Frasier this morning."

My cheeks warmed. "How did you find out about that?"

Frasier said he'd keep it quiet!

Arch unbuckled his belt, pulled it off his waist, wrapped it around my throat to use as a collar, then yanked me closer to him with the leather. "It doesn't matter how I found out," he growled, his hand coming around my chin, his fingers squeezing my cheeks and making my lips pout. "You're all ours now."

"No, I'm—"

Before I could finish my sentence, Arch bent me at the hip, and my tits bounced forward, swaying underneath me. Rush placed his palm on my forehead, pushing it back and gripping his cock through his jeans. He undid his belt and zipper, then pulled out his dick.

"These big, fat fucking titties," Rush said, grabbing one and bouncing it around in his free hand.

Arch shoved my skirt to my ankles, moved behind me, and lined himself up at my entrance. "I've wanted this for so"—he wrapped his hands around my waist, the head of his cock brushing against my entrance—"fucking"—thrust—"long."

My toes curled, and I willingly opened my mouth to moan out

in pleasure. Rush shoved his fat cock between my lips and grunted, thrusting in and out of me slowly at first.

"Good girls like you are never innocent," Arch growled. "You're all dirty whores."

Heat exploded in my core, and I tightened around Arch. "I-I'm not!"

"Dirty little whores who'll do anything to feel good," Rush murmured, pushing some hair out of my face and shoving his dick back into my mouth. "Astrid, I know you better than you think. Have watched you touch your drooling little pussy more than once. Who do you think told Calix to take you last night?"

My watery eyes widened, and I clenched even tighter on Arch. *Fuck!*

"You're just a desperate little slut," Arch said, reaching around my torso and groping my tits. "Desperate for attention …" He pounded into me from behind. "But even more desperate for some cock."

"Make her pussy cry," Rush mumbled, taking a better hold on my head and matching Arch's pace but inside my throat.

I sank my fingernails into his thighs and cried out in pleasure. The pressure built higher and higher and higher inside me, until I was about to …

About to …

Body trembling, I choked on Rush's cock and came hard. Wave after wave of ecstasy rushed through my body, and I curled my toes, barely able to stand upright. Arch suddenly pulled out of me, leaving me empty, and I fell to the ground, Rush's cock still down my throat.

Rush sank his hand into my hair, grabbing it roughly as he bucked his hips forward. Warm cum shot down the back of my throat, and he forced me to drink it down and swallow. I stared up at him hazily, pussy pulsing.

When Rush finally pulled out of me, Arch stepped forward. "Clean my dick off with that filthy mouth."

In a daze, I opened my mouth and stuck out my tongue. Arch

shoved himself into it, forcing me to suck my juices off his hard, throbbing cock. I whimpered when he hit the back of my throat.

"Please come," I mumbled, words muffled by his huge dick. Spit rolled down my chin and onto my swaying tits. My pussy was still aching from the orgasm from a few moments ago. "Please …"

Arch pulled himself out of me and decorated my face with his cum, getting it all over my lashes and cheeks and lips. I stared up at them, licking what I could off me, feeling exactly like what he had called me—a dirty little whore.

Arch and Rush began stuffing themselves back into their jeans, grabbing their belongings from the floor.

"What am I going to do about a shirt?" I asked, holding my arms over my tits and smooshing them to my chest. I stared at them both through hazy eyes, licking the last few drops of Arch's cum from my lips. "I don't have an extra change of clothes."

"Don't worry," Arch murmured, reaching into his backpack. "I brought something from home." He tossed me a bikini top that was way too small to be mine. It definitely hadn't come from home because I didn't have bikinis this small. They'd barely cover my tits. "It's yours."

"It's mine, my ass," I growled, finally coming to my senses. "Give me a shirt."

Rush snatched my phone from the floor and slipped it into his pocket, a smirk in those usually grumpy eyes. "Have fun figuring it out."

And with that, they both stepped out of the boys' bathroom, leaving me with a torn shirt and a skimpy little bikini that would maybe cover my nipples. That was … if I was lucky.

CHAPTER SEVEN

CAIRO

ASTRID WAS LATE FOR CLASS.

Nervously, I bounced my heel on the ground underneath the table in our Physics class. The classroom buzzed with the chatter from other students, awaiting the arrival of our teacher, who stepped into class the minute it started.

But Astrid always, always, always arrived ten minutes early.

I glanced at the door for the umpteenth time, hoping to catch a glimpse of her brown hair, tied up in her high ponytail. My heart raced inside my chest. Why did she make me feel like this? It wasn't like we were best friends, but we had hung out a couple of times …

For a project.

Still, we had spent time together outside of school, and I hadn't had the balls to push it any further. The Crew had though, last night, at that stupid party that I'd convinced them all to go to because I wanted to take my mind off her.

What a surprise to find a drunk Astrid riding Calix's dick.

Nerves zipped through me as the bell rang. Mr. Gosche

stepped through the door and blew out a low breath, shaking his head and muttering that he didn't want to be here today, like every day.

I tapped my fingers against my textbook, rehearsing what I wanted to say to her a dozen times in my head. Just a simple *hi* and maybe a comment about the latest Physics homework? No, Calix definitely hadn't convinced her to get together with some Physics homework.

My gaze dropped from the door to my phone nestled on my lap, lighting up with messages from Arch and Rush, insinuating that they had met up with Astrid sometime after—or during—lunch. They had both run out after she did.

Jaw twitching, I averted my gaze. Everyone had been with her except me.

Goddamn it.

All this time, nobody in The Crew had spared her a second glance until I showed interest in her. Not Frasier, who slept with any girl he could. Not Arch, who fucking lived with her. Not Rush, who had *said* he had been interested in her. And especially not Calix.

Suddenly, the door opened, and I snapped my head up. Astrid walked into the class with her head hung low, holding a torn shirt closed over her chest. Or at least trying to. But her tits were too big, or maybe the shirt was just too small. Why was it even torn anyway?

"You're late, Astrid," Mr. Gosche said, not looking up from his computer.

"Sorry," she whispered, practically running toward our back table.

Her arms were smooshed against her huge, bouncing tits. She glanced up at me and gave me a small smile as she slid onto the stool beside me, finally letting her torn shirt fall open so I could see the tiniest bikini that she wore.

Holy fuck.

My dick stiffened inside my jeans, and I readjusted myself so she wouldn't see how hard I was. Last night, when I'd finally gotten home, I had stroked so many out at the thought of her being wrapped around *my* cock and not Calix's.

God, I wanted her so fucking badly.

"What, uh, happened to your shirt?" I asked.

"Shit," she muttered to herself. "You noticed?"

I swallowed hard and scratched the back of my neck. "It's hard not to."

She scooted closer to the table, hiding her tits behind it so nobody in front of us could see, but I had the best fucking view of them all as her tits swung in that tiny little bikini, her nipples barely covered by the cloth. All I wanted to do was rip it right off and suck one into my mouth.

My dick stiffened even more that it began to hurt, to *ache.*

"Your idiot friends left me without a shirt," she said, glancing over at me.

I snapped my gaze up from her tits to her eyes, pretending like I hadn't been looking, like I hadn't been daydreaming about bending her over and fucking her senseless. She probably already thought so poorly of The Crew; I didn't want her to think I was just like them.

Even though … I wanted to fuck her too.

"Oh, yeah?"

She blew some hair out of her face. "Yep. You wouldn't happen to have an extra, right?"

Fuck. I had an extra pair of clothes for gym in my bag, but I really, really, *really* didn't want her wearing them. I wanted her to sit in class, brushing those big tits against my arm every time she moved, wanted her to beg me to touch her.

"Yeah," I said out of the goodness of my heart. "Want it?"

"Please," she said, turning toward me. "I will love you forever."

I grabbed the shirt out of my bag and handed it to her, trying not to seem too pissed off about it. Calix, Frasier, Arch, and Rush would've never given her a shirt to wear so they could watch her bounce around. But me? I couldn't let her be embarrassed during the entire class.

"You're the fucking best," she said, slipping her arms into the sleeves.

When she pulled it over her head, her tits bounced out of the bikini, completely bare for a split fucking second. I placed a hand against my hard dick and averted my gaze down to my textbook, which I hadn't opened yet.

Fuck. Fuck. Fuck. Fuck. Fuck. Fuck. Fuck.

I wanted her so badly. So fucking badly. My dick was throbbing.

Once she finally pulled it over her head, she placed a hand on my elbow. I gulped and peered over at her, seeing her nipples pressed hard against my shirt, which was too small for the size of her chest.

"I owe you one," Astrid said. "How can I repay you?"

"Oh," I whispered so Mr. Gosche wouldn't hear. "You don't have to repay me."

Fuck, why did I say that?! Of course, there are many ways she can …

"But I want to," she said, gently squeezing my elbow. "You're the only one who helped me. I'm sure there is something I can do for you, right? Maybe I can do your homework one day or buy you a coffee before school or … *anything*."

"Anything?" I repeated.

"Anything," she said, but I couldn't tell what she meant by it.

"I, uh …" My gaze dropped to her nipples. "Fuck, you're so hot."

Astrid's eyes widened almost as wide as mine did as the words left my mouth.

What the absolute fuck did I just say that for?!

I was supposed to be the nice guy out of the group, and here I was, sexualizing her as much as they all did.

"I mean," I said, pulling my arm away from her and turning

back to the class, "a coffee before school sounds good. How about six thirty Monday morning at Dunkin' on Granite Road?"

Astrid giggled nervously and straightened herself out beside me. "That sounds great."

CHAPTER EIGHT

ASTRID

HUGGING my backpack to my chest, I hurried to the student parking lot after school. Students—and teachers—had kept staring at me today after *some people* ripped my shirt and left me in a tiny little bikini. It didn't help that Cairo's shirt was way too small for me either!

I hurried past Jace, who leaned against his Maserati, one arm slung around his stepsister's waist as he whispered something into her ear that made her red. Arch flashed me a smirk from his car parked next to Jace's.

Nostrils flaring, I averted my gaze and continued to my car that I had left here yesterday before the party. I *had* planned on coming back to retrieve it before the night was over.

When we got home, I would actually kill Arch for what he had done today! How dare that asshole give me a little bikini and tell me that he had wanted to see me in it for a while. *Yuck!*

Diya bounced on her toes near my car, gaze dropping to my backpack. "What are you—"

"Long story," I said, not knowing how I could explain myself. "Long, long, looooong story."

She giggled and leaned against my shitty car. "I have time."

Fuck.

I blew some brown hair out of my face and unlocked the car. "Let's just say that my shirt ripped down the middle today, and I barely had anything on underneath. Cairo from Physics let me borrow his."

"Cairo?" Diya hummed. "The cute one?"

My stomach tightened, jealousy twisting at my insides. She thought he was cute?

"Yeah, the cute one," I said.

Diya might be my best friend, but she had never expressed interest in Cairo before, but I had never expressed interest in her hot brother. I dumped my backpack in the backseat and regathered myself, pushing the jealousy away.

Why was I even jealous anyway? Cairo was too sweet for my liking, but the way that he had told me that I was hot and even gotten so hard for me ... *God,* it'd really made me feel things that I shouldn't.

"Wanna take a ride down the beach?" Diya said, opening my passenger door.

"Down the beach?" someone said from behind me. "I don't get an invite?"

My entire body tensed, and I swallowed hard, immediately recognizing the voice. Calix propped his forearm on top of my car and leaned against it, right beside me, his playful gaze on me, right in front of Diya.

"You're not invited," I said, ignoring his smoldering eyes.

With his free hand, he brushed his fingers against mine behind the car. "No?"

I shivered as the memories of last night flooded through my mind. Calix's hands had been all over my body, his huge cock sliding in and out of me in front of so many people. Part of me wanted it to happen again and again and again.

But it couldn't.

I couldn't do that to my best friend.

"No," I said, tugging my fingers away. "We're meeting boys down there."

Calix's playful stare turned deadly, and he clenched his jaw. "Oh, yeah?" he asked coldly.

"Yep."

"Diya, get out of the fucking car," he growled, his gaze on me and only me. While he might have directed his voice at Diya, he wasn't talking to her. No, he was talking to me. "You're not going to meet any boys."

Diya rolled her eyes. "We're not meeting boys."

"You're a bad influence on my sister," Calix said to me.

"*I'm* a bad influence?" I asked, poking him hard in the chest. "*You're* the bad influence."

"Says the girl who got drunk at a—"

I kicked him as hard as I could in the shin, making him grunt. The next kick wouldn't be in such an easy place for him if he kept running his big mouth. I'd make sure he could never have babies—ever.

"Oh shoot!" Diya said, shutting the passenger door. "I forgot something in Math. I'll be right back." She hopped onto the sidewalk and threw me a wink. "Then we can dump this loser and meet all the boys you want, A!"

When Diya was out of earshot, I twirled on my heel toward her brother and crossed my arms over my chest. "Keep quiet about last night! It didn't happen, and I didn't even enjoy it, so you can forget all about—"

"You didn't enjoy it?" he hummed. "Not when you were moaning and begging for more?"

I glared up at him through my brows. "No."

He scoffed. "Yeah, right."

"I'm being serious."

Instead of taking my word for it, he moved closer and slipped his hand underneath my bottoms and cupped my pussy. A low growl left his mouth, and a smirk danced across his lips. "Hellcat, your pussy betrays you."

"Get off me," I snarled, shoving him away. "It doesn't matter anyway."

"Yes, it does."

"No, it doesn't."

"I want to make sure you have a good time."

"No, it—what?" I asked, realizing what he had said.

Calix moved closer and curled a finger around a strand of my hair. "I don't care who you are to my sister, Hellcat. You are *mine* now—all mine—and I will do what I want to you, where I want, in front of whoever I want."

My heart pounded so hard that I could hear it in my ears, my cheeks burning. "Wh—"

"Never mind!" Diya called from a ways away.

I shoved her brother away as she approached.

"The doors are locked. I'll just get it tomorrow …" She paused and furrowed her brow. "What's going on here?"

"Tell him to stop being an ass," I said to her, slipping into the car, my mind racing.

Diya said something to her brother that I couldn't hear over the sound of my clunky car starting, and I gripped the steering wheel so, so, so hard. If I wasn't careful, my best friend would find out that I'd slept with her brother.

CHAPTER NINE

CALIX

SITTING in the corner booth of Galaxy Grub, I absentmindedly swirled my straw through the last of my strawberry milkshake. The leather booth was worn in multiple places, scratching against the back of my legs.

Rush and Arch played pool near the bar, where Frasier flirted with a cheerleader. We weren't supposed to be in here, but Rush's dad knew a guy who knew a guy who owned this place, so they let us—and most Redwood seniors—slide.

Cairo sat across from me, finishing up some Physics homework, quieter than usual tonight. But I didn't mind because I was so fucking lost in the thought of Astrid from last night and this afternoon by her car.

"Hey, asshole," Arch shouted.

I snapped my gaze up to him and nodded. "You talking to me?"

"Get your mind out of the fucking gutter and play a game with me."

Rush retrieved the balls from the table and placed them in the center, his jaw tight. Once he handed me his pool stick, he snatched his food from the bar and then collapsed in my spot in the booth. Cairo peered up at him through his glasses and grabbed a fry off his plate, then returned to his work.

"You daydreaming about fucking my stepsister again?" Arch asked, lining up for his turn.

"Shut the fuck up."

"Her pussy's good, isn't it?"

"You should know," I said, trying not to sound too annoyed.

Last I knew, Rush and Arch had had a bit of a *meeting* in the bathroom with Astrid. Apparently, they had left her in a tiny bikini to wear for a top. I didn't know what pissed me off more—that they'd fucked her or that I hadn't gotten to see her bouncing around Redwood like that.

"She's an annoying little bitch, but—*God*—her head is the best in Redwood."

I sank a ball into the hole. "That good, huh?"

Arch threw me a smirk. "Jealous?"

"Of a dick like you?" I chuckled. "No."

When Arch missed his shot, he cursed and laid his stick across his shoulders, holding on to it with both his hands. He shuffled backward a couple of steps, watching the balls roll across the table. "Your mom getting any better?"

"No."

"Fuck, dude," he murmured, shaking his head. "She has to."

I blew out a breath and pushed a hand through my hair. "I still don't think Diya knows that she has cancer. I told her that she should tell Diya, but she doesn't want her to worry. It just fucking sucks that I can't help her."

"I can ask Astrid's dad if—"

"No," I said. "You know how much your family loves drama. You tell one of them something, then the entire family knows within five minutes. Besides, he's not a cancer doctor, so I doubt he could help at all."

"Well, let me know if—"

Before Arch could finish his sentence, the door slammed against the wall in the front of the bar.

"Calix! I know you're here!" a high-pitched voice called, followed by heels clacking against the tiled floor.

I growled under my breath, "Fuck."

Blonde hair pulled into a tight bun on top of her head and a black dress clinging to her body, Mira strutted into the bar and made a beeline for me. There went any fun I'd hoped to have tonight. Now I had to deal with this bitch.

"Mira," I murmured, ignoring her approach and taking my turn. "What do you want?"

My ex-girlfriend slid onto the pool table, knocking the balls all over the place.

"Get a fucking life," Arch growled, tossing his stick onto the table and storming to the booth while muttering, "Always have to ruin the fun."

Frasier and the girl he was flirting with looked over, arching a brow at me. None of the guys liked her, and I honestly didn't know how I'd put up with her for so long while we were dating. She was someone I wanted to forget. A three-year-long mistake.

After rolling my eyes, I tightened my grip on my stick. "What do you want?"

"We need to talk."

"Well, I don't have all fucking day."

She crossed her arms. "We're getting back together."

"Who the fuck do you think you are, telling me what to do? Move on."

An annoying laugh left her mouth. "You don't get it."

"No, I don't get anything you do."

"If we don't get back together, then I'll show Diya your little *mistake* from the party last night. And I don't think your sister is going to like seeing pictures of you fucking her best friend, especially after what happened with me."

I gritted my teeth and tossed the pool stick down beside Arch's. "I don't know what you're talking about. Take your crazy ass back to wherever you came from. I didn't go to any party last night."

"Oh, no?" she asked, whipping out her phone. "What's this?"

She showed me a picture of Astrid on top of me last night, every single one of The Crew members sitting around, watching. I lifted my glare to her beady little eyes.

I fucking hate this bitch so much.

"What's it with you and your sister's best friends?" she asked, shaking her head.

"Where the fuck did you get that?" I snarled.

"A friend."

"So, you're planning on blackmailing me?"

"If that's what you want to call it," she hummed, kicking her legs back and forth. "But Diya would be devastated if she found out, and you know you'll lose Astrid, just like you lost me. So, what's it going to be, Calix?"

"I didn't lose you," I clarified. "I broke up with you because you're fucking psychotic."

She hopped off the table. "Guess I'll show your sister."

I snatched her wrist before she could walk away. "Wait."

"Want me that badly?" Mira giggled.

"Tell me what you want from me."

"I already told you," she said. "I want you back."

As much as I hated Mira, Diya couldn't find out what happened. Astrid didn't want Diya to know; she had made that clear today. I needed to get those pictures off Mira's phone, one way or another. And while I usually wouldn't care about who knew what about me, something deep inside me ... didn't want to hurt Astrid.

I'd do anything to keep her safe.

CHAPTER TEN

ASTRID

I SANK into the plush pink velvet of Ruby's enormous king-size bed, my fingers tracing the embroidery on her throw pillows. Astrid was a pink girl—pink hair, pink clothes with the occasional black to spice things up, pink decor, pink everything.

Diya and Seraphina giggled on the couch about some meme that a freshman had created with our old principal's head flying across the football field with the caption *You had to be there* 🤣 or something like that.

Seraphina usually couldn't hang out with us after school because she was busy tutoring the worst of the worst students at Redwood. She loved it though … a bit too much if you asked me. But I was happy we could all finally hang out.

I really needed it after the past day I'd had. I couldn't go home and get fucked again. My raw pussy was aching from how many times that I had done it today with all the guys in The Crew. All except Cairo.

Warmth gathered between my legs at the thought of him again. He might be on the nerdier side, but, God, why did I feel like he was hiding something sinister underneath that facade?

The innocent ones were never quite innocent. I would know.

A chandelier cast a soft yellow glow across the room. I shifted my focus from my best friends to the window that overlooked a blooming garden with perfectly trimmed bushes. God, to have Ruby's life …

Well, every part of it except her nonexistent family.

But maybe a nonexistent family was better than my asshole stepbrother.

Bella and Jade were sprawled on the fluffy rug near the bed. Jade was leaning back on her forearms, dressed in all black, while Bella was on her stomach in a frilly white dress, batting her lashes at Jade.

They'd always been too close to just be friends. I was sure they liked each other.

"Okay, but tell me why Marc's dad is so hot?" Ruby asked.

A giggle escaped my mouth. "Marc, as in your boyfriend?"

Ruby hopped up onto the bed next to me and showed me her phone. A zoomed-in picture of Mr. Henders, the baseball team's coach and a doctor who worked with my father, was plastered on the screen.

Excitedly, Ruby kicked her legs back and forth. "Look at those muscles!"

I offered her an exaggerated eye roll. "Oh my God."

"What?" she asked, smacking my arm. "It's better than you."

After sending her a death glare, I returned to looking at the phone, feeling Diya's gaze on me. I told Diya everything, especially anything and everything boy-related, but I didn't want her asking about this. Not now!

"Okay, but what about Diya and Mr. Garcia?" I asked to take the attention off me.

Diya's face turned red, and she shot up, waving her hands around. "I don't like him!"

"Oh my gosh, you totally do." Jade giggled from the rug, holding a hand over her face.

"No, no, no, no!" Diya continued to wave her hands like a

madwoman while shaking her head and glaring at me. "I don't like him!"

"Wait," Bella asked, giggling too. "Isn't he your stepdad?"

"No!" Diya said, cheeks turning redder. "Well, he is, but I don't like him!"

"You always stare at him in class," I teased.

"Do not!!!"

"Do too."

"I do not!"

"Do—"

Diya grabbed a pillow from the bed and smacked me hard in the face with it, sending me back against the mattress. The girls broke out into a fit of laughter as Diya crawled on top of me and began beating me with the pillow.

"Okay, but real talk …" Seraphina hummed. "Have you fucked him yet?"

"No!" she exclaimed a bit too loudly and too quickly. "I definitely have not."

"You"—*smack*—"definitely"—*smack*—"have."

Ruby placed a hand on Diya's shoulder. "Diya, it's okay to like your men a little bit—"

Diya swung the pillow around, and I ducked out of the way so it hit Ruby right in the chest. Ruby doubled over all dramatically, as if the swing actually hurt her fragile body. And before I could react, pillows were suddenly being swung everywhere.

Pillows hit me from all directions, and suddenly, Seraphina smacked the shit out of Diya and sent her down onto the bed. She landed on the mattress beside me, clutching her belly and wiping away the tears from her eyes.

"Don't tell anyone," Diya said between giggles. "Especially my brother."

"I promise I won't," I said.

Because there was a secret that I was hiding from her too …

CHAPTER ELEVEN

ASTRID

WHILE WAITING for Cairo in the Dunkin' parking lot on Monday morning, I fiddled with the black T-shirt that he had lent me, the fabric soft against my fingers. If it hadn't been for him, I would've probably had to walk around Redwood Academy all day with my tits hanging out.

Besides, who knew what perverted teachers would've jerked off to me afterward?

Cairo pulled into the lot and parked next to me, giving me a soft, small smile through the window. My heart pounded inside my chest, and I exited my car, grabbed both our coffees from my cupholders, and opened his passenger door.

He furrowed his brow. "You already got them?"

"Yep," I said. "I wasn't going to chance you not letting me pay. I know how you are."

His smile widened a bit, and he undid his seat belt to relax. "Well, thank you."

"No, thank *you,*" I said, tugging his shirt out of my bag. I held it out for him. "I washed it, so no need to worry about my cooties."

A low chuckle left his mouth. He sipped his coffee and shook his head, his cheeks the lightest shade of pink. "You can keep it." He shrugged, another laugh leaving his mouth, but this one wasn't as smooth as the first. "It looks better on you anyway."

My heart raced, and I pressed my thighs together. "You think so?"

Cairo's gaze drifted from the dashboard to my legs. "Yeah, I think so."

I curled my fingers around the hem of my skirt. *Why am I so nervous?* I wasn't sure. I had no problem back-talking any of the other guys in The Crew, but Cairo seemed so precious, and I didn't want to corrupt him.

"What about it looks better on me?" I whispered, my pussy pulsing wildly.

Cairo swallowed hard and sipped his coffee again, glancing out the windshield. "You know ..."

He wiped a hand down his right jean pant leg and shifted in his seat. I dropped my gaze to his lap, noticing how hard he was.

Fuck.

Fuck. Fuck. Fuck. Fuck. Fuck. Fuck. Fuck.

He was hard. So, so hard. And he was trying to hide it from me.

Warmth exploded through my cunt, and I pressed my thighs closer together. God, I needed him so badly. All I wanted was to crawl across the center console, pull his huge cock out of his pants, and ride him like I had with Frasier Friday before school.

"What's the reason?" I asked. "I didn't quite get that ..."

Cairo swallowed hard and peered at me once more, struggling to keep eye contact. "Your tits looked fucking amazing in it."

My eyes widened slightly at how straightforward he had been. Cute and shy Cairo?!

Nipples hardening through my top, I shifted toward him. "You think so?"

He placed his coffee down in the cupholder and looked down at them. "They look good in everything."

God, he is so shy, and it's so hot!

"Do you want to play with them?" I asked, heart and pussy pounding. "As a thank-you?"

After his cheeks tinted a deeper shade of red, he swallowed. "Come on, Astrid ..."

"It's okay," I whispered, peering at him through my lashes. "I kinda maybe want it."

Cairo reached over and squeezed one of my tits with his hand. I didn't quite realize how big his hands were until he was groping and kneading my breast. His fingers ... God, they were so long. I bet he could—

Without hesitation, Cairo pinched my nipple, and my body jerked in surprise. A moan left my mouth, and I moved toward him, placing my hand on his thigh.

"More, Cairo. Do it again, please ..."

"Astrid," he murmured, his voice shaky, "don't beg."

"Don't beg?" I whimpered, moving my hand further up his leg toward his hard cock in his jeans. "But it feels so good. Please, do it again."

"Astrid," he repeated again, "I'm warning you that ... if you don't stop ..."

"What?" I asked, pulling him out of his jeans. "What are you going to do about—"

Cairo seized both my nipples between his fingers and tugged me forward, out of the seat and leaning over the console. I placed my hands on either of his thighs to steady myself, coming face-to-face with a Cairo that I had never seen before.

He had been so soft, but nothing on his face screamed soft right now.

"You're a bad girl," he growled at me. "Bad girls get punished."

Fuck.

"What did I do to—" I started before he pinched my nipples harder.

"You're lucky I don't bring you back to my place. I don't think you'd be able to take it."

"Take it?" I scoffed, loving his current demeanor. "I can take any—"

Before I could say another word, he took a handful of my hair and shoved my face down toward his cock, my back arched over the center of the car. My pussy clenched as I wrapped my mouth around the head of his cock, willing and desperate for it.

"That mouth is going to get you in trouble," he murmured, pushing my head all the way down to the base of his cock.

I gagged on it, but didn't pull back, sticking my tongue out and licking his balls.

"*A lot* of trouble ..."

He reached around me, slipping his hand up my skirt and finding my entrance with his fingers. I clamped around their length and choked more on his dick, bobbing my head up and down on him.

Holy—how is he so deep already?!

"More!" I cried, my voice muffled on his dick. "Please, more!"

I swallowed as much of his cock as I could with every bob of my head, desperate to please him. I hadn't stopped thinking about him all night. I touched myself when I knew that I shouldn't, wondering what he'd be like in bed.

I'd thought he'd be shy, reserved. But this? *This?!* Fuck.

After pulling his hand out of my hair, he wrapped it around the base of his cock and balls, feeding himself to me while he was knuckle deep in my pussy with his other hand, massaging my G-spot with those long fingers.

"Cairo," I cried on his cock, spit running down my chin and between his thighs, probably staining the driver's seat. I dug my fingernails into his thighs and whimpered, the pressure rising quickly inside me. "I'm going to ... I'm going to ..."

Cairo lifted his hips off the seat, pushing himself deeper into my throat, and grunted. His cum shot into my mouth, and I came hard on his fingers, my pussy exploding, pulsating, clenching, and tightening on them.

"Oh my God!" I cried, pulling back, my legs shaking uncontrollably and cum rolling down my chin.

Cairo sat back in the driver's seat and stuffed himself back into his jeans, breathing heavily. "Maybe we can do this more often? You know, coffee before school …" He paused and glanced down at his lap. "Or this."

I wiped the spit off the corner of my lip. "Maybe we can."

CHAPTER TWELVE

ASTRID

"DON'T you usually meet The Crew in the mornings?" I asked, walking with Cairo into Redwood Academy.

It was ten minutes before the first bell, and normally, the halls were dead until five of seven, but not today.

Students were bustling in the corridors, chatting with each other about the baseball game tonight. Baseball wasn't huge in our school, but we were playing against our rival, and usually, the entire senior class got wasted on game days.

"Sometimes," Cairo said, glancing around—back to his nervous, shy self. "Not today."

"Why not? You're all—"

Before I could say another word, ask another question, or let him answer anything for me, my gaze landed on Calix down the hallway. He was leaning against a set of lockers, his gaze on his ex-girlfriend.

This was why they hadn't hung out this morning, wasn't it?

I gritted my teeth and stared at Mira. That bitch had once been in our friend group until she went crazy and began fucking Calix.

My gaze shifted back and forth between them for a moment, and I balled my hand into a fist.

How could he be with her? *Why* was he with her? They had broken up so long ago, and as soon as we had gotten together, they were suddenly back together? No, that couldn't be right. Something was up.

Mira wrapped her arm around his and pressed her breasts against his chest, beaming up at him. Jealousy twisted my insides, and my mouth dried.

Fuck. I hate her. I hate her. I hate her. I hate her. I hate her.

As if she knew I was looking at them, she peered over at me. Calix remained still, looking down at her, but his body tensed a bit. He knew that I was watching, and this fucker didn't care.

"Oh," I hummed to Cairo as nonchalantly as I could, "Mira and Calix are back together?"

Cairo scratched the back of his neck. "Oh, yeah …"

My heart dropped, and I dug my nails so deep into my palms that I swore I drew blood. Really? Was this all just to make me jealous? It didn't matter because all we had done was fuck. That was all. Nothing else.

After tearing my glare away from him, I continued with Cairo through Redwood's halls. Students were laughing, fighting, screaming, and shouting at each other, but I kept my lips pressed tightly together and didn't say a word.

I don't care what Calix does.

Down the hall, I spotted Frasier with his arm wrapped around some pretty cheerleader's waist, and I paused for a moment.

What the fuck was wrong with me? Why did I care what The Crew did? I couldn't. *I didn't.*

Frasier was a man-whore, so I expected nothing less from him, even after our time in his car Friday morning. He wasn't someone who could only be with one woman. Never mind with me. I was just that nerdy girl he used.

But why did it sting so badly to see my best friend's brother with another girl? Why was I this furious? Fuck. No, I wasn't catching feelings. I couldn't catch feelings. I had already promised Diya that I would never betray her like Mira had.

I'd vowed never to do that. She didn't deserve it. She was too sweet.

Rush shouldered me from behind, shoving me into the locker and storming down the hall. His fists were clenched by his sides, and I honestly didn't think that he realized what he had just done. Still though, that shit pissed me off.

"What's Rush's problem?" I asked Cairo, straightening myself out.

"You know Rush … he's always like that."

"Why? Why is he always grumpy?"

Cairo paused for a long moment, looking over at Rush about to turn the corner. The muscles in his back were flexing against his gray T-shirt that hugged his body, and all I wanted to do was drag my nails down his—

No, Astrid, we're done fucking these guys. Everyone except maybe Cairo …

I wouldn't catch feelings for Cairo. Not at all. He wasn't my type. Not even a little bit.

The bell rang, and Cairo shuffled backward. "I got to get to class. I have an exam."

"Okay." I waved. "I guess I'll see you in Physics."

He scurried away, and while he was a bit scrawnier than the others—*God*—this morning had been so fucking sexy. I hadn't thought that sweet and shy Cairo had it in him to be that … dominant. And what had he meant about getting in his bed? Was he more dominant there than this morning? I pressed my thighs together.

I would do *anything* to find myself in his bed. I turned on my heel. *Anything*—

"Hellcat," Arch murmured as I bumped straight into his hard chest. I craned my head up to look into those dark and vicious eyes. His lips were curled into a smirk, and he snatched my upper arm. "We have to talk."

"Get off me," I said, trying to push him away. "I have to get to first period."

"Oh, I don't think you're going to make it to class today."

CHAPTER THIRTEEN

ARCH

"YOU DIDN'T COME HOME last night," I said, squeezing Astrid's upper arm and tugging her through the hallway.

She tried yanking herself out of my hold, but I wasn't letting her go anywhere. No, she was my little plaything now. Almost all the others had spent time alone with her, even Cairo, for fuck's sake. It was my turn.

"Let me go, you asshole," she hissed, glaring at me.

I shoved her into an empty classroom. "Sleeping around?"

She cradled her arm and flared her nostrils at me. "You like to get on my very last nerve every single day of my life, don't you?! Ever since our parents got married, you haven't gone a day with something stupid coming out of your mouth."

My lips curled into a smirk. Angry Astrid was the sexiest.

"I know how you like to get around," I hummed.

She grabbed me by my collar and stepped closer. "I do *not* like to get around."

"Hellcat," I purred, curling a finger around a strand of her hair, "don't lie."

"I hate you," she sneered between her teeth, "so much."

I twisted her around and shoved her up against the classroom door, pressing her face against the small window to see out into the hallway. I drew my nose down the column of her neck and bit her shoulder. "You sure you hate me that much, Hellcat?"

This bitch slammed her elbow back into my ribs and ground her ass against me in one movement. A low growl left my mouth, and I pulled up her skirt and shoved her panties to her ankles, my fingers finding her sopping cunt.

"You were out with Cairo this morning," I snarled. "Frasier Friday morning."

"Is that what this is about?"

I undid my pants and pulled out my cock, lining it up with her entrance. "I don't look good jealous, baby." Then I slammed myself deep, deep, deep into her pussy, a grunt leaving my mouth and pleasure rushing through me.

"You're disgusting," she said back at me, nose scrunched up in disgust but a dark haze in her eyes. "You're my stepbrother." *Thrust.* "I hate you." *Thrust.* "Leave me alone." *Thrust.* "Go fuck yourse—holy fuck."

"It doesn't matter who I am, Hellcat." I smacked her clit, making her clench. "You love coming. I hear you with your toys every night, those soft moans drifting through the walls. You love fucking taunting me."

This was payback.

Astrid opened her mouth to protest, but the only things coming out of her mouth were breathy moans. I gripped her waist tighter with one hand and smacked her clit again with my other, sinking my teeth into her shoulder, desperate to leave marks all over her.

To claim her.

To *own* her.

She was mine.

"You're going to walk into second period with my cum staining your legs because your cunt is too tight to hold all of it inside," I growled into her ear, pumping into her roughly. "A pretty little whore, decorated with cum."

"Arch," she cried, her fingers white on the door, "don't you dare—"

I slammed deep into her and grunted, exploding inside her tight little pussy. She tried to waggle away, but she had nowhere else to go. Every inch she moved forward, I moved with her, making sure that I shoved my cum as deep as I could get it.

With my hand cupping her quivering pussy, I slapped it and made her tighten even more, milking more cum out of my balls. I wrapped my free hand around the front of her throat and pulled her head back, my mouth on hers from above.

"Thank me for my cum," I said.

"Fuck you," she growled, her pussy only clenching harder.

"Don't be a fucking bitch. Thank. Me."

After a moment of no response, I smacked her clit once more, forcing her over the edge.

Her pussy clenched over and over and over around me, and she cried out into my mouth, "Thank you for filling up my pussy! Thank you for filling up my pussy, Arch!"

I kissed her hard on the mouth, then pulled back and spit in it, pressing her lips closed with my hand on her chin. "Good fucking girl." When the bell rang, I pulled out of her, stuffed myself back into my pants, and tugged the door she was leaning against open. "Looks like I'm going to have to teach you manners more often, Hellcat."

CHAPTER
FOURTEEN

ASTRID

THAT ASSHOLE.

With my nostrils flared, I stormed down the halls of Redwood Academy with my hands balled into fists. The scent of hot dogs and nasty cheese fries drifted through my nose from Culinary up ahead. I stopped in front of my locker and undid the lock.

"Stupid piece-of-shit Arch," I growled under my breath.

How dare he make me miss my first class! There goes my near-perfect attendance.

My thighs were still coated with his cum. I had gone to the bathroom and tried to wipe as much of it off as I could, but I could still feel him pressed between me, his cock pulsing inside me, his mouth on mine.

Fuck, that was so—

No, Astrid. It wasn't hot. So, stop thinking about it!

Someone cackled to my left, and I peered over to see Mira tugging at Calix's collar in front of his locker. I gritted my teeth—because it didn't bother me—and grabbed my books for next period. I had Calc, and I hated Calc.

That's why I was pissed. Not because of these irritating boys.

"You're so funny," Mira giggled, beaming up at Calix.

They were looking at each other in a way that made my blood fucking boil. All I wanted to do was rip her away from him and tell him to stop ruining Diya's—*and my*—life.

"Where were you first period?" Diya asked from my right, looping her arm around mine.

I snapped my gaze away from her brother and forced a smile. "Oh, you know …"

"She was getting fucked," Ruby hummed, walking by with Seraphina to their next class.

"Don't listen to her," I said, rolling my eyes and hoping that Diya didn't pick up on my jealousy with her brother and Mira. I didn't need her thinking that I was into him—or any of the boys in The Crew for that matter.

"Mmhmm," Diya said, a small smirk on her face. "I know what you've been up to."

My grip tightened on my books, my insides twisting. *Fuck.* "You do?"

"Yep," she said. "I saw you parked at Dunkin' this morning with Cairo."

Oh, thank God.

She playfully smacked my arm. "When were you going to tell me?!"

Cheeks warming, I looked down so some hair fell into my face. "It's nothing. We're just friends … I was just thanking him for letting me borrow his shirt the other day. Nothing more than that, promise."

"Oh, yeah?" she asked, wiggling her brows. "Was that why you got all defensive when I said he was cute the other day?"

"No!" I exclaimed. "When did that happen?"

Honestly, so much had happened in very little time with The Crew that I couldn't remember it all. Did Diya really think Cairo was cute? I could've sworn that Cairo really wasn't her type.

Diya rolled her eyes at me. "You seriously don't remember?"

"Okay," I said, pointing a finger at her. "I don't wanna hear it,

Miss I Wanna Sleep With My Teacher Turned Stepfather. It's really fitting, coming from you, who can't keep her tits in her shirt."

"Me?!" Diya exclaimed, her cheeks rounded and red. "Weren't you walking around Redwood in a tiny little bikini just the other day?! And you have the nerve to tell your best friend that she's being a whore?"

"I did not say that." I giggled, feigning anger at her still. "But you are one."

Diya crossed her arms and matched my fake anger. "If I'm one, then you are too."

"Deal," I hummed, closing my locker as the bell rang.

She stepped a few feet backward and waved me off. "Get to class, slut."

Once she disappeared into a different hallway, I blew out a breath and turned toward her stupid fucking brother to see Mira running her hands all over him.

God, why is she so annoying? It is almost like she purposefully wants me to suffer.

"Astrid," someone hummed from behind me, slinging an arm over my shoulders.

I looked to my left. "Frasier."

A sly grin decorated his playboy lips. "Someone on your mind?"

"What do you want?" I asked, narrowing my eyes.

"Relax ..." He held up his arms. "I'm just here to help."

"Help?"

"It's obvious you have a thing for Calix."

"I do not."

"Well, if you ever need someone to help get his attention—"

My gaze cut to him, and I arched a brow. "Why do you want to help me? You're more into fucking and dumping girls, only to find more, aren't you?"

Especially after what he had done to me the other morning.

All those sweet little promises for nothing.

"I know what you're like, Frasier," I said.

"Do you?" he asked. "I don't think you know the first thing about me, and you really don't know how to get the attention from a guy like Calix. But I can help. All you have to do is play along with me."

"And how do I do that?"

"We make him jealous," he said, as if it were that simple. "You and I hang out at school, after school. I'll blow him off and tell him I'm with you. Trust me, he won't be able to stand it, especially if we make it seem like we're more than friends."

I held out my hand for him to shake. "Deal."

He stared down at my outstretched hand, and instead of shaking it, he pulled me closer until my body was pressed against his and his lips were brushing against mine. "If we're going to be more than friends, then you have to act like it, baby."

And right there, in front of Redwood Academy and Calix, he kissed me on the mouth.

CHAPTER FIFTEEN

CALIX

I BALLED my hands into fists and watched Frasier kiss my girl. I mean, Astrid.

What the fuck is he doing? And why is she kissing him back?

Mira had her hands all over me, trying to pry my attention away from my little sister's best friend and *my* best friend, all fucking over each other in the middle of Redwood. Frasier was a player—Astrid knew that.

Why is she—

He clutched her by the waist and pulled her closer until her tits were flush against his chest, garnering stares from other students. A girl like Astrid with a guy like Frasier was bound to be all over school by next period.

When Astrid pulled away from Frasier, her cheeks were flushed, her eyes were wide, and her lips were swollen. He tucked some hair behind her ear, released his grip on her, and sauntered away, leaving her staring breathlessly at him.

After a moment, she straightened herself out and tugged her books to her chest. A wide grin was painted on her face as she began walking toward me to her next class—Calc. She didn't even spare me a fucking glance either.

A low growl escaped my lips, and I released Mira to follow Astrid.

Who the fuck does she think she is? Was that to make me jealous?

"Astrid," I called, pushing past students. "Astrid!"

Yet she continued to ignore me while giggling to herself and stepping into Calc. When I made it to the door, she was already seated. I flared my nostrils and walked in her direction, trying to keep my anger to myself.

But honestly, what was she thinking?! Being with Frasier at *Redwood?!*

It was bad enough that I had found out they'd slept together in his car the other morning. Had he schmoozed her that much? Had she really fallen for his charm? She knew how many girls he had been with.

"There's my baby," Mrs. Dawson cooed at me, pushing herself up from her seat and sauntering over to me. She was all dolled up in an ugly neon Lilly Pulitzer dress, like usual. She grabbed my arm before I could walk down Astrid's aisle. "How are you doing?"

Mrs. Dawson was a fucking predator, always flirty with the guys in her class.

"Good, Mrs. Dawson," I hummed, keeping my glare focused on Astrid.

Astrid glanced up at me.

"Will I see you at the baseball game tonight, sweetie?"

"No."

"If you do decide to show up, I'll need a hug."

Once she finally let me go, I walked down Astrid's aisle and squeezed the shoulder of the guy who was sitting behind her. "Get up."

He readjusted his glasses. "But this is where I always—"

I leaned down, sneering in his ear, "Get. Up."

After scrambling to gather all his belongings, he hurried to another seat at the other side of the room. I sat down behind Astrid and waited for her to turn around to talk to me. She had to have something to say.

One moment passed. Then another.

Silence. Complete fucking silence.

"All right, kids," Mrs. Dawson said. "Settle down."

I ran a hand through my hair, unable to fucking believe that she was ignoring me now. After what had happened at the party the other night?! Did it mean nothing to her? If it had, then why had she kissed Frasier back?

I leaned forward and grabbed a lock of Astrid's hair, tugging on it.

"Ow!" she hissed, grabbing the back of her head and turning around. "Can you not?"

"What's going on between you and Frasier?" I asked.

"What do you mean?"

"You know what I mean."

She furrowed her brow and tilted her head like I was crazy. "No, I don't."

After balling my hands into fists underneath my desk, I sat back and attempted to act like this didn't bother me. Why was I asking her this anyway? Why did it matter? I didn't like Astrid like that. I couldn't.

"Don't play dumb," I said, keeping my voice steady. "You fucking him?"

"Why does it matter to you?"

"It doesn't." *Lie.*

"Sure seems like it."

"It. Doesn't."

"Okay," she said, turning back to the front.

I clenched my jaw and glared at the back of her head. It didn't bother me. My body relaxed—as much as it could—on the seat, and I turned my attention to Mrs. Dawson. No, it didn't bother me at all.

We'd just fucked.

Nothing more.

When I finally calmed down, Astrid leaned back slightly so her hair was dangling all over my desk, then tilted her head to the side so I could see a smirk painted across her lips.

"You know," she began in a whisper, "I should be honest with you."

I tapped my fingers on the desk, grinding my teeth together. "About?"

"Well, Frasier's your friend, so I'm sure you'll find out sometime."

"What?" I snapped. "What is it?"

Why all the fucking dramatics?! I can't handle it!

"We're just ..." She paused and shrugged. "You know ..."

"No, I don't know, Astrid. Tell me."

"Seeing each other a bit"—she peered back at me—"as friends."

As friends?! As fucking friends?!

"Friends," I scoffed. "That's not what it seemed like in the hallway."

"Yeah, well, you know how Frasier is ..."

"He's a fucking pig who sleeps with everyone," I growled. "You know that."

"Oh, come on. He's not that bad. Can actually be really sweet sometimes."

I leaned forward again, heart pounding so hard that I could hear it in my ears. "Are we talking about the same fucking person? Frasier. Frasier Crane. Same guy who had an orgy with the softball team last year?"

She scrunched her nose. "Ew, I don't want to hear about that."

"That's the guy you're dating."

She turned around. "We're not dating."

"Then what the fuck are you doing kissing him in the middle of Redwood?"

A smirk crossed her face again, and then Astrid turned back around. "Okay, you caught me. I'm fucking your best friend, Calix. What are you going to do about it?"

CHAPTER
SIXTEEN

ASTRID

AS SOON AS the bell rang, I shot up from my seat and hurried to the exit of Mrs. Dawson's Calculus class. After I had asked Calix what he was going to do about me kissing his best friend, he had gotten so mad. And I mean, so, so, so mad.

Angry. Furious. Jaw clenched. Eyes dark.

I bit a whimper back. *God, it was so hot.*

"Excuse me," I said, shoving my elbow into Carter's ribs. He was the quarterback of the football team, so he could take it. I pushed past him and moved my legs as fast as they'd go. "Please, get out of my way!"

Students crowded the halls. I glanced over my shoulder to see Calix inside the room, stalking toward me slowly, like I was his prey. Heat coursed through my body, and I ducked through the crowd, dodging students and desperately trying to make an escape.

Man, I am in so much trouble with him.

"Sorry," I muttered, shoving past a group of freshmen who walked way too slowly.

I needed to find somewhere to hide. Anywhere.

Someone grabbed my hand and tugged me into an empty classroom, away from the mess of students. I glanced over at my kidnapper to see Frasier standing there with the widest smirk on his face. A moment later, Calix entered the room.

He halted when he saw Frasier. "What the fuck are you doing here?"

"About to eat my girl for lunch."

Holy—

"You guys aren't fucking dating," Calix growled. "Don't bullshit me."

Frasier curled his hands around my waist and pulled me closer to him, grinding his hard cock against my backside. I pressed my thighs together, nipples hardening inside my bra.

Oh God. Oh God. Oh God.

"Not bullshitting you, dude," Frasier said, burying his nose into my hair but staring at Calix, a smirk on his lips and against my bare neck.

I shivered and slumped my shoulders forward, the sensations making me feel *things*.

"Look at how she melts for me." He bit down on my neck gently. "I bet your pussy is soaked for me, isn't it, baby?"

Jaw clenched and nostrils flared, Calix locked the door and pulled a chair from one of the desks, setting it right in front of us and sitting down in it. He drew his tongue across his teeth. "Let me see then."

"Wh-what?" I whispered.

"Pull up your skirt and let me see how wet you are for him."

I clenched and shuffled from foot to foot. *This is* not *how I expected this to go!*

Frasier pulled away from me, took a few steps back until he leaned against the desk, and began undoing his belt. "Show him how wet you are for me, baby," he murmured. "Before I make him listen to how wet you are."

Pussy exploding with pleasure, I turned back toward Calix, whose eyes hadn't left mine. I whimpered and curled my fingers around the bottom of my skirt. Usually, I wasn't this nervous around these guys, but right now …

God, I just want to—

"Skirt up," Calix growled. "Now."

With my heart pounding rapidly against my chest, I lifted up my skirt, inch by inch by inch, further and further up my thighs until I reached my soaked panties. I bunched the skirt up around my hips, showing him how ruined I was for his best friend.

After a moment, Frasier bent me over Calix, so I was face-to-face with him, my hands on his thighs. He reached around me, pulling down the front of my shirt and letting my tits bounce out of it, hanging down.

Calix grabbed me by the throat and glared at me as Frasier swiped my panties to the side and shoved his huge cock into my tight, wet pussy. I bit my lip to hold back a moan and furrowed my brow, staring into Calix's dark eyes. Frasier slammed into me again, my tits bouncing against Calix's chest.

Fuck. Fuck. Fuck. Fuck. Fuck. Fuck!

"You hear how wet she is for me?" Frasier said to Calix, his fingers curling into my hips as he continued to pound into me over and over and over.

The pressure built up higher and higher inside my core, but I didn't break eye contact with Calix. I couldn't. He had me locked into him. My pussy clamped down on Frasier's cock, my fingers digging into Calix's thighs.

"Huh?" Frasier mocked. "You hear that pussy? What about you, baby? You hear it?"

I nodded, a whimper escaping my throat. "Yes, I hear it."

"Tell him who you belong to," Frasier said, loving every fucking moment of this.

Calix's jaw twitched, and he suddenly tugged on my nipples. Hard. "Tell me."

"You!" I cried, the pleasure exploding through my body. My legs shook uncontrollably. I didn't even know which one of them I was talking to anymore because—*God*—it felt too fucking good! "I belong to you!"

"That's right, baby," Frasier murmured, slowing his pace and stilling inside me.

Dragging his gaze up my body to my eyes so agonizingly slowly, Calix drew the pad of his thumb across my lower lip. I clenched around Frasier, milking the cum out of his cock, and stared down at Calix's lips. The only way this could get any better was if he kissed me.

"You're mine," Calix said so softly that only I could hear it.

I furrowed my brow and pressed my lips together. "Calix ..."

"Say it, Astrid. Say it for me."

Frasier pulled out of me, then wrapped a hand around my body and my throat to tug me away from Calix. His hands were all over my body, teasing my nipples, my clit, my body, everywhere that Calix hadn't.

"Your body is mine," Frasier murmured into my ear.

Oh my fucking God! Two guys telling me that I belong to them!

My life couldn't get any better than this.

After Frasier kissed my neck, he pulled my shirt down to cover my breasts, then did the same with my skirt to hide my naked body from Calix, who looked extra fucking pissed now. And it made me even wetter.

I had just come, but I desperately wanted to again. And again. And again.

Especially while they fought over me.

"Come on, baby," Frasier said, tugging at my hand. "You can sit with me during lunch."

And with that, Frasier pulled me out of the empty classroom with cheeks flushed and his cum running down my thighs. I didn't know what Calix was thinking, but I did know that as soon as he had me alone ... I would be punished.

Punished hard.

CHAPTER SEVENTEEN

ASTRID

FRASIER'S HAND didn't leave my lower back as we walked all the way through the cafeteria toward The Crew's table. Every pair of eyes was locked on us, and I listened to the slow stir of whispers whirling around the room.

"Why is he with her?"

"Another good girl gone. RIP."

"Bagged another one."

My stomach twisted, and I peered at my friends, who sat at my usual table with their eyes wide. Thank God that Diya wasn't here yet because I didn't know how I would explain this to her. She'd find out soon, but maybe I could play it off.

If I really wanted to make Calix jealous, then I had to continue this little … game.

"Relax, baby," Frasier murmured into my ear.

"Everyone is staring at us," I whispered back.

He curled his arm around my waist, a smug smirk playing on his lips. "Let them."

Heart pounding inside my chest because Frasier was so good at this fake-dating thing and making me feel all these emotions that I really shouldn't, I forced a confident smile on my face and slid onto a seat next to Cairo. Frasier sat beside me, his hand on my thigh. Cairo took note and looked away. Arch glared at Frasier from across the table, his lip curled up in disgust.

A few moments later, Calix walked into the cafeteria, his gaze cold, just like Rush's, who hadn't looked at me since my last encounter with him. He ate his lunch, his phone on the table, face down. Did he hate me that much?

"Hey, Astrid," Cairo said, acknowledging me before anyone else.

"Hi," I whispered, looking around at all the students gawking at us.

My gaze locked on to my friends' table. Ruby smirked at me and pointed down to her phone, and suddenly, my phone was buzzing in my pocket. I tugged it out and stared at the bright screen from under the table, reading texts in our group chat.

Ruby: Shut. Up.

Bella: Someone is busssssy today. 😏

Jade: Frasier though? 🤮

Bella: Hey, Frasier is cute!

Jade: He is, but he's a man-whore.

Bella: I bet he has some good 🍆

Jade: Not better than I can give you 😉

Seraphina: Wait, LOL. Frasier?!?! You're fucking him? Since when?!

Me: No, I'm not fucking him!

Another message came through in a private thread from Ruby.

Ruby: Don't tell me that you're sleeping with all of them!!!

Before anyone could see my chat—especially Frasier—I turned my phone upside down and slipped it back into my pocket. I didn't need him to get a bigger ego than he already had if he saw Bella's message.

Or maybe I just didn't want him going after her next.

Jealousy twisted at my insides. Of course I didn't want that. I liked … his attention.

Not him.

"Everything okay?" Frasier asked, moving his hand further up my thigh.

I pressed my thighs together in an attempt to stop him from doing this *again* in the middle of Redwood. One of these days, someone was bound to see it. It was bad enough that we were sitting together.

"Just my friends," I murmured, staring at my lunch. "And everyone else ..."

The entire table sat in a tense silence, Arch and Calix both glaring at Frasier while Rush continued to stare down at his lunch, jaw clenched tightly. Cairo shifted beside me, playing with the food on his tray.

"So, finally decided to sit with us," Cairo said, breaking the silence.

"I don't think I had much of a choice," I said, taking a peek at him, cheeks warming.

"You always have a choice," Cairo said, only loud enough for me to hear.

Heat coursed through my body as the memory of this morning flooded through my mind. Cairo had told me that I wouldn't be able to handle all of him, especially not if he brought me home.

Was this his way of giving me a warning?

A warning not to get on his bad side? A warning not to be with Frasier so he could have me to himself? A warning that if I went against his orders and refused to be a good girl for him that he would punish me?

"Oh, yeah?" I whispered, brushing my leg against his. "You think so?"

Cairo glanced down between us for a moment. Then, to my surprise, he squeezed my thigh, his fingers lightly digging into my skin. He leaned closer. "Don't make the mistake of thinking that I won't ruin you the next time we're alone."

Then he stood from his seat, grabbing all his belongings, and walked away from the table, muttering something about having to get to class before the bell because he had to redo an exam, which was a lie. Cairo never had to make up any exams. He was a straight-A student.

"Slutting around with The Crew," Arch noted. "Fits you, Hellcat."

I cut my glare to him. "I am not slutting it around with you guys!"

"Seems like it."

"Well, maybe your mom needs to buy you glasses," I said. "I just made my choice."

For the first time today, Rush looked over at me. That seemed to get his attention.

"Your choice?" Arch growled. "What the fuck does that mean?"

"It means that Frasier and Astrid are together," Calix said.

"No, they aren't," Arch said.

Frasier smirked. "Yes, we are."

"Bullshit," Arch said.

"Call bullshit all you want," Frasier said, tugging me closer by his grip on my thigh.

Rush slammed his palms onto the table and stormed out of the cafeteria, leaving four of us. I swallowed hard and looked from Arch to Calix, who mirrored each other's pissed facial expressions.

Frasier placed his mouth on my ear and kissed it, way slower than I wanted him to. More and more eyes shifted to us. "She's mine, boys. All mine."

CHAPTER EIGHTEEN

CAIRO

ASTRID LEANED against the Physics table, strands of her hair falling into her face. I averted my gaze away from her and took notes in my book to look busy. Ever since I had found out that she was dating Frasier—*Frasier, for God's sake*—I couldn't stop thinking about it.

Did this morning mean nothing to her? Is she actually *dating him? What does she see in a playboy like him?*

Honestly, I had thought that if a good girl like her was going to date anyone in The Crew, it'd be Calix or me.

I desperately wanted it to be me. And only me.

"What is it?" Astrid whispered.

I snapped out of my trance, realizing that I had been staring at her again, and cleared my throat, my shoulders shrugging. "Nothing …" *Just that you're dating one of my best friends, even after our coffee date this morning!*

With my pencil, I outlined all the diagrams in my textbook. The equations meant nothing to me right now, as I couldn't focus. I hadn't been able to focus since Mr. Gosche sat Astrid next to me a few weeks ago.

"We still doing coffee?" she asked, leaning closer, her breasts brushing against my arm.

"Coffee, huh?" I asked, stiff—*everywhere.* "Is that what you want?"

Astrid batted her lashes at me. "Of course. What else could I want?"

After drawing my tongue across my teeth, I peered back at my textbook. "I don't think Frasier would like that much." I balled my hand into a fist around my pencil. "Why don't you get coffee with him tomorrow morning?"

When she scooted her seat closer to me, my dick twitched. Her thigh pressed against mine, along with her upper arm, the scent of her shampoo wrapping around me like a snake. "Are you jealous, Cairo?"

"Jealous?" I repeated. "Why would I be?"

"Because of this morning." She nudged me. "You know, you can be honest with me."

"About what?"

She looked back at her notebook. "About your feelings."

My feelings? Like this ache in my chest whenever I think about her and Frasier after I spent time with her alone this morning? I can't tell her about that! She obviously doesn't care anyway …

"Feelings?" I scoffed. "For what? You?"

Ouch. That came out worse than I had expected.

The brightness in Astrid's eyes faded, and she straightened herself out and tucked some hair behind her ear, turning back toward the front of the class. "Oh … yeah, I was actually just, you know … talking about your feelings for … how boring this class is."

Fuck, I screwed up.

I turned back to the front and rubbed my arm. "You know how I feel about this class …"

"Do I?" she whispered.

I opened and closed my mouth a handful of times, then nodded. "The same way you do."

"Oh, I don't think so …" Astrid tapped her fingers. "You don't know how I feel."

Our gazes met for a moment, until we both looked away at the same time. I dropped my eyes to the textbook and stared at the pages with a handful of equations that I had learned last night, but seemed to forget about since Astrid had walked into the room.

"If you don't want to get coffee again, it's okay," she said, playing with her fingers.

"I do," I said. "But we shouldn't."

"Why not?"

"Frasier."

She shifted in her seat uncomfortably. "He doesn't have to know."

"He's one of my best friends."

"So?"

"So, I'm not going to do that to him."

"He had no problem doing it to you."

"What's that mean?" I asked.

"You know what it means," she said, spitting my words back at me.

Frasier knew that I liked her—that *all* the guys in The Crew liked her, except maybe Rush, as I didn't quite know what he was thinking most days—and still decided to make a move on her in a romantic way.

Fuck Frasier.

"You want to get coffee tomorrow?" I asked. "We can go."

Astrid peered back at me, eyes wide. "Really?"

"Yes."

"Just us … by ourselves?"

"Just us."

Underneath the table, she pressed her legs together. My dick twitched again inside my pants as I thought about how her mouth had felt around it this morning. I peered over at her, gaze dropping to her lips. She was such a good girl sometimes, a brat at other times.

I leaned closer to her and dropped my voice. "Only if you're a good girl for me."

A smirk crossed her face. "And if I'm not?"

"If you're not," I murmured, gently brushing my fingers over her exposed skin, "then we won't get coffee anymore together."

Suddenly, all the mischief was gone from her eyes. "How do I be a good girl for you?" she asked.

"You can start by"—I leaned my elbow on the table and moved toward her, tucking some hair behind her ear—"crawling underneath our table."

One moment, she stared at me through wide eyes from above the table, and then the next, she was underneath it, tugging on my belt. I tensed and looked around to make sure that nobody was watching.

Holy fuck, I wasn't expecting her to actually—

She pulled out my cock and wrapped her lips around my head. "Am I a good girl, Cairo?" she murmured, wetting it with her mouth. "Tell me I'm a good girl." She sucked more and more of my dick into her mouth until she reached the base and choked softly.

When she came back up for air, my dick and her lips were covered in spit.

"Tell me I'm a good girl. Please, tell me I'm a good—"

I laced my hand into her hair and guided her back down onto my cock. "You're a good girl, baby. You're such a good girl for me."

CHAPTER NINETEEN

ASTRID

DIYA SAT cross-legged on my bed with a textbook on her lap. "Did you see Sakura's belly in History today?" She tapped her pen on the pages, the afternoon sun flooding into the room. "She's so petite that it's kinda obvious she's pregnant."

We were *supposed* to be doing homework, but did we ever when we were together?

"I know, right? But who can blame her? She's dating Mr. Avery."

"Avery?!" Diya explained. "The hot Literature professor?! That's who got her pregnant?!"

"How did you not know that? Oh, right. I forgot that you've been too busy with those extra tutoring sessions with your step-daddy." I stifled a giggle and shot her a wink. "You know with tits *that* nice, you're going to end up pregnant by a teacher next."

After narrowing her eyes at me, she shoved me. "I will not."

"Famous last words."

"Astrid!" she exclaimed. "He's my stepdad!"

"Your hot stepdad." I lay back on the bed, pretending like I was reminiscing about being in his class before when I had only ever met him at her house. "You know I'm a sucker for hands, and he has a nice pair of them. Don't you ever imagine them squeezing your—"

"Okay, that's enough!" Diya shouted, cheeks reddening. She slammed her book closed.

"Gonna go get some extra help?" I asked, eyeing the time on my phone. "He's probably still at school, waiting for you to slip into his classroom, slide up onto his desk, and tell him to eat your pussy."

Diya pushed her books into her backpack and glared. "Excuse me while I gag at that thought."

"The only thing you're going to gag on is his huge cock."

"You're the absolute worst," she murmured, but there was a smirk inching onto her lips.

While I might be able to hide that I'd fucked her brother, she couldn't hide anything from me. She was an open book, and I loved to read. *Fuck, that sounds like something in a cheesy romance novel.*

"Anyway ..." Diya started. "He's actually cooking dinner tonight, and I really want a taste."

I dramatically rolled my eyes at her. "Oh my God. Cooking, huh? Is that what you're calling it now? Shall that be our code word in case we ever need to talk about your sexy stepdaddy in front of your brother?"

The sound of the front door slamming echoed through the house, followed by the thud of heavy footsteps that belonged to the one and only Arch.

Diya smirked and tossed her backpack over her shoulder. "Saved just in time," she said.

A couple of moments later, my door swung open, and Arch glared at me from the hallway. His dark hair was tousled, his jaw clenched and sharp. He crossed his arms over his chest and drew his tongue over his teeth.

"What do you want?" I asked him.

"Diya, don't you have a home?" Arch growled. "Leave."

"Diya does not have to leave."

"Yes, she fucking does," Arch snapped, his gaze still on me. "Because we have to talk."

"Talk?" I asked, sitting up on the bed. "About what?"

"Diya, leave. Now."

Diya shot me an amused look, mouthing something about how I deserved this for putting her through hell about her stepdad. She walked past Arch and stepped into the hallway. "Have fun. See you tomorrow, *slut*."

I narrowed my eyes at Arch. "Bye, Diya."

As soon as the front door closed, Arch slammed mine shut and stalked toward me, his gaze low. I didn't move a muscle because I refused to let him believe I was scared of him or that I cared at all about him.

"You're lying about Frasier," he said at the foot of my bed.

"No, I'm not."

"You're not dating that asshole."

"Yes, I am."

"Bullshit," he growled. "The only one who believes that shit is Calix."

"Seems like you believe it, too, with how jealous you've been."

Arch grabbed my ankle and yanked me across the bed toward him. My textbooks slipped off the bed and dropped onto the ground. I grabbed on to the mattress in an attempt not to fall off the damn bed, but Arch pulled me right off it.

I landed on my ass with a thud. "What is your problem?!"

"I'm not jealous," he growled from above me.

I rubbed my backside. "You sure about that? Because it seems—"

Before I could say another word, Arch pushed his thumb between my lips and into my mouth. My eyes widened, and I shut up really quick, my mouth wrapping around his finger almost instinctively.

"It doesn't matter who you date or who you say you're dating," he said, crouching down until we were face-to-face. He tilted his head to the side, his gaze dropping from my eyes to my lips, then further down to my tits.

Right as I thought he was about to spit something else out at me, he pulled his thumb out of my mouth and smacked me on the cheek. Heat coursed through my body, and I stared up at him through wide eyes, taken aback.

"All you want is someone's cock, don't you?" he asked, snatching my chin. "Stick out your tongue."

Instead of fighting him, I stuck out my tongue. He spit into my mouth, then shoved four of his fingers into it.

"You need cock and a good, hard fuck. Frasier's too vanilla to fuck you the way you need. Frasier can't fuck you the way that I can."

"Is that a promise?" I said, voice muffled by his fingers. Spit dribbled down my chin.

"A vow, Hellcat."

CHAPTER TWENTY

ASTRID

ARCH BENT me over the bed and shoved my skirt down to my ankles. I stared back at him, debating whether I wanted to make a break for it to piss him off or to let him take me.

He yanked his shirt over his head, and in the mirror behind him, I saw scars decorating his muscular tan back. My pussy tightened before he even thrust into it when I saw how the sunlight flooded into the room and bounced off his skin.

God, he is so ho—

Arch slammed into me and took a fistful of my hair in his hand. "Fucking bitch." He pulled me up to him and ripped off my top, his hands all over my body. "You *need* me to treat you like the dirty little whore you are."

"I don't need—"

Before I could finish my sentence, I heard the front door open. "Astrid?"

"Fuck!" I said. "They're home already?!"

Footsteps began ascending the stairs.

"Arch! You have to stop," I exclaimed, grasping the bedsheets in my fists. "Please!"

I stared at the door in horror, waiting for Dad to open it and see his stepson fucking his daughter—and not in a nice way either! Arch had been absolutely wrecking every single part of my body, and I was sure that I looked … *used.*

"You have to hide," I whispered, heart pounding.

"Who am I hiding from?" he growled into my ear, one hand around the front of my throat as he ruthlessly pounded into me. "Huh, Hellcat? Who am I hiding from? Your dad? What's he going to do to me?"

My pussy tightened around Arch, and I whimpered out. After seeing all those scars on his back, I knew that not many people stood a chance against him. Out of all the members of The Crew, he was definitely the most psychotic.

"Astrid!" Dad called from down the hall, his footsteps becoming louder.

"Please, Arch," I bargained. "I'll do anything."

He smirked against my neck. "Anything, hmm? Fine."

Instead of pulling out of me, like I'd thought he would, he turned me toward my closet and bucked his hips forward, shoving me toward the door. I moved quickly, his cock deep inside me at all times. If he wasn't going to stop, then we both had to hide. And fast.

I yanked the closet door open and shuffled inside, pushing clothes out of the way and pressing myself up against the wall. Arch stepped in behind me and shut the door, his hands immediately back on my hips, thrusting in and out and in and out.

Tightening around it, I pushed my fingers against the wall until they turned white. My tits were smashed up against my clothes, my head to the side so I could look back and make sure the closet door wasn't open a smidgen.

Arch pulled my hips back so my upper body came off the wall just a bit, and then he slid his hands up my belly to my tits and squeezed. Hard. I clenched around him and bit my lip to hold back a moan.

God, this is so, so, so wrong!

"These fucking tits are mine," he growled into my ear.

He pulled out of me and twirled me around so I faced him, tugging one leg up in the air and shoving his big, fat cock back into me. He captured one of my nipples into his mouth and bit down hard, sucking and sucking and sucking.

"Arch," I whispered. "It hurts!"

"You fucking love it," he murmured against me, his voice quieter than it had been. He moved his mouth up my tit and sucked on the skin so hard that it would definitely leave a mark. "Your pussy is so tight; it's about to snap off my cock."

Just then, my bedroom door opened, and I slapped a hand over my mouth to stop my whimper. Arch thrust into me harder and faster, the sound completely audible and wet. So, so, so wet.

"Astrid?" Dad called. "You home?"

"Fuck," I whispered into my hand, the pleasure too much. "Fuck!"

Arch moved over to my other breast, capturing my nipple and biting down this time. I clenched around him and dug my fingernails into his muscular shoulder, my toes curling. He pulled back on it, then released it, letting my tits bounce together.

"Tell your dad how much of a slut you are," he whispered against my chest.

"I'm a slut," I murmured quietly, the pleasure too much.

"Louder."

"Astrid?" Dad called again. "Your car is out front, and your keys are on the counter."

I pressed my lips together and shook my head at Arch, but he took my tit in his mouth again and bit down even harder, this time causing me pain.

Then he pulled back just as hard and smacked me on the mouth. "Say it."

"I'm a slut," I cried softly. "Arch, please ..."

"She's not here?" Arch's mom said from what sounded like the hallway. "I can't find Archie boy either."

Arch growled at the nickname and pinned me to the wall with

his hand around my neck. He placed his forehead against mine, picking me up with both arms now, and slammed into my pussy as deep as he could get.

I cried out into his mouth in pure pleasure, wave after wave of ecstasy rushing through my body. My pussy clenched on his dick repeatedly, and he grunted into my mouth, his warm cum spilling deep into my cunt.

"Maybe they're downstairs," Dad said to Arch's mom.

Once the door closed and I finally came down from my orgasm, I pushed Arch away from me. His cum dripped down my thighs, coating my legs. He leaned against the wall, peering back at me with his eyes glazed over, lids half shut.

"Just what you needed, Hellcat, wasn't it?"

"No," I said, lying through my teeth and pulling open the door. "Better luck next time."

CHAPTER TWENTY-ONE

ARCH

I GLARED at Astrid's retreating figure and stuffed my cock, still wet with her juices, back into my jeans. That one had a goddamn fucking mouth on her. From the moment she had told me that she was dating Frasier, I had known it was a lie.

But that didn't make me any less pissed.

Once I redressed and grabbed all my shit out of Astrid's room, I followed the sound of voices down the stairs to the kitchen. Astrid leaned over the kitchen island. Her dad was at the stove, cooking a steak on the skillet. Mom sat across from Astrid on a stool, watching her new husband.

"What do you think, kiddo?" her dad asked Astrid, back still turned.

"When is it?" Astrid asked, nose scrunched.

"Next month."

Astrid peered at Mom and plastered a small smile. "Maybe. Let me think about it."

"Think about what?" I asked, stepping into the kitchen.

Astrid's dad peered over his shoulder, offering me a half smile. "A cruise. Wanna go?"

"No," I said. *And neither does Astrid, it appears.*

"Come on, Archie," Mom said, hopping up from the stool and walking over to me. She wrapped her small arm around mine and smiled up at me. "I think it will be good to get away once you graduate. You know, to celebrate."

"Celebrate what?"

"You graduating school."

"Not interested. I have plans."

"Please think about it," Mom said. "For me."

I gazed down at her, spotting her wedding ring glimmering underneath the overhead light. It looked perfect, except for …

I furrowed my brow, tugged my arm away from hers, and pulled her hand closer to my face.

"Why the fuck are your knuckles scraped?" I asked.

Mom pulled her hand away from mine and walked back to the stool. "Oh, don't wor—"

My gaze snapped to Astrid's dad. "What the fuck did you do to her?"

His eyes widened. "I didn't do—"

"Don't give me excuses," I snarled, lunging toward him.

Astrid stepped between us and shoved me back a few feet. "What is your problem?!"

"Archie …" Mom took Astrid's place. "You know Oscar wouldn't do that."

"No, I don't," I said between clenched teeth. "Why are your knuckles scraped?"

Astrid's dad and my mom shared a look, and then Astrid's dad turned back to the steak cooking on the stove.

"I told you that you shouldn't hide it from him, honey. He's bound to find out one way or another."

Mom blew out a breath and set her hands on my chest. "Promise you won't be mad?"

I glared at the back of Astrid's dad, then Astrid herself. "No."

"I ran into your father yesterday," she said.

My gaze dropped down to her, blood boiling. "You. What?"

"I was out shopping, bringing groceries to my car, and he—"

I stepped past her and stormed toward the front door. "I'm going to kill him."

Before I could race around all of Redwood to find that fucker, Mom grabbed my wrist and tugged me backward. "You're not going to go anywhere near him. I don't know what he'll do to you if he finds you."

"He should be worried about what I'll do to him when I find him," I growled.

Cut him up into tiny little pieces. Feed him to his awful dogs. Decorated his living room with his blood, like he used to do with us. That fucker didn't deserve to live, and he knew that. That was why he targeted her and not me.

If he showed his face around me, I'd murder him with my own two hands. I wasn't that little kid anymore that he could push around. I had the same fucking fire inside of me for him that he'd had with us while I was growing up.

"Please, Archie," Mom pleaded, using her soft voice on me.

I flared my nostrils and turned around toward her and the others. Astrid stared at me through wide eyes. I pursed my lips and gritted my teeth, wishing that she weren't in the room. I didn't want her overhearing our business. It didn't matter to her, and she shouldn't care.

"Fine." I averted my gaze from Astrid. "I'll drop it."

Still turned toward the food, Astrid's dad cleared his throat. "Leave me alone with Arch for a second, okay, honey? You too, Astrid."

Astrid and Mom both left the room, but not before Astrid shot me a glare for trying to attack her dad.

She mumbled, "Watch it," to me, as if I were afraid of her, then followed Mom up the stairs.

After adding some more butter to the pan, her dad turned around, one hand around the skillet's handle, masterfully tossing the steak in butter. "I would never lay a hand on your mother, Arch. I'm not like your father."

"Just because she trusts you doesn't mean I do."

I did trust him. But I'd seen the way people who appeared nice could snap so easily.

"I know," he said, peering out the door to make sure the girls weren't listening in, and then he lowered his voice. "But I wouldn't be angry with you if you did go after him, as long as nobody knows it's you and as long as you don't put yourself, your mom, or Astrid in harm's way."

I raised my brows, then furrowed them, still not sure of his motives. "That all?"

"If you need help—"

A low, empty chuckle escaped my mouth. "What's an old man like you going to do?"

"An old man?" he asked with a more lighthearted chuckle than mine. "Is that how you see me?"

Arms crossed, I turned away from him. "I don't need your help with that."

"There's something you do need my help with?" he asked. "What is it?"

After a moment of debating whether I wanted to tell him or not, I decided that if he would help me with this, then maybe I could begin to trust him with Mom, maybe he could be useful with dealing with Dad.

"Calix's mom is sick," I said. "Cancer. Find her a better doctor who can fix it."

"Cancer's not that simple, Arch."

"You want me to trust you?" I asked. "Then do what I ask."

Then I stormed out of the kitchen and through the front door, slamming it behind me.

CHAPTER TWENTY-TWO

ASTRID

I SAT IN THE DUNKIN' parking lot, tapping my fingers on the steering wheel and bobbing my head to the music playing throughout the car. Morning light flooded into the car, casting a golden hue on my fingers.

Cairo had better show up.

If he didn't, then I would be sitting here alone until school started, looking like an idiot. And there was no doubt in my mind that if any of the other Crew members saw me here alone, waiting for him, then they'd make fun of me for it.

Especially Arch.

My hand tightened around the wheel. *Fucking Arch.*

Chest tightening, I glared out the windshield. While he had always been psychotic—that had been established multiple times—I had never seen him turn into such a vile animal as when he saw his mom's scraped knuckles. Lunging at Dad like that?!

He had quickly—*and wrongly*—assumed that *my* dad would do something like that. Dad was a doctor who healed people, for fuck's sake!

The only time I had seen him remotely violent was after he

found out that someone murdered Mom. After that, he had turned into such a quiet guy, barely speaking a word to anyone, barely *looking* at anyone else, until he met Arch's mom. There was actually some light in his eyes now, and he wouldn't dare think about hurting her.

So, I didn't know why that fucker had thought he would.

Fuzziness from the radio filled the car, and I switched the station, peering into my rearview mirror to see the main road. *Where the hell is Cairo?* This was the same time we had met here yesterday morning. *Is he really not going to show?*

Mind wandering back to Arch, I gritted my teeth.

What had driven him to make such a wrong assumption? From what I had gathered from their conversation, Arch's father was a monster, and Arch was protective of his mom. Had he hurt them both? For how long? What had he done?

Last night, Arch's eyes had been wild and filled with intense rage. So much hatred.

I blinked a few times, trying to push the thoughts away. I should've been focused on when Cairo was actually going to get here. My gaze cut to the clock on my dashboard. *Time is ticking.* But I couldn't get Arch out of my head.

The way he had looked at Dad … it was like he was barely holding himself together, like he was on the brink of losing it completely. And, damn, did I want to fix him. I mean, what girl wouldn't want to heal a broken, psychotic red flag of a man?

Obviously a sane one.

In my rearview mirror, I saw Cairo pulling into the Dunkin' parking lot. After pushing Arch from my mind, I sat up taller and straightened myself out. Despite Cairo thinking that Frasier and I were together, he'd actually shown up.

He pulled up next to me and looked over, a small smirk tugging at the corner of his lips, and then he nodded me over. I smiled back, both my heart and my pussy racing at the thought of him having me again and again and again. Every morning before school.

Instead of slipping into his car, I stayed in mine, a bit of my brattiness coming out this morning. But something about Cairo … made me feel so comfortable, like I could be a brat with him and he would punish me.

But not in a way that Arch did. Arch was violent and rough.

Cairo was … *stern.*

Warmth exploded through my pussy, and I matched his stare through the window. The cute, shy guy in my Physics class clenched his jaw and stepped out of his car, shutting the door behind him. He walked over to my side and leaned down to look into the car.

I rolled down the window and smiled sweetly. "Yes?"

"Get out of your car, Astrid."

To hide a smirk, I pressed my lips together. "And if I don't?"

A low, sadistic chuckle left his mouth. "You'll see what happens when you disobey."

Fuck! My pussy pulsed uncontrollably.

"Get. Out. Of the car."

While I so desperately wanted to brat it out and see what this punishment really was, the tone in his voice made me want to obey. I grabbed the door handle, then stopped myself, trying to regain control of my body.

Stupid body betrayal syndrome!

Cairo pulled the door open and took my hand. "Come with me."

"No," I whispered, standing. I met him eye to eye; his gaze was so intense that I had to look away.

"No?" he hummed, moving toward his car. "You want to be a brat with me, but you can't this morning, can you?" He opened his passenger door for me and stepped to the side, allowing for me to sit if I wanted. "Why is that?"

"Because," I said, pussy pulsing. I didn't know what I wanted from him right now—someone hard but stern or someone soft but stern. I wanted all sides of him to see which one was my favorite. "Because …"

"Hmm?" he murmured, pushing some hair behind my ear, his mouth dangerously close to mine, lips millimeters away. His warm, minty breath fanned my face, making me feel things in places that I shouldn't. "Do you want to be my good girl today?"

I stared up into his dark brown eyes, heart racing, opening and closing my mouth.

"Is that what you want?" he asked again, his gaze softening. "Is that who you need to be?"

I furrowed my brow and pressed my thighs together. "Yes," I whispered.

"Then sit," he ordered. "We can go for a drive."

"A drive?" I repeated, suddenly lost for words, in a headspace that seemed so … calm.

"Sit."

Not having to be told again, I sat down in the passenger seat. He buckled me in and walked around the car to the driver's seat, sitting beside me.

He swiped his thumb across my jaw, making me look at him. "You're going to be my good girl today, aren't you, Astrid?"

"Yes," I whispered. "I'll be your good girl."

CHAPTER TWENTY-THREE

ASTRID

WHAT. The. Fuck?

I stared with wide eyes as Cairo pulled into the driveway—*gated* driveway, to be exact—of the biggest house I had ever seen. *House* wasn't even the right word for how huge the mansion and the entire estate was.

My heart raced so hard that I could feel it beating against my rib cage. I peeked over at Cairo, who continued to drive up the hedge-lined driveway, which was longer than my street, toward the mansion.

How is he so unbothered?! Is this normal for him?!

"Where are we going?" I asked, shuffling my feet.

"I told you that we were going on a drive."

"But … where is this? What is this place?"

He looked at me, one hand on the steering wheel. "This is my house."

What did his parents do for a living?! My dad was one of the top doctors in the state, and he didn't even earn this much money to have an estate this large. It almost didn't seem possible that this was someone's *house*.

"Oh," I whispered, heat growing between my legs. "What are we doing here?"

I didn't know why I was suddenly all shy with him. I had been a brat in the car when I thought I had the upper hand over him, when I thought that there was no way innocent little Cairo would *actually* bring me to his house to treat me how I needed.

After Cairo parked out front, a small smirk tugged at the corner of his lips. "You know why we're here, Astrid. This was what *you* wanted, wasn't it?"

"But we have school," I said.

Cairo placed his forearm on the center console and leaned closer to me, his brown eyes glowing underneath the sunlight. "First time skipping school?" he asked, his smirk turning into a small, innocent smile. "Me too."

Warmth flooded through my chest now, making me feel all gushy and gooey and … God, he was only supposed to be the cute, innocent guy in The Crew that I could take advantage of, and now he was making me feel all these weird things. If he was—

Mid-thought, I jumped up when someone suddenly opened my door.

"Miss, right this way," a tall man in a suit said, holding out his hand for me.

What the hell is this?! Talk about old money …

Cairo didn't seem bothered or, you know, like, amazed by any of this. I peered over at him to see him stepping out of the car himself and handing off the keys to someone else. I scurried out of the car, feeling so out of place here, and Cairo took my hand from the man.

"Do you actually live here?" I asked. "Like *here*, here?"

With my hand engulfed in his, Cairo led me up the center stairs to the double-door entrance. "It's my grandparents' old house. Back in the day, they did something with oil. My parents inherited it. Anyway …"

Something with oil? Anyway? We can't just skip past that entire part ...

But Cairo didn't seem like he wanted to talk about it. He might live like a king—no, like an emperor—but he definitely didn't tell anyone about it or even show off his money at school, like a lot of filthy rich students did.

"Where are your parents now?" I asked, spotting several cars in the driveway.

"Probably in Europe somewhere. I don't know."

Wow, rich people problems ...

"Oh," I murmured, stepping into the house and trying to play it off like these enormous rooms were completely normal for me, like it didn't look like I was trash inside a golden castle.

If Cairo didn't want to talk about money, that was fine with me. I didn't care that much about it because we had come here for one thing.

"So, it's just us here?"

Cairo shut the door behind us and dropped his head to look at me through his brows, that innocent expression suddenly gone. He stepped closer to me, and I moved backward, heart racing and pussy pulsing.

"It's just us," he said.

"Oh, yeah?" I whispered, nipples so hard that they *hurt*.

When Cairo finally closed the distance between us, he wrapped one hand around the front of my neck. "Us and a couple of the staff," he murmured against my lips, his dark gaze locked on mine. "But I don't mind if they see you bent over the couch with my collar around this pretty little neck."

Holy fucking shit.

"Would you like that?" he asked.

A whimper left my mouth, and I pressed my legs together.

"Words, Astrid. I need you to use your words."

I clenched and nodded. "Yes, I would like that."

"Good girl," he praised, dipping his hand between my thighs. "That's my good girl."

He moved his fingers in effortless circles against my clit through my pants, and my knees nearly buckled. Yesterday morning, he had been so rough with me as he pounded into my mouth, and now he … was so soft.

"Wait here," he said, releasing me. "By the time I return, all your clothes should be off, and you should be bent over this couch." Cairo stepped backward, his gaze soft but stern. "Do you understand, Astrid?"

I looked over my shoulder at the room we had just walked through, knowing that there had to be more staff. Wouldn't they see me?

"Do. You. Understand?" he asked again, snatching my nipples through my shirt.

Pleasure exploded through my body, and I moaned softly. "Yes, I understand."

"Tell me what you're going to do."

"I'm going to be naked and bent over the couch by the time you come back."

He squeezed on my nipples. "And if you are, you'll be rewarded, understand?"

I stared up into those brown eyes that had always, always, always been so innocent. "Yes, I understand. I'll be naked and bent over the couch by the time that you come back, Cairo. I promise."

CHAPTER TWENTY-FOUR

CAIRO

WITH A COLLAR DRAPED across my palm, I walked back into the room where I had left Astrid to find her completely naked and bent over the couch for me. My dick stiffened inside my jeans, and I bit back a grunt.

Holy fuck.

I expected to have to punish her for not listening, for being a brat, but it really did seem like she needed to be treated like a good girl today. All this time, since that party, I had thought she wanted it rough, thought she *liked it* rough. That was how everyone else treated her.

And maybe she did, but not with me and not all the time.

When I approached her, she tensed, her back toward me and her ass on full display.

I gathered her hair to the side and leaned over her naked body, my lips against her ear and my bulge against her backside. "What a good girl you are for me, Astrid."

She whimpered softly, her tits grazing against the couch cushion. "Please …"

"Please, what?"

"Please, collar me." She pressed her thighs together. "I need it."

Fingertips skimming down her back, I wrapped my arm around her hip and sank my hand between her thighs. Her cunt was dripping with her juices, *with anticipation*. I pushed my fingers between her pussy lips and found her clit. Her knees buckled, but I held her in place.

"How badly do you need my collar?" I murmured.

"Really badly," she cried, gently bucking her cunt against my hand. "Please, Cairo."

"You have to show me," I ordered, grinding my bulge against her ass. It was becoming harder by the second, and I was becoming too desperate to really wait for her to show me anything. "Prove how much you want it."

But patience and delayed gratification were always rewarded. *Always*.

"I'll do anything," she said in a breath, peering back at me, her eyes in a daze.

She reached behind herself and found my bulge with her hand, stroking me through my jeans, as if she *needed* it. And, God, did I want to give it to her.

My dick throbbed. "Turn around and touch yourself for me."

She widened her eyes, as if she was surprised by my request, yet she turned around and sat on the edge of the couch, staring up at me through her lashes. "You want me to … to …" She dropped her gaze to her pussy, then looked back up.

I dropped to my knees and placed the collar on the cushion next to her. "Touch yourself."

After a small whimper, she spread her legs. I placed my hands on her knees to move them apart even more and guided her feet up onto the couch. She pushed a hand between her legs and rubbed her clit, her brow furrowed in pleasure.

"Cairo," she whined, moving her fingers faster and faster. "Please, collar me."

I peppered kisses up her inner thigh as she pleasured herself, and when I reached her cunt, I gently pushed two fingers inside her. Her legs jerked upward, and she moaned. I found her G-spot and massaged it.

"You're doing so well, baby," I murmured, my breath on her cunt. "Can you come all over my fingers for me?" I placed another wet kiss on her inner thigh, grinding my dick against the couch. "If you do, I'll buckle the collar around your throat."

When the words left my mouth, she clenched around me and moved her fingers faster against her clit. She held her breath, cheeks becoming flushed and body tensing. I pushed her left knee to the side to climb up her body, fastening my mouth to her nipple and sucking.

She sank her fingers into the cushions and cried out in pleasure, her pussy pulsing around my fingers and her legs trembling uncontrollably. Her eyes were shut, her brows knitted, her mouth ajar.

Fuck, she's so sexy.

"Am I a good girl for you?" she cried through the orgasm. "Please, tell me that I'm a good girl."

"You're a good girl," I murmured, keeping my fingers buried inside her. "My good girl."

For another few moments, she rode out the orgasm, then slowly fluttered her eyes open and stared up at me through a haze. I pulled my fingers out of her pussy and grabbed the collar, unfastening it.

"Turn around and bend over the couch again," I ordered.

Astrid twisted onto her stomach and pushed herself up onto her knees, leaning her upper body against the couch back, pulling her hair to the side. Her legs were spread, her pussy glistening with her juices.

I tugged myself out of my jeans and positioned myself at her entrance. I had never been inside of anyone before, didn't have experience like the others in The Crew did, but I had a craving for Astrid, one so primal that I pushed all my nerves to the side and became another man when I was with her.

"God, please," she cried. "I haven't been able to stop thinking about you being inside—"

Before she could finish her sentence, I slammed myself into her and wrapped the collar around her throat. Her pussy clamped down onto my cock, harder than it had with just my fingers, and I began pumping in and out of her.

"Oh my God!" she said, clutching on to the couch for support. "Oh my fucking God!"

As steady as I could, I buckled the collar around her throat and grabbed her by it to thrust her toward me. Her tits bounced against the couch back, her moans getting lost in the empty house.

My dick slid in and out of her with ease, my balls becoming heavy with pressure.

"You're doing so well for me," I murmured into her ear, the words barely audible. I sank my arm around her waist and found her clit with my fingers, rubbing it in a steady rhythm. "So well. So, so well ..."

"Call me your good girl."

"You're my good girl, baby." I took her hand and placed it against her collar with mine guiding it across the leather. "This collar means you belong to me, *my property*, my good girl. Only mine."

"Cairo"—she dragged my name out—"if you don't stop, you're going to make me—"

A low grunt left my mouth, and I buried myself as deep into her as I could get and came inside my good girl's tight pussy.

CHAPTER
TWENTY-FIVE

FRASIER

I LEANED against the entrance to the cafeteria, chatting up some cheerleader. I didn't know her name, but she was cute, I guessed. Though she hadn't stopped talking probably since middle school.

"Mmhmm," I murmured to her, keeping her attention just enough while I scanned the hallways for any sight of *her.* I brushed my hand against the girl's hip and nodded along. "Is that right? That's crazy."

"Are you even listening?" she asked, crossing her arms.

My lips curled into a smug smirk, and I looked back at her. "Of course I am."

"Doesn't seem like it."

"Chelsea told Nicole, who told Allie about the D you got in History," I said.

She giggled and looped her arm around mine.

God, sometimes, women were so simple. *Just pay attention to them, buy them food, and indulge in their drama when they tell you about it. Too fucking easy.*

After another moment of lingering by the door, expecting

Astrid to finally walk down the halls because I'd seen her car in the lot last period, I pulled my gaze away from the girl on my arm and narrowed my eyes down the hall.

Cairo hadn't been in school either all day. *Very* unlike him.

I swore, if they had been—didn't matter. I wasn't waiting for Astrid anyway.

I was here for someone else.

A second later, Cairo turned the corner with Astrid following right after him, a small smile on her face.

And what was that around her neck? Was that a collar? That asshole had put a collar on her? When? This morning? That was what they had been doing all this time?!

If Calix saw this ...

"All right, I'll see you. Go wait for me in there," I said to the girl, shrugging out of her grasp and gesturing for her to meet me in the cafeteria. Once she was gone, I headed down the hall toward Cairo. "Someone's walking in late."

"Class ran a bit over," Cairo said, scratching the back of his head and lying straight through his teeth.

Astrid stared up at me through huge eyes, tugging at the collar around her neck, as if she wanted me to see, *wanted* me to say something to her. I relaxed my clenched jaw as best as I could and grabbed her hand.

"Good. I'll take my girl from here then," I murmured, pulling her down the hall.

"Frasier," she said, shuffling after me out Redwood's double doors, "where are we going?"

"You already missed half the day. Who cares about the rest?"

"I do!"

"Should've thought about that before you left with Cairo this morning," I said, trying to keep my voice steady. I didn't have feelings for Astrid like that, but something inside me had really snapped when I saw her leaving with him this morning.

"Left with Cairo? I didn't even get to school this morning," she said.

"I know. You went to *get coffee* with him earlier, didn't you?"

When we reached my car, she released my hand and arched a brow at me. "How did you know that? Stalking me now, Crane?" A smirk crossed her lips, and she rocked back onto her heels. "I thought that wasn't your style."

"Stalking you?" I repeated in a low chuckle. "You wish."

"Oh, yeah? Then how'd you know that I was with him, getting coffee this morning?"

I opened up the passenger door for her and stepped closer, tilting my head down slightly. "You know, babe, there is a thing called driving on one of the busiest roads leading to Redwood, where the Dunkin' you were at this morning is located. Hate to break it to you."

"You know, *babe*," she said, her sassiness finally coming back, "there's a thing called that same busy road isn't one that *you* should be on in the morning. Your house is in the complete opposite direction."

"How do you know where my house is?" I asked.

Astrid opened and closed her mouth a handful of times, and I seized her waist, pulling her flush against my body, my lips millimeters from hers.

"Hmm? Who's the stalker now?"

She stared up at me, cheeks reddening, but gaze never leaving mine. "You wish."

"Baaaabe," I said, dragging the word out, pushing her up against the car. My gaze dropped down to her full lips, and I swallowed hard, my throat suddenly dry. I swiped the pad of my thumb across her lips. "Don't start with me."

After sucking in a sharp breath, she looked from eye to eye, the sassiness leaving her. I stared back, wishing for her to continue the banter, but, God, how I desperately wanted her to be more than just a—no. No, I only wanted her to make Hazel jealous.

Yeah, that's right. Hazel was one of the reasons The Crew had been at that party. I had dragged them there, flirted with every girl to get some reaction out of her, and then … then Calix brought Astrid over to our section of the house and that was it.

That was fucking it. It had been over.

Over for only that night.

"If you want to make this"—I gestured between her and me—"believable, you can't be hanging out with Cairo. Don't want Calix to think you're so easy that he can have you too. He likes the chase."

Now? This was a mutually beneficial thing.

She used me to make Calix jealous. I used her to make Hazel jealous.

It definitely wasn't anything more than that.

CHAPTER TWENTY-SIX

ASTRID

"YOU DIDN'T BRING me here to kill me, did you?" I asked, staring out into the forest.

Frasier had parked his car in the same place he had when he brought me to school the other morning, where we … had fucked.

Memories of that morning flooded through my mind, and I pressed my thighs together.

A low chuckle left his mouth, and he exited the car. "No, I just like it here."

"Here?" I repeated, following after him. "You like it *here*?"

"Why is that so surprising to you?"

"Because you just seem more like a downtown guy, where all the hustle and bustle are …" *And all the cheerleaders.* I leaned against his car and closed my eyes, enjoying the sounds of nature around me. "It's so quiet here."

"It's not quiet," he said. "If you listen closely, there's a stream to the east. It's a bit of a hike, but there's a small waterfall about thirty minutes southeast of here too. Maybe when it's warmer, I'll take you."

Butterflies spread through my chest, and I had to remind myself that this was all fake.

We wouldn't even make it as a fake couple until late spring, early summer.

"Maybe," I hummed. "But I don't hike."

"You'd hike with me."

I opened my eyes and glanced over at him. "Oh, yeah? What makes you so sure?"

"Babe," he murmured, leaning against the car beside me, his body heat radiating off him in waves and making me hot in places that I really shouldn't be. Yet I couldn't stop thinking about the last time that he'd brought me out here. "I can't give away my secrets."

After crossing my arms, I faced him. "That's because you don't have any secrets."

He mirrored me, crossing his arms and craning his head down at me. "Is that right?"

"Mmhmm."

His gaze traveled across my face, from eye to eye, then down to my lips, lingering for a moment more than it should've. I nervously licked my lips, heart pounding heavily inside my chest.

Stay in control, Astrid! This is fake. F-A-K-E!!!!

"You're coming with me tonight to the race," he said when his hazy gaze met mine.

"Race? What race?" I asked, trying to snap out of the trance this man had me in.

No wonder why he was a player. I knew that we were fake dating, and he still made me feel like the most important, most desired girl in the entire world. God, what was wrong with me?! If I let this continue …

"Rush is racing," he murmured, releasing his crossed arms and pulling me closer, his hands on my hips.

"Racing? Like … cars?" I whispered, heat exploding through my body.

"No, racing ice cream trucks."

I playfully rolled my eyes. "God, you're so sassy today."

"I'm not sassy today."

A small giggle escaped my mouth. "Yes, you are."

"It's not a today thing. I'm like this all the time."

I arched my brow. "No, you're not. You're a flirt all the time."

"Look at you, putting me in a box," he murmured. "Stereotyping."

"Look at you, the player using metaphors and big words."

An unreadable expression crossed Frasier's face. "Player?"

I poked him hard in the stomach, trying to lighten the mood that had suddenly dropped out of nowhere. "You know that you're one."

Frasier stepped back and stuffed his hands into his pockets, leaning against the car and finally looking away from me and into the forest. "Yeah, yeah. So, I'll pick you up at ten tonight. The race starts at eleven thirty."

Pausing, I stared at him for a few moments and then glanced at the ground. *Did I say something that he didn't like? Why the sudden change in mood?* It was a complete one-eighty from just a moment ago.

"Who's going to be there?" I asked.

"Me," he said, jaw clenched. "Doesn't matter who else."

Rush hated me. Would he want me at his races? Probably not.

Was that the sole reason why I wanted to go? Of course.

"Okay, I'll be ready at ten then."

After a moment, Frasier lifted his gaze back toward me, the harshness suddenly gone and replaced with those curious, flirty, familiar eyes. "Make it nine." He took my hips again in his large hands and pulled me closer. "For me?"

Fuck! How does he do it?!

Frasier tilted his head to the side, his nose gently brushing against mine. I swallowed hard, breathing in his minty breath, my heart racing.

"Nine," I repeated in a breathy whisper.

"We can grab dinner beforehand."

I sucked in a sharp breath and swallowed hard as his fingers rubbed circles on my exposed skin. "Yeah, we can do that."

I peeked up at him, catching his gaze on my lips again. And we were so close ...

Kissing my *boyfriend* was normal, right? That was the most logical thing to do in a situation like this, wasn't it?! Except he wasn't really my boyfriend and I wasn't sure which of these feelings inside me were fake and which ones were real anymore.

Besides, I couldn't fall in love with one of the guys from The Crew. I wasn't even supposed to have a crush on any of them—*cough, cough, Calix*. But I was doing this because of Calix ... to make him jealous.

If I didn't practice kissing Frasier, how would it look real, right?

My heart pounded so hard that I could hear it in my ears. *Right?*

I lifted myself onto my tiptoes, our lips grazing against each other's. *Right.*

CHAPTER TWENTY-SEVEN

ASTRID

WHEN MY LIPS collided with Frasier's, butterflies bubbled up from my stomach. I placed my hands on his shoulders to hold myself up on my toes, heart racing inside my chest. Why did I feel like I was thirteen again and having my first kiss with Arch in my basement?

Frasier placed his hands on my hips, lifted me into the air, and sat me on his car.

I spread my legs and allowed him to come closer, my pussy exploding with pleasure. After moving my hands up his chest, I gently sank my fingers into his muscular shoulders, deepening the kiss.

He placed his hands on either side of my thighs, bending down and leaning closer. The faint scent of his cologne drifted through my nostrils, and I whimpered into his mouth.

God, what is wrong with me?

If it was fake, then why did it feel so real? Why was I getting butterflies and suddenly wanting to spill the tea to all my friends?! I couldn't tell them zilch, never mind that I was actually falling for one of the biggest players in school.

Or maybe a couple of them …

As I parted my lips, Frasier slipped his tongue into my mouth. I tilted my head to the side, moving my tongue against his. A low grunt left his mouth, making me even warmer between my thighs.

"Baby," he said, dragging it out into the kiss.

A low rumble of an engine drifted through my ears, but I couldn't care. I rested my hands behind me on his car, my lips dancing against his, eyes closed. The sound of the engine became louder and louder, until Frasier finally pulled away and looked up at the car pulling up to the side of the forest beside us.

I stared up at him through a haze, admiring how handsome he was.

"Astrid?" Ruby called.

After cursing under my breath, I looked up to see Diya and Ruby getting out of the car.

Thanks for ruining the moment! If they hadn't shown up, who knows what would've happened here with Frasier?

God, I am turning into such a slut.

"What are you guys doing here?" I asked, tucking some hair behind my ear and wiping spit off the corner of my mouth. I slid off the car and straightened myself out, barely able to look at my best friends.

"Someone skipped out on the first half of the day," Ruby said.

"And then your phone showed that you were in the middle of the woods, so we came to investigate in case you were …" Diya looked over at Frasier, then back at me. "You know, getting murdered."

"And you think *I'm* sassy," Frasier said into my ear, his minty breath fanning my neck.

My cheeks reddened, and I walked toward my friends. Diya wrapped her arm around mine, eyeing Frasier as if she didn't trust him. And honestly, she probably shouldn't. *I* shouldn't.

"I'll see you tonight," Frasier called, leaning against his car, huge arms crossed over his chest, just the sight making me feel things all over my body. His lips were curled into a small smirk. "Don't be late, babe."

Once I slipped into the backseat of Diya's car, I bit back my smile and tried to suppress all the *gross* feelings that I had for him. Diya and Ruby climbed into the front seat.

"You're actually dating him?!" Diya shouted once we made it a safe distance down the road and back toward Redwood.

I stared in the rearview mirror at Frasier's departing figure and tried to hold back a smile.

"No," I said, lost in my own world. "Just trying to make Ca—I mean, someone jealous."

Fuck, that was close.

"Who? Cairo?" Diya asked with a grin.

Ruby smirked at me through the rearview mirror. "*Definitely* Cairo."

"Maybe," I said, shooting her a playful glare.

Ruby looked over her shoulder from the passenger seat. "Going to the race tonight?"

"You know about it?"

"Of course," she hummed. "I'm going too."

"Since when?"

"Since now. We're going to make sure that *Cairo* is *really* jealous tonight."

CHAPTER TWENTY-EIGHT

ASTRID

THE SCENT of Ruby's hair spray and perfume filled Diya's bedroom. I stared into the mirror at Ruby, who twisted my hair back into a messy braid for tonight's race, then toward Diya, lying on her mattress on her stomach, kicking her legs back and forth, her gaze glued to her phone.

A small smile crawled onto her face, and I snickered.

"What are you up to, D?"

She cleared her throat and turned her phone over on the bed. "Nothing."

"Mmhmm," Ruby said, arching a brow into the mirror. "Sure you're not texting with ste—"

"Can you guys not?!" she hissed quietly. "Calix is still home."

"Still home?" I asked. "He's going out tonight?"

"Yeah, to the race tonight too. Probably to eat some girl's face off."

My chest tightened with jealousy. When I had passed his bedroom earlier, it had reeked of cologne, but I hadn't seen him. While I had thought he'd be there tonight, it seemed like Diya knew more about his attendance than I did.

"Ew," I murmured as Ruby gave a gentle tug on my hair. "Which girl?"

"Wouldn't you want to know?" Ruby murmured quietly to me.

"I don't know," Diya said, rolling onto her back and letting out a sigh. "He has so many."

I balled my hands into tight fists in my lap, my nails digging into the skin on my palms. *So many?* Who were they? How did she know? Did he have them over every night? Sleep with a different one every day?

"So many what?" someone asked from the hallway. "You talking about me?"

Diya hurled a pillow through the door, and then a moment later, Calix walked into the room with it in his large hands. His hair was tousled to the side, his stubble tracing his sharp jaw, and the light from the hallway was hitting all his tattoos just right …

Goddamn it! What is he looking so good for?!

Calix tossed the pillow at Diya, shooting me a smirk. "Ruby, Astrid, you girls going tonight?" While he mentioned Ruby's name, he didn't spare her a glance. His gaze was locked on to mine, eyes filled with mischief.

He already knew that I was going.

"Yep, we're going," Ruby said, tugging on my hair tighter.

Just as quickly as his gaze met mine, he turned back to his sister. "You going too?"

"No."

"She's busy studying," I said, desperate for his attention.

"You should be studying too," he said, but didn't look over. "Shouldn't she, Diya?"

I glared in his direction.

"I told her to," Diya said, back on her phone. "We have a big test coming up next week."

Calix looked back over at me, his smirk even wider. "The race isn't going to be any fun for you, Astrid. You should stay over tonight. I'm sure Diya could use some company."

Oh, so he could go flirt with every girl there?

"Diya's good. Busy actually, with more than just books," I added so she wouldn't worry about how much Calix was actually talking to me tonight. She could worry about if I was going to hint about her and her stepfather. Obviously, I would never, but she couldn't know about my crush. "Aren't you, Diya?"

Diya glared at me and jumped up, shooing her brother to the door. "Yes. Now get out."

After a moment of pushing him back into the hall, she slammed her door closed. Ruby held her hand out to me for an elastic, and I placed one into her palm.

"Don't worry, D. We're not going to tell your brother about your crush."

"He's not my crush," Diya said.

"*Sugar daddy* is more like it," I said playfully.

Diya hated it, but she loved me.

"There you go," Ruby said, grabbing the hair spray. "Now just ..."

Once she sprayed way too much hair spray on my head, I swiped my hand through the air, coughing, and moved closer to the mirror.

"You don't think this is going to fall out tonight? It's kinda—"

"With the amount of chemicals that I put on your head, no. But if it does, you'll look hot."

I listened to the sound of Diya's garage door opening and shot up from my seat in front of the vanity. *Calix is leaving already?! It is only seven o'clock. Where is he going at an hour like this, looking how he does?*

"I have to get home," I half lied. "Frasier is going to be picking me up soon."

Ruby gathered all her makeup supplies and shoved them into her bag. I grabbed my backpack and headed toward Diya's door, heart racing. I didn't know *why* I was reacting as I was, especially not after feeling all those things with Frasier earlier.

Diya followed us into the hall and through the kitchen, where her stepfather was drinking some whiskey and reading something on his phone. He peered up when we passed, his eyes lingering long on Diya.

"You sure you don't wanna come, D?" Ruby asked, stepping out.

Diya played with the doorknob and peered to the side. "No, I'm busy tonight."

"Well, your loss," Ruby hummed, looping her arm around mine. "No hot boys for you."

When her stepfather cleared his throat, Ruby tugged me down the front steps toward our cars. If there was one thing that I loved about Ruby, it was that she loved making guys jealous—of her, of her friends, it didn't matter.

And I had a feeling that tonight would be no different.

CHAPTER
TWENTY-NINE

CALIX

ENGINES ROARED THROUGHOUT THE NIGHT, rumbling beneath my feet. I leaned against Rush's car with my arms crossed over my chest and scanned the crowd. There must've been hundreds of people here, drinking and mingling before the race.

And yet I couldn't find Astrid.

Rush played around on the inside of the car, double-checking everything. I cleared my throat and tapped my shoe on the concrete.

Where is she?

She had left right after I did. I'd watched her peel out of my driveway through the rearview mirror.

Is she actually dating Frasier? I didn't believe it. She was smarter than that.

I loved the dude, but …

"What're you so nervous for?" Rush asked.

"I'm not nervous."

"Your eyes are darting around like you're looking for someone."

"No, no one," I said. "Just tryna find some pretty girl to take home tonight."

Rush scoffed, still adjusting something inside the car. "Yeah, right."

After a low growl, I drew my tongue across my teeth and peered into the crowd once more. I wasn't nervous about Astrid showing up. I was *pissed* that she might potentially show up with that dickhead.

If she showed up with him, I wasn't going to stand and watch. I knew that she liked me.

A flash of pink hair caught my eye. Ruby—who had been with Astrid a couple of hours ago—flirted with some guy from another school, a cup of beer in her hand. Mid-conversation, her gaze met mine, and she smirked.

Once she waved him off, she strolled over to us. "What's up, Calix?"

"Ruby," I said with a nod, trying to keep my cool.

If Ruby was here, then Astrid had to be here too, right? And if Astrid was alone somewhere in the crowd, what if she was doing the exact same thing that she had done the last time we met her at a party?

"Astrid should be here soon," she said to me. "Astrid *and* Frasier actually."

I clenched my jaw. "Cool."

"You know," Ruby hummed, "they're really into each other."

"Sure."

"You think I'm lying?" she asked. "Frasier picked her up for dinner before this."

"Dinner?" I repeated, gaze snapping to her. "Where'd they go?"

Ruby's smirk widened. "Wouldn't you like to know?"

"Ruby," I snarled, "I'm not in the mood."

She peered down at her phone. "They should be done by now, but you know how horny they both are. Probably decided to sneak off somewhere, like they did this afternoon, and fuck like—"

"I don't care," I snapped, hands balling into fists.

"Sure you don't," Ruby hummed, looking into the crowd and sipping on her beer. "I bet you don't care that she told me that Frasier is better than you too, huh?"

She said what?!

"Better than me at what?" I said through my teeth, facing her now, seething.

Ruby peered over at me innocently. "You know …"

"You're fucking lying," I said, pulling my gaze away. "Stop it."

"You know what I think? I think you should make her jealous tonight," Ruby said. "Find yourself a pretty girl to hang on you during the race and afterward. Astrid won't be able to handle seeing you with someone else."

"Get the fuck out of here."

Ruby chuckled and walked away, tipping her plastic cup at me. "See ya."

A low growl left my mouth as she disappeared into the crowd. I turned back to Rush, who stepped out of his car and shut the door behind himself.

He peered over my shoulder, his eyes shifting from neutral to hard. "What the fuck is she doing here?"

"Ruby? She came over to piss me—"

"Who the hell is Ruby? Why is Astrid here with Frasier?"

I followed his gaze and spotted Frasier with his face buried into the crook of Astrid's neck, his arm around her waist, guiding her forward. Her nose was scrunched up, and a big, wide grin decorated her face.

The better question was, *What is she doing? No, what* the fuck *is she doing?!*

With anger rushing through me, I stormed in her direction—knowing that she saw me—and right in front of her, I grabbed a girl with long brown hair and a flirty smile. She had been giving me looks since I'd arrived, and maybe … Ruby was right.

Maybe I should make her jealous.

I gripped the girl's waist and pulled her closer to me, pressing my lips against hers.

CHAPTER THIRTY

ASTRID

MY NAILS SANK into my palms, my stomach twisting. *What the fuck is Calix doing?!*

With Frasier's hand on my hips from behind, guiding me toward Rush's car, I had to physically hold myself back from stomping forward and ruining someone's face tonight. Calix had his lips locked with some bitch.

And, yes, she was a bitch to me because she was kissing the guy I liked.

This little fucker knew what he was doing too. This was probably his plan since he had found out that I'd be here tonight. Get dressed up nice, find a pretty girl that he *knew* would piss me off, and kiss her in front of me.

God, I want to wring his neck!

As we approached, Calix pulled away and wiped the spit off his lips, his hazy eyes meeting mine. "Oh, hey, Astrid, Frasier. Didn't think you'd both be here so soon. You know, with dinner and everything."

I flared my nostrils and glared at Calix. *How dare this motherfucker …*

I should've been able to handle this. I *did* have a boyfriend, right? Frasier was right beside me now, his arm nestled around the small of my waist. We had just gone out for the best—and first—dinner that I had been on with a guy.

Calix wrapped his arms around her waist, and she leaned into him, her head on his shoulder as she stared up at him. I gritted my teeth at him, only to have him smirk in return.

Why is he like this?!

Yet I had been doing the exact same thing *to* him.

After forcing a smile at Frasier, I turned toward him. "I'm going to get a drink." I stood on my toes and kissed him on the cheek, making sure that Calix saw. "I'll grab you something too. Be right back."

Frasier gently moved his hand off my waist, his fingers warm against the exposed portion of my skin. My heart skipped a beat, and I wrote all these emotions off as hormones because I was *supposed* to be getting my period soon. Who knew when that ho would come?

"I'll be waiting," Frasier said, his eyes softer than usual.

I wasn't sure *what* it was, but ever since he had picked me up tonight for dinner, he'd seemed a bit different. He had almost been ... nervous. But I had quickly brushed that off because I knew how he was. I knew *who* he was.

That was why Calix had such a problem with me seeing him.

While the crowd of people was thickening by the moment, I ducked underneath outspread arms, shoved some elbows into ribs, and scurried around bodies to get away from the mess inside my head.

These hormones are going to kill me!

Everything between Calix and me had been so complicated already. Then, once I added these feelings for Frasier, Arch, who had introduced me to all these guys; and cute and dominant Cairo into the mix ... I was screwed.

Near a parked truck, I found a cooler of beer and sank my arm into the ice-cold water to grab one. Once I cracked it open, I took a long-drawn-out sip, closed my eyes, and blew out a breath. This had to do the trick. I didn't have any other options right now.

After another sip, I rolled my shoulders forward, and I decided that I was as good as I was going to get. The jealousy still boiled inside me, but I had to ignore it by ignoring Calix. He would get pissed if I didn't spare him another glance tonight.

I chucked the rest of the beer into a trash can and headed around the crowd this time because I wasn't interested in accidentally getting groped right before the real action started. Besides, I had—

Someone slapped a hand over my mouth and wrapped their other arm around my waist, tugging me into a back alleyway. I hurled my elbow back into their ribs, only to be pushed flush against the brick building.

"You shouldn't be here," the man murmured into my ear.

I peeled his hand off my mouth and turned around to face him. "Rush?!"

He clenched his jaw. "Go home."

My gaze traveled across that angry man's face, his features hooded from the way light cast on them from above. I drew my tongue across my teeth and crossed my arms over my chest. "No. I'm here on a date with Frasier."

"*Exactly* why you should go," he said through his teeth, his hand closing around my throat.

I sucked in a sharp breath, feeling every part of his body against me, his huge bulge pressing on my stomach.

"You don't want me here with Frasier?" I whispered, staring up at him.

"No."

"What about without him?"

He got even harder against my stomach, and I pressed my legs together. I uncrossed my arms and drew my fingers down his muscular chest through his shirt, and warmth exploded between my thighs.

"What if I was here for you?" I asked.

"Astrid," he growled.

I moved my fingers further down his chest, down his abdomen, to the front of his waistband, playing with it. "Would you like that?"

Rush placed his forearm against my throat to hold me in place, and then he slipped his other hand inside my skirt. I sucked in a breath, eyes widening, and froze in place, my body anticipating his next move.

His fingers immediately found my clit, and he rubbed it gently. "You're not here for me."

"Yes, I am," I whispered, nipples hardening.

He moved his fingers faster. "No, you're not."

"Yes, I ..." The pressure rose quickly inside me. "Yes, I ... I ... *fuck*."

"You're here to make Calix jealous with your fake boyfriend."

My heart raced inside my chest, and I shook my head. "N-n-no, I'm—"

When his fingers slowed, my hips unintentionally bucked against his. He pulled his fingers away slightly, and I moved my pussy closer toward them, desperate for him to continue, aching for him to touch me again. And again. And again. And again.

"Yes, you are," he said, his gaze on my lips. "Say it."

"No."

I could feel the heat of his fingers millimeters from my clit.

"Say it," he ordered again.

A whimper left my mouth. "No."

"Admit to it, Astrid, and I'll give it back to you."

I pressed my lips together and stared at him, every single part of my body aching. I didn't want to give him the satisfaction of saying it out loud. Everyone might know it or think it, but nobody said it aloud.

When I went to scramble out of his hold, he pushed his forearm harder against my neck so I couldn't move anywhere. The only place I was going to go was where he'd let me. Rush was much bigger than me and probably more muscular than anyone else in The Crew, even if he hid it underneath his sweatshirts.

"Astrid," he started, "sa—"

"That's exactly why I'm here," I cried out, digging my fingers into his huge biceps. "Now, please, touch me. Please, Rush. I need it so badly. I'm stressed out, jealous, anxious, and I need you to make me come."

Rush placed his fingers back onto my clit and massaged it quickly. I bit back my moans and squeezed my eyes closed, the pressure rising quickly inside me. The closer I came to the edge, the more I tightened my grip on his biceps.

"B-b-but I'm here for you too," I said, almost at the tipping point. "You don't say two words to me, ignore me half the time I see you, yet you touch me like you own me. Maybe I'm using Frasier to make you jealous t—"

Before I could finish my sentence, Rush pulled his fingers away and slapped my clit hard. My eyes rolled back into my head, and I cried out, my moans being drowned out by the crowd just feet away.

My legs trembled uncontrollably, and I gripped harder on to him for support. He rubbed my clit in a couple more small circles, then released his grip on my neck. I doubled forward into him, breathing heavily.

Suddenly, the roar of engines erupted around us. Rush's gaze traveled from me back to the crowd, and he stepped away from me, posture shifting. The race was about to start.

After one more glance, Rush shoved people in the crowd and headed to his car. I took a deep breath in an attempt to regain my focus, yet my feet were glued to the ground. Rush slipped into his car and gripped the steering wheel with one hand, his biceps flexing. He tilted his head to the side just slightly, and he looked at me. Then the flag went down, and he hit the gas.

CHAPTER THIRTY-ONE

ASTRID

CARS RACED down the makeshift track, which was mostly the roads near the beach, abandoned during the winter and early spring months. I stood at the edge of the crowd, heart pounding inside my chest as I listened to the roar of engines.

According to a conversation that I overheard, the drivers drove around the track twice, and on Rush's second pass, he was neck and neck with another racer, both whizzing past us so fast that the wind unraveled my messy braid.

The tension between the two cars was deadly. A game of speed and control.

And Rush must have a lot of control after what he had just done with me. If I were him, I would've lost the second I left my car. But Rush? God! Warmth was exploding through my legs right now.

One minute, they flew down the straightaway, and then the next, the other racer served to cut Rush off. I sucked in a sharp breath, my eyes widening, as Rush veered to the side and into a sand dune. For a split second, it looked like the car was about to spin out of control.

But somehow, someway, he straightened his car back out and jerked it into control, the sheer skill making me gush. How was he so good? He raced like his life depended on it, or maybe like he was trying to impress someone …

What an egotistical thing to think.

Though I couldn't shake the look he had given me after I told him I wanted to make him jealous.

For a second time, Rush and the other racer were inches from each other while the others just passed by the crowd around me. I stood on my tiptoes, trying to see the outcome as the two drivers closed in on the finish line.

A rush of adrenaline burst through me, and I clutched my chest, heart beating rapidly.

Come on, Rush. Come on, Rush. Come on!

Suddenly, Rush kicked it up a notch, forcing the car to accelerate and braking past the finish line just a second before his competition did. I jumped into the air, breathless and cheering. Rush had won. He had really won! I stood back, trying to process it all.

"That was wild, wasn't it?" Frasier said to my right, his arms curling around my waist.

"My God," I whispered, staring as Rush's car slowed to a stop. "It was."

Out of all the guys in The Crew, Rush was the most mysterious to me. Yet watching him dominate like that, pulling himself out of what should have been a disaster, especially right after he had made me into a puddle … God.

"And my drink?" Frasier murmured, drawing his nose up the column of my neck.

My entire body shuddered in pleasure from all the sensations I was feeling right now, and I pressed my thighs together.

"Oh, um … right. I kinda … forgot about it. Got a bit … distracted."

With Rush's fingers rubbing me in places they shouldn't have.

A crowd of race fanatics and girls hurried toward Rush's

parked car, one that he hadn't gotten out of yet. I stared for a couple of moments, wondering if he would actually get out of it because as far as I knew, he didn't like people.

Or maybe he had wanted to give off the impression of not liking me.

I waited, heart slowing as the adrenaline wore off. From inside the car, Rush scanned the crowd, and then he stopped when we made eye contact. I sucked in a sharp breath, faintly listening to something Frasier said. Rush's face remained emotionless, but he didn't look away.

One moment, he was staring at me, and then the next ... the other driver was flinging Rush's driver's door open and hurling his fist into the car at him.

CHAPTER THIRTY-TWO

ASTRID

BEFORE I COULD PUSH my way to the front—stupidly thinking that I could help—a crowd formed around the cars. A heavy thud echoed over the noise, and my stomach twisted. If he hurt Rush, then he would have another thing coming …

I elbowed people recording the fight and slipped between bodies in an attempt to get a better view. The crowd roared in excitement as another thud rumbled through the night. I shoved the last tall person out of the way and stood three people deep from the fight to catch Rush stumbling back and wiping blood from the corner of his mouth.

His opponent stormed toward him, hurling his fist at Rush. Rush stepped back and slammed his fist into the guy's jaw, immediately sending him to the ground. My eyes widened, and adrenaline exploded through my body.

Rush hadn't even hesitated.

As the guy tried to stand, spitting some vile words at Rush that I couldn't hear over the noise, Rush slammed him back onto the ground, straddled his waist from behind, and bashed his head into the concrete.

Oh my God.

Where has this Rush come from?! I had never seen him like this before.

All that thick muscle, covered in sweat, pounding his opponent into the ground over and over and over again. I pressed my thighs together and sucked in a sharp breath, desperately trying to push the thought away because ... I couldn't be thinking this now.

When another guy stepped in and grabbed the back of Rush's shirt, Frasier was suddenly in the fight, hurling the guy off Rush and shoving him backward. Frasier didn't seem like the type to fight, but he would protect his friends.

In a moment, the fight turned into a brutal, messy brawl between the two sides.

"Aw, *that's cute,*" the pretty blonde girl said in front of me. "Frasier is up there."

Frasier? They knew Frasier? They don't go to our school.

Her friend stood on her toes. "Where? With Rush?"

"Yeah. You know that he brought a girl here to make me jealous?" She giggled, holding on to her friend to steady herself, as if it were the funniest thing in the entire world. "She's not even that pretty either."

My chest tightened, and I dropped my gaze to the ground, fingers tugging on the insides of my sleeves. I mean, I knew that I wasn't Frasier's usual cheerleader, pageant-queen type, but I didn't think I looked *that* bad. Had he really brought me here to make someone else jealous?

I didn't think so because we'd had such a nice date earlier, but ...

The more they giggled, the tighter my insides squeezed in on themselves. Tears filled my eyes, and I wrapped my arms around my stomach to make myself smaller, hoping that they didn't see me right behind them.

"I can't believe he thought he'd make you jealous with *her*." The friend laughed.

I shuffled back a few steps, tears heavy in my eyes, and slammed into someone's hard chest. In a hurry to get out of there, I turned around and brushed past him. When he grabbed my arm, I hazily looked up at him.

"We need to get you out of here," Calix said, his hands finding my waist as he guided me through the rowdy crowd toward the back alleyway where Rush had taken me earlier tonight. "Things are about to get bad."

I dug my heels into the ground and stopped, not turning around to face him again. The tears were about to fall, and I didn't even know why. From the very beginning, Frasier had known that I was using him. I should've known he was doing the same with me.

Why am I so stupid?!

"Where's your girlfriend?" I asked. "Why don't you get her out of here instead?"

Calix tightened his grip on my hips and pushed me forward. "We don't have time for this, Astrid. Move."

"No."

Once Calix released me, I crossed my arms and glared at the ground. *Was it really that easy to get him to go away? Do any of these guys actually like me, or are they all using me? Of course, they are using—*

Suddenly, Calix picked me up and tossed me over his shoulder as if I weighed nothing.

I yelped in surprise and punched his back. "Let me down from here! I want to go home. I'm tired of hanging out with you guys!"

Instead of responding, Calix continued to push through the crowd with a tight grip on me. I punched him harder and kicked my legs back and forth, realizing that no matter how hard I tried, I wouldn't be able to escape his grip.

"Calix!" I shouted when we reached the alleyway. "Let me down!"

"No."

"Calix! Now!"

"No, because you're going to get your ass hurt."

"I'm not."

"You are."

"No, I'm not. I promise that I won't go anywhere."

"I'm not letting you down."

I flared my nostrils. "I hate you."

Instead of entertaining me, Calix continued to walk until we reached his car. He opened up the passenger door and deposited me on the seat. After he buckled me in, he crouched beside me, his features softening.

He tucked some hair behind my ear. "You ok—why are you crying? Who hurt you?"

I opened and closed my mouth a handful of times, the tears beginning to fall down my cheeks. I bit my lower lip to stop it from trembling and tried my best to hold back a sob. But every part of my body was shaking.

"N-no-b-body."

"If someone touched you, tell me," Calix said, jaw clenched tightly. "Now, Astrid."

A sob left my mouth, and I gripped on to his wrist because I didn't want him to leave me here in his car. I didn't want him to go back out there and learn that stupid little Astrid had gotten herself played by the guy who was *supposed* to be her boyfriend.

Calix had warned me, and I had thought that I had it all under control.

"Please, don't go," I sobbed. "Please, bring me somewhere else. Anywhere but here."

CHAPTER THIRTY-THREE

ASTRID

"ARE you sure it's smart to bring me here?" I whispered as I walked up the walkway with Calix's hand on my lower back, guiding me. It was the first thing I had said to him since I'd slipped into his car. "Diya was here when I left."

When we reached the front door, Calix pushed his key into the lock and quietly turned it. "I'm not leaving you anywhere alone, especially with how you are right now."

"I'm fine," I said.

"You were sobbing in my car."

"No, I wasn't."

"Yes, you were."

"No, I was—"

The door clicked open, and Calix shushed me. He took my hand and stepped into the house. I swallowed the lump in my throat and followed in after him. If Diya saw me here with her brother, I would never hear the end of it.

We made our way to the stairs, and the first one creaked.

"Shit," Calix cursed under his breath. "Stay quiet."

"You're the one swearing!" I said into his ear.

Another step, another creak.

"I have a plan, so we don't make too much noise," Calix said, releasing my hand and pulling me into the air. He tossed me over his shoulder, one arm draped around the backs of my thighs, the other resting on my ass.

I narrowed my eyes and held myself back from kicking and screaming this time.

Stupid Calix, looking for any reason he can to have his hands all over me.

Once we made it to the second floor, where his and Diya's rooms were located, he paused and peered down the hallway. Then this asshole smacked me hard on the ass. I bit back a yelp and kneed him in the chest.

What does he think he's doing?!

"I don't think anyone is home," he said in his normal tone.

I waited a moment before responding to make sure. "Then set me down!"

He moved his hand across my ass, getting a good feel for himself. "Or what?"

"I'll tell you what," I muttered, hitting him in the back again. "I'm going to ruin your life."

"Can't get much worse than being here with you," he said.

"Oh, buddy," I said. "You have another thing coming to you if that's what you think."

A low chuckle left his mouth, and he smacked my ass again. "I'm *so* scared."

"You just wait until you set me down."

After walking into his room, he kicked the door closed with his foot, smacking me again. "Guess I won't let you down then. Can't have the *big, bad* Astrid coming to ruin my life. I'll never recover."

Tired of his jokes, I wrapped my arm around his neck from behind, putting him into a choke hold and squeezing as hard as I could. I didn't know if I was doing it right, but those jiujitsu classes that my parents had made me take when I was five were really paying off now.

I locked the choke on tight and squeezed harder, wrapping my legs around his waist, too, to really squeeze his body and make him think twice about teasing me again. This man was going to get everything he deserved.

Calix leaned against the bed with his knees, grabbing at my arm in a *measly* attempt to pull it away, and then he dropped me down, falling on me with his entire body weight. All the air got knocked out of my lungs, and I released my death grip. When he pulled back, we both began gasping for air.

"I hate you," I said between breaths, glaring up at him.

His body was still nestled between my thighs as he leaned over me with one hand posted beside my head, coughing to catch his breath. One moment turned into two, and soon, our ragged breaths turned into short, softer ones.

His gaze traveled from one eye to the other, then slowly down to my lips. I sucked in a sharp breath, my gaze following the same pattern—both his eyes and then down to his full lips that I remembered had been all over me at the party.

I swallowed hard. "Calix ..."

"Astrid ..." He dragged out, eyes hazy and fixed on my lips. "*My Hellcat.*"

Warmth exploded through my thighs, my heart racing. "Won't your girlfriend be mad at you"—when he moved a couple of inches closer, I bit back a desperate whimper—"for bringing me home?"

"Girlfriend? That girl at the race? She was just a random girl to make you jealous."

He *had* been making me jealous with her. Did he want me as badly as I wanted him?

Almost instinctively, I tilted my head to the side, drawing my nose against his. "Not her. I'm talking about Mira, my ex-best friend." I curled my fingers around his collar. "You know, the one you're supposedly dating."

"Mira?" he said in a low chuckle. "We're not really dating, just like I know you're not really dating Frasier."

I closed my eyes, heart tightening at the sound of his name. "That's not true."

Calix's lips curved into a smirk as he drew his nose up mine. "Don't lie to me, Hellcat." His breath was warm against my mouth. He moved his lips, and when I went to close the distance, he pulled back. "We both know it's not real." He moved them toward me again, then pulled away when I got near. "Admit it."

I lifted my head in an attempt to close the distance again. "Calix ..."

He pulled back just enough. "Admit it."

"Okay," I murmured, drawing my hands up his chest and around the back of his neck to bring him down toward me. "I'm only seeing him to make you jealous." And then I kissed him hard on the mouth.

CHAPTER THIRTY-FOUR

CALIX

AFTER THOSE WORDS left Astrid's mouth, I couldn't help myself. I pressed my lips against hers, my hands sliding down her body. I had known it the entire time, yet hearing her say that she had been using Frasier to make me jealous …

Fucking hell, my dick was throbbing.

She laced her fingers through my hair and tugged, a small moan leaving her mouth as I ground myself against her cunt. All these years, I had wanted her. All these years, I had used other girls to make her jealous, her ex–best friend even.

And now? She was mine. All mine.

I peppered wet kisses down her jaw, then down the column of her neck, then down her chest and between her cleavage, pulling away her clothes. My dick was hard and aching to be buried deep inside her.

Once one of my hands reached her pussy, I sprawled it across her cunt. Astrid's legs fell outward, like she was pudding for me, and another breathy moan left her lips. She arched her back, brows knitted together.

"Calix," she whimpered, "oh my God."

With my fingers finding her clit, I rubbed it in circles and sucked one of her nipples between my teeth. Her entire body tensed, and she tugged on my hair harder, pressing as much of her body against mine as she could.

God, I loved when she was desperate like this.

"Please," she cried. "More."

I sucked on her nipple harder, drawing my tongue around the sensitive bud, back and forth, up and down, then bit it softly. She cried out in pleasure, bucking her hips against my hand and clawing at my clothes.

"So desperate for it, Hellcat," I murmured, tugging up on her breast with my teeth until her nipple popped out of my mouth.

Her mouth was ajar, hazy eyes staring at me.

"My desperate girl."

"Calix ..." she whined.

Fuck, every little moan made me harder.

When I moved over to her other breast, she pushed down on my shoulders.

"Calix, I can't wait any longer. I need you inside of me. Please. I know I'm desperate. So, so desperate, but I need it. Calix, pl—"

Before she could finish her sentence, I sucked her other nipple into my mouth. Her eyes rolled back into her head, and I moved my fingers faster around her swollen clit. Her legs began shaking, and she sank her nails into my skin.

I ground my cock against the mattress. "Patience, Hellcat."

Once I was thoroughly satisfied with torturing her tits, I kissed down the center of her stomach and nestled my body between her thighs. She lifted her hips, but I made sure my lips stayed millimeters away so she could feel the heat of them.

She wasn't going to rush this because I wanted to savor every bit of her.

I drew my rough fingertips up her inner thighs, making them tremble even more. Then I let a wad of spit drip from my lips onto her pussy. It rolled from her clit down her lips.

She lifted her hips again off the mattress, a breathy whisper leaving her mouth. "Please …"

After pushing myself up to my knees because I didn't even think that *I* would be able to handle the torture of her moans any longer, I pushed the head of my cock between her pussy lips and rubbed it across her clit in torturous circles.

Pre-cum dribbled out onto her cunt as she reached down and grabbed my cock from me. She moved it down so my head pressed against her entrance and stroked me, *teased me* the way I had been torturing her.

"Please, fuck me," she cried. "I can't handle it anymore."

A low growl left my throat. I seized her hips and slammed my dick into her tight pussy. She arched her back and screamed out, her walls squeezing my dick so much harder than they ever had.

"Fuck," I growled.

"Oh my God!" she moaned, hands up on the headboard to push herself down every time I thrust up into her. "Oh my God. Oh my God. Oh my fucking God, Calix! Please, don't stop! God, please, don't ever stop!"

"Fuck," I hissed, pounding into her harder. "You're so tight."

"More. More. More!"

"My desperate little Hellcat." I rested the backs of her thighs on my shoulders, then leaned forward and placed my forearms on either side of her head, my mouth against hers. "I knew you were doing it all for me. How long have you wanted this?"

She whimpered again.

"How fucking long, Astrid?" I grunted into her mouth.

Her pussy tightened more and more around my dick, and my balls became heavy. I slammed into her harder and faster until she was clawing at my back so hard that she was definitely drawing blood.

"For so long!" she cried against me.

When her pussy began pulsing around my dick, I buried myself inside her and stilled. Pleasure rushed through my body, and I slipped my tongue into her mouth. She trembled underneath me, crying out into me.

"After tonight, Hellcat," I murmured, "you're all mine."

CHAPTER THIRTY-FIVE

ASTRID

A SHARP KNOCK at the door jolted me awake. I jerked my eyes open and stared out into an unfamiliar room, heart racing. Oh my God. I'd accidentally fallen asleep at Calix's place last night and not left before Diya got home.

"Go away, Diya," Calix murmured groggily into my ear, pulling me closer.

My body was nestled against his, his arm wrapped tightly around my waist from behind. His sheets were tangled around us, and I swore if Diya walked right in, I wouldn't have an explanation ready.

Hell, she wouldn't *accept* an explanation at that point.

"Calix!" Diya called from the hallway. "I need to talk to you."

Breath hitching, I stiffened. Where was I going to hide? How would I get out of here?

I shifted in the bed to face Calix, who was still fast asleep, his mouth ajar.

I smacked him in the chest quietly so Diya wouldn't hear and kept my voice low. "Calix, wake up! Diya is at the door."

He blinked a couple of times, wiping his eyes, then smiled. "Morning, Hellcat."

After widening my eyes, I slapped a hand over his mouth. "Shush it! Diya is outside."

"So?" he murmured against my hand, tugging me closer. "You're in my bed."

"This is serious! She can't find me here."

When Diya knocked again, he rolled his eyes and slowly sat up, leaning against the headboard. "Relax," he whispered, peering around his room until his gaze locked on to the closet. "Hide in there for now."

Hiding ... that was my only option. If I tried to climb out the window, I'd surely hurt myself.

"Calix!" she shouted. "Open the door."

"Shut up, Diya," he growled back. "I'll be out in a sec, unless you want to see me naked."

Suddenly, the knocking and shouting stopped from the hallway. I grabbed what I could find of my clothes and hurried to the closet, completely naked, slipping inside it and staring out through the crevice.

Once Calix pulled on some sweats, he opened the door just a crack. "What?"

"What took you so long?" she asked. "And why's your door locked?"

"Didn't think you'd want to see the baddie I'd bagged last night when you decided to barge into my room this morning like a fucking maniac," he said. "What do you want? Why are you knocking on my door this early?"

While I couldn't see Diya, I could only imagine her scrunching her nose right now. "Baddie? Which one did you bring home last night? Another one of my friends?" *Shit.* "Doesn't matter. It's about Mom."

My eyes widened. Diya and her mom never really got along, even more so now that she had remarried. Her mother had always been jealous of Diya—it was so obvious that it was sickening.

Always trying to pull one over on her own daughter, to the point where Diya just didn't talk to her anymore. So, hearing her seem almost anxious saying her mom's name was new.

From the small gap, I watched Calix tense, his shoulders going rigid and his jaw clenching. Usually, he only got that way when he was pissed or jealous over Frasier. Otherwise, he was carefree.

"What about Mom? Where is she?" he asked.

"Apparently, she's in the hospital," she said. "She called this morning, asking for you."

Calix pressed his lips together, then nodded. "Okay. Thanks for letting me know. You going to go see her?"

"No," Diya said. "She said that she didn't want me there. Only you."

After a couple more heavily exchanged words, Diya walked down the hall, and Calix shut the door behind her. He ran a hand through his hair and opened the closet. I blew out a breath and tugged on my clothes because his closet was too small for me to do that in there.

"That was way too close," I whispered. "What would she have done if she'd seen me?"

He shrugged, but didn't smile this time. "Probably killed me. But I'm used to it."

I released a shaky laugh in an attempt to lighten the suddenly dull mood.

"She didn't find out though," he said. "We're good, but we have to get you out of here."

While I knew that I had to go, I didn't think *he* wanted me to go. But he was suddenly cold and uninviting, like he had the entire backstory about why his mom was in the hospital and it wasn't sitting well with him. He hadn't even asked Diya any questions.

"Is your mom okay?" I asked.

"She's fine."

"You look worried."

"I'm fine," he snapped, then sighed and ran a hand through

his hair. "She just has some shit going on and doesn't want to tell Diya. Diya thinks that she doesn't love her. God, it's a fucking mess in this house every fucking day."

And it doesn't make it any better that Diya is sleeping with her stepfather ...

Calix peered over at me, then looked away almost shyly after making eye contact. "I should take you home before Diya finds out that you're here. I know that you don't want her knowing about us."

I looked down and nodded. "Okay. Let me find my phone first."

After looking on the nightstand and behind the bed, I flipped up the blankets on the mattress and spotted it underneath the sheets at the foot of the bed. I grabbed it, wondering how the hell I was going to get out of here unseen if Diya was literally in the house.

My phone buzzed in my hand, and I stared down at the flood of missed messages.

Frasier: Where are you?

Frasier: You okay? You disappeared.

Frasier: I've been looking for you. Call me.

Ten missed messages from Frasier and a handful of calls too. For someone I was just fake dating and for someone who had just been using me to make that pretty girl at the race jealous, he seemed a bit too worried.

Guilt settled heavily in my chest, but I decided not to text him back.

I had been using him, like he had been using me, and that was that. I had gotten what I wanted.

When my phone buzzed again, Calix peered over at me, halfway through putting on a shirt. "Who's that? Diya?"

"Frasier."

Calix clenched his jaw. "Why is he texting you?"

"Because I'm dating him."

"*Fake* dating him. Tell him to fucking stop."

"He's your best friend. You tell him."

"He's texting you."

"Well, maybe I don't want him to stop texting me," I said.

My eyes widened for a moment. Did I … did I really like Frasier like that?

God, my life is a mess. I was fake dating someone to make my best friend's brother jealous, only to finally snag him and get jealous that the guy I had been fake dating had been using me to get with another girl. And maybe now I had feelings for both of them, but also Rush, and who could forget cute, *innocent* Cairo?

What am I doing?!

"It doesn't matter," I said. "Get me out of here."

After staring at me for a couple of moments, Calix drew his tongue across his teeth angrily and opened the door to look out into the hallway. A moment later, he shut it. "Diya is probably in the kitchen. I'll distract her. Sneak down the stairs and get into my car."

"Isn't there another way?!" I whisper-yelled.

"No," he said, then slipped out the door.

I gave the finger to the door and gathered my belongings. When I finally heard them spark up a conversation, I snuck out of Calix's room and down the hallway, peeking my head around the corner of the door to the kitchen.

Diya's back was turned toward me, and I quickly shuffled down the stairs before she could see me. Once I reached the foot of the stairs, I smacked hard into someone. My eyes widened, and I looked up to see Diya's stepfather.

"What are you—"

I slapped a hand over his mouth. "If you say anything to Diya about me being here, I will tell Calix about you and Diya sleeping together," I said before I could stop myself.

His eyes widened, but he pressed his lips together and put up his arms in defense. Then I scurried out the back door and made a break for Calix's car.

God, what am I getting myself into?

CHAPTER THIRTY-SIX

ASTRID

CALIX DROVE me down another side road in Redwood. I leaned my back against the passenger seat, my mind lost in thoughts of everything that had happened last night and this morning. Kissing Calix? Sneaking behind my best friend's back? Almost getting caught?

It shouldn't have given me the thrill that it did.

One of his hands was on the steering wheel, the other on the center console and dangerously close to my thigh. We had been driving for at least twenty minutes. I should've been home by now. But it seemed like Calix didn't want to bring me home either.

Crazy how one night could change everything.

Every time we came to a stop, he peered over at me. "You thinking about Diya?"

"A bit, but more like how we almost got caught. My heart is still racing."

"Yeah, sneaking past her"—his lips curled into a smirk—"was wild."

"Wild is an understatement." I giggled.

He didn't know about my run-in with his stepfather or about him and his sister sneaking about while their mom was apparently sick. So many secrets that I had to keep to myself, but that I so desperately wanted to tell.

Though it wasn't just Diya and Calix that were on my mind. That race and Rush, Frasier, Cairo … and then my asshole of a stepbrother who was supposed to be at the race last night and hadn't shown up.

All of it felt so wrong …

"Have you talked to Rush?" I asked, rubbing my palms together. My phone buzzed in my hand—*Frasier again*—but I ignored it for now. "Is he okay? I mean, after everything that happened last night."

Calix's hand tightened on the wheel. "He's fine—or at least, he says he is."

"Why so mad about that?" I asked, noticing his clenched jaw.

"I'm not mad about him being okay."

"Then why are you clutching the steering wheel like you hate him?"

"Because …"

"Because why?"

"He was asking about you."

My eyes widened, and I turned my gaze toward the windshield, trying to bite back a smile. *Rush was asking about me?* Heat flooded through my chest, and I swallowed a giggle. *Me?!*

"Just wanted to make sure that you got home after the fight," Calix continued.

I could feel his gaze burning into the side of my face, and I nodded, pretending like this was nothing, like I didn't like anyone else except him, like Rush asking about *me* didn't make me the giddiest girl in the world.

God, I am the biggest slut ever, going after this group of best friends.

"That bothers you?" I asked. "That he was asking about me?"

"Yes."

Screaming!!!

"Why?" I whispered, peeking over at him.

While driving, he grabbed my thigh. "Because I want you all to myself."

Pleasure rushed through my entire body, and I pressed my legs together. This was bad. So, so, so bad. Why were they all so jealous of each other and possessive over me? I was a nobody! But, *oh Lord,* was I really going to make these guys fight over me? Yes.

One hundred percent yes.

"Do you think that Rush is really okay?" I asked, trying to change the subject.

Not because I wanted to change the subject, but because I knew it would drive him wild for me to tell him that I didn't just want him, that I really wanted the entire friend group. He'd go fucking insane.

"We'll see," he murmured, hand still on my thigh.

"We?"

Calix took another side road and drove until we came to the main street, and then he turned into Galaxy Grub, a run-down bar where some kids from Redwood hung out. It was known that the owners gave out free drinks to underage kids.

In the parking lot, I spotted not only Rush's car, but Cairo's, Arch's, and … Frasier's.

While I liked all the guys, my stomach was twisting. I had been ignoring Frasier's messages all morning and afternoon. If he saw me walk in with Calix, I didn't know what would happen. Besides … he had really been using me to get with that girl.

He couldn't be mad, right?

No, he didn't deserve for me to be faithful to him. He had known I was using him.

Yet, still, guilt churned in my belly.

"They're all here," I muttered, more to myself than to Calix.

Calix parked in an empty spot near the back, beside Frasier, as the silence began stretching between us. I knew I had to go inside, face the questions from Frasier about why I was with Calix … but this was what we had both wanted, right?

After another moment, Calix exited the car. I hesitantly followed after him, heart racing. When we approached the entrance, he grabbed my hand like I was his. And while we had spent last night together, we never really put a label on it.

The inside of Galaxy Grub was exactly as I'd thought it'd look—the warm glow of the lights, the faint smell of greasy food, and the low hum of conversation toward the pool tables in the back. Arch was hunched over in a booth by the window, complaining about something to Cairo, who sat there so innocently with a textbook. Rush was at the bar, grabbing a beer from the bartender, one eye completely swollen closed.

Calix tugged me along toward the back, not even saying a word to anyone. His hand was wrapped tightly around mine, keeping it warm. But then my gaze locked on to Frasier's intense, jealous one.

CHAPTER THIRTY-SEVEN

FRASIER

I SPOTTED Astrid as soon as she walked into Galaxy with Calix, hand in fucking hand.

What the fuck is she holding his hand for?

My fists tightened by my sides, and I gritted my teeth, glaring at them from across the bar. I had spent the whole night wondering where she'd gone, texting her, looking around for her, *worrying* about her. And here she was, with Calix.

Was she with him the entire night? Is he *the reason that she ignored my texts?*

When her gaze met mine, she stiffened and dropped Calix's hand. I drew my tongue across my teeth and flared my nostrils. Maybe she had been seeing him behind my back and didn't want me to find out.

Is that what she is doing? Using us?

Calix placed his hand on her lower back and continued guiding her toward Arch and Cairo, who sat at our usual table. Sipping on a beer, Rush sat beside Arch and didn't look at Astrid once. I walked over to them and pulled up a chair from a table.

"Where were you?" I asked Astrid.

"You didn't come home last night. Thought you might've died," Arch said.

She shuffled her feet and tugged on her sleeves, peering at the ground. "I was …"

"With me," Calix said, meeting my gaze with a smirk.

I raised my brows at him. He really didn't want to do this here.

"Yeah? With you?" I spit back. "That why she doesn't look satisfied?"

He dropped his smirk and replaced it with a disgusted grimace. "You don't know what she looks like when she's satisfied, you fucking asshole. All that sleeping around, and she came back to me."

A low chuckle left my mouth. "Is that so?"

"You bet, dickhead."

My gaze traveled to Astrid, who stayed at his side. She peeked at me, then looked away, her nipples hardening underneath her shirt. She got off on this shit, didn't she? Did she like that we fought over her?

I stretched out my legs, making myself big, and patted my knee. "Come here, babe."

Her eyes widened, and she looked at my lap, then at Calix, then back.

"Babe," I purred, tilting my head down to look at her through my brows. "Come. Here."

A moment passed, then another. Nobody said anything, not even Arch. She shuffled her feet a couple of steps, then finally walked over to me, but didn't sit. I seized her waist and pulled her onto my lap so she faced the other guys, my nose in her hair and my smirk on her neck.

"You're so good for me, baby," I murmured against her skin.

"Astrid," Calix growled, "get off him."

"What the fuck are you going to do about it?" I growled at him, sliding my hand up Astrid's bare thigh. I pulled her skirt up so Calix could see how wet her pussy was for me. "Huh, Calix? What are you going to do about me touching *my girl's* pussy?"

When a small moan left Astrid's mouth, I pushed two fingers between her pussy lips and rubbed her clit. She squirmed in my hold, but I fastened one arm around her body like a seat belt, holding her neck in my hand to keep her steady.

I readjusted her so my bulge was nestled right against her pussy.

"Tell him who you belong to," I murmured into her ear, my dick hard as fuck.

"Please …" she whimpered softly, glancing around the empty bar. "Not here."

"Right here."

"But … we're in public …" She peered over at Cairo, and I glided my fingers across her swollen clit. Back and forth and back and forth. "Cairo, please, tell them to stop. Someone is going to see. Please, Cairo."

"Cairo isn't going to help you," I said, tightening my hand around her throat.

She squirmed harder on my lap, but I held her in place. She wasn't leaving me.

"Who do you belong to?" I asked her again, rubbing her pussy faster and faster and faster, building her up in front of all the guys the way that I knew she loved. "I'm not letting you go until you tell me, so you're going to—"

"I belong to The Crew," she cried.

My eyes widened for a moment, and I thought I had misheard her.

"The Crew?" I repeated.

She nodded, bucking her hips against my fingers. "The Crew. I belong to all of you."

CHAPTER THIRTY-EIGHT

ASTRID

ONE MOMENT, Frasier was grinding his bulge against me, and the next, he was inside me. It happened so quickly, but my skirt was off, my shirt was ripped, and my tits were bouncing for all to see. He slammed up into my pussy, and Calix undid his zipper, lining up right beside him.

For them hating each other so much, I didn't think they would fuck me in the same hole—

Holy shit!

Calix shoved his fat cock into my pussy too. When I went to open my mouth to cry out in pain and pleasure, his lips connected with mine, and I ended up crying and moaning into his mouth, my pussy stuffed full.

They pushed into me at different intervals—slow, fast, erratic paces.

"Oh my God," I said, their hands all over my body. "Fuck!"

We were in public. There were people here in the bar, watching us, for fuck's sake! I shouldn't like this as much as I did. Someone from school was bound to see, record it, post it online for the world to watch.

Except all I cared about right now was being filled ... by all of them.

I peered over at Rush, who now sat back in a seat beside us, one hand on his bulge, his eyes on my pussy.

"Please," I whispered, staring up at him through my lashes. "Please, fuck me too."

Out of all the guys, Rush hadn't fucked me like this yet. He had fingered me, shoved his fat cock into my mouth, made me come so many times, but he hadn't been inside my tight little pussy, and I didn't know how much longer I'd be able to take it.

"I'm not going to fuck you today, Astrid," he said, reaching over and rubbing my clit as Frasier and Calix pushed into me.

My pussy tightened around them, and I whimpered out, desperate for him, "Please."

"No."

"Why not?" I cried, head lolling back against Frasier's shoulder. "Everyone else has."

"You sound like a dirty whore," Frasier growled into my ear. "Being used by us."

Clenching even more around them, I moaned out in pleasure and came on their cocks, my pussy pulsing over and over. Calix cursed under his breath and stilled inside me, his warm cum filling me up. I curled my toes, and he and Frasier pulled out of me.

Pussy drooling with their cum, I held my legs apart in the middle of the bar and stared at Rush through desperate eyes. "Please, fuck me, Rush. Please, my pussy is begging for you to fill it up! Why won't you fuck me?"

He wrapped his free hand around the front of my throat and pulled me closer, his warm breath fanning my ear. "Why not? Because when I fuck you, I want you alone in my car, crying out *my* name and my name only, Hellcat."

Then he slipped his fingers from my clit to my pussy, catching their cum and pushing it back into my pussy. I curled my toes, feeling him push his fingers all the way to my G-spot and then further, until he almost reached my cervix.

"Someone, fill her cunt," Rush said. "Push their cum deeper. Get her pregnant."

I clamped down around his fingers, my body exploding with pleasure and my eyes rolling back into my head.

Holy fucking—

Wave after wave of ecstasy rushed through me, and my legs trembled uncontrollably.

"Please," I cried. "Please, someone ..."

Arch pulled me off Frasier's lap and sat me on the pool table, spreading my legs and immediately pushing his huge, throbbing cock into my tight pussy. I clutched on to his huge biceps and continued crying out in pleasure.

"Oh my God," I moaned. "Oh my fucking God. Don't stop. Please!"

He slammed into me repeatedly. "You love being fucked by your stepbrother, don't you?"

"Sh-shut up," I stammered out, my tits bouncing. "And fuck me harder."

He slapped me hard on the cheek, and I clenched around him, so he smacked me again. I tightened around him and anticipated another, but instead, he grabbed my chin, forced me to look up at him, and spit on me.

"You dirty fucking whore. Tell me what you are."

But he didn't give me a chance to as he rubbed the spit into my face and slapped me again.

"I'm a"—*slap*—"dirty"—*slap*—"whore!"

"You're a dirty *fucking* whore," he growled, pumping into me. "Say it again, and don't fuck it up this time."

"I'm a"—*slap*—"dirty"—*slap*—"fucking"—*slap*—"whore!"

As the last of my words left my mouth, I came all over his cock. He stilled inside me, grunting lowly. Then he shoved me onto my knees, and I grabbed at his dick to lick off his and Calix's and Frasier's cum off him. I wrapped my hand around the base to keep it still and swirled my tongue around his head, then sucked all of him into my mouth.

"You're fucking nasty, Hellcat," Arch growled, wrapping one hand in my hair.

I stared up at him through my lashes and sucked the last bit of cum from his cock.

He pulled my head back. "Look at you, you dirty slut. Don't forget about Cairo."

I licked my lips and glanced over my shoulder at Cairo, who still sat in the booth. To anyone else, he'd look so innocent, so inconspicuous, but I had seen the real him. I knew how he really wanted to treat me …

Like the brat—*the good girl*—that I was.

"Come fuck me," I murmured, daring him because I knew he wouldn't do anything in public. He might be a dom, but he was still cute, innocent little Cairo to the guys and to Redwood. "Here."

Cairo's eyes darkened, and he cocked his finger. "Come here."

"Don't you want to fuck me?" I asked from my knees, leaning over onto my arms.

Arch pushed his foot against my ass cheek, shoving me forward. "Don't be a brat."

"Crawl to him," Rush growled, leaning against the pool table beside Arch, arms crossed.

While the others were *trying* to discipline me for him, Cairo didn't seem fazed by it. He hadn't moved his gaze away from mine as he cocked his finger again in my direction.

"Don't make me say it again, Astrid."

Fuck, my real name.

I gulped, my pussy warm. *If I kept this up …*

"Now, Astrid. Come here."

It felt like the entire bar was watching me, but I knew that tone of voice … I had heard him use it during our time at his house. He was stern, but made me wet and warm in so many different places.

So, I crawled over to him on the dirty floor of Galaxy Grub, my ass swaying back and forth, my tits swinging underneath me. I stopped at his feet and stared up at him, suddenly desperate to be his good little girl.

"What do you say?" he murmured.

"I'm sorry."

"Sorry for what?"

"Being a brat to you."

"You know what happens when you're a brat to me, right?"

"Yes," I whispered.

"What happens?"

"I get punished."

"Do you want me to punish you here?"

My nipples ached, and I pressed my thighs together. Part of me thought that Cairo really wouldn't punish me here in front of everyone, not this publicly. But by the way he was staring at me, silently noting how my body reacted to the thought of being punished, I knew he would.

So, I shook my head.

"Words," he demanded. "I need words from you."

"No," I whispered.

He patted his lap, and I crawled on up, reaching to undo his zipper and then pulling out his huge cock. I rubbed it up and down, positioning him at my entrance. With his hands on my hips, he pulled me down onto him. I curled my fingers around his shoulders.

"You won't like my punishments as much as you like my rewards, baby," he murmured into my ear, pumping up into me. The others were still watching, but he was talking too low for them to hear. "I promise you that."

"I like punishments," I said.

"You won't like mine, but you won't see them because you're my good girl, aren't you?"

I curled my toes. "Mmhmm."

He seized my nipples and tugged. "Words."

"Yes, Daddy! I'm your good girl!" I cried as he pulled my head back slightly so my lips were millimeters from his. I bounced on his dick, pushing Arch's, Frasier's, and Calix's cum further into my pussy. "I'm your good fucking girl."

And just like that … I had been claimed by The Crew.

CHAPTER THIRTY-NINE

ASTRID

"HOW ARE YOU FEELING?" Cairo asked from the driver's seat.

I glanced over at him and turned my body into his direction, my head resting against the passenger seat headrest. He slowed down at a yellow light as Rush and Arch blazed past us, heading to Cairo's place.

"Okay," I whispered.

Cairo tucked some hair behind my ear. "Do you want me to run you a bath when we get to my house? I'm sorry we couldn't do proper aftercare." He gently rubbed my inner thigh. "I didn't expect them to take it that far there."

"Maybe later," I hummed, admiring the way the moonlight bounced off his dark eyes.

While I wasn't used to aftercare—at least not with any of the other guys because our relationship wasn't like that—I had asked Cairo specifically to drive me because my body … seemed so connected with him.

I couldn't explain the feeling. I wanted aftercare, but not with any of the others tonight.

"Once everyone leaves?" he asked.

"If that's okay," I said.

"Of course. I can—"

Before he could finish his sentence and as soon as the light changed to green, Frasier beeped his horn behind Cairo. *So impatient.* The car accelerated, and Cairo peered in the rearview mirror.

A long silence filled the car as he turned off the main road and continued driving.

"You were with Calix last night?" he asked.

"Yes."

"Alone?"

I paused, then nodded. "Maybe ..."

He drew his tongue across his bottom lip and nodded too. I stared at him for a couple more moments, waiting for him to say something, to continue, but instead, he drove in silence.

Was cute little Cairo ... *jealous* too?

When we pulled up the driveway, Rush's and Arch's cars were parked out front without them inside. After we stopped, someone opened my door, and I stepped out of the car. Cairo guided me inside with Frasier and Calix behind us.

"Where are they?" Cairo asked the staff.

"In the cinema," one of the ladies said, flashing me a smile. "We'll bring you some hors d'oeuvres as we prepare dinner for you boys and for you, Miss Astrid."

"Chips are fine," Frasier called over his shoulder as he disappeared down the hallway with Calix. For them hating each other less than an hour ago, they sure were quiet now. He turned around and flashed one of his smirks. "Please."

"You have a cinema?" I whispered to Cairo as we headed down the hall.

"It's just a big room with a TV," he said, opening the door.

It was not, in fact, just a big room with a TV.

It was just an enormous room with a huge TV and several aisles of reclining seats.

I settled into a seat between Frasier and Cairo, eyeing Rush and Arch a couple of aisles ahead, who were talking about something and looking back at me. Heat rushed through my body, and I pressed my thighs together.

They were so good at tag-teaming. I couldn't stop thinking about it happening again. Hell, I couldn't stop thinking about what had just happened in front of all those people. Being used and abused by these guys.

God!

But then my stomach twisted at the thought of Diya finding out. She could've walked right into Galaxy Grub this afternoon. Someone could've recorded what we had done in public—it had happened before in this town.

What was I thinking?!

Our ex–best friend—I didn't even like saying her name—had done the same exact thing to Diya, and Diya hadn't talked to her since. If she found out about me being involved with her brother in *any* way, she'd never even look at me again.

Sooner or later, Diya would find out. I couldn't hide it forever, though I desperately wanted to. How could I explain it to her? She was the one person who understood me better than anyone. But how could she understand this?

I peered at Calix, who leaned back against the seat, watching a movie. His eyes were heavy, his features so much softer than they were earlier. Even though he might've been fighting with Frasier over me today, these guys were his peace.

It didn't matter which one of the siblings I chose; someone would get hurt.

Frasier's knee brushed against mine, and I glanced over to catch him staring at the screen, too, almost as if he didn't realize his skin was touching mine. I kept it there and looked back at my lap.

Frasier had been using me. I still hadn't told him that I knew. How could I? I didn't want it to be true. The way he had claimed me today in front of everyone, before they all had their way with me, I'd just ... I'd thought that ... maybe he was a bit possessive.

A bit jealous? And if he was, then why had he used me?

Buzzing from my phone jolted me out of my thoughts.

Diya: Where are you?

My eyes widened, and I swallowed hard and racked my brain for any reason that she could be texting me without her usual excitement or craziness baked into her texts. Had I missed something? Were we supposed to study together tonight?

Then came those four dreaded words that everyone in trouble loathed to read.

Diya: We need to talk.

CHAPTER FORTY

ASTRID

MY STOMACH DROPPED.

Diya knew. She had to know. Why else would she message me now, after I had spent the night at her house with her brother, then decided that it was a hell of a good idea to go to a bar and sleep with The Crew *in public*?!

God, what is wrong with me?!

"Who's that?" Frasier asked, almost a tinge of jealousy in his voice. He clutched my knee and glanced over, gaze dropping to my phone for a couple of moments before they met my face. "Another boy?"

"No, just Diya," I said, as if it wasn't the biggest thing ever. "It's nothing important."

Just Diya? Nothing important?! She is going to kill me when I see her!

I needed a cover. I needed an excuse. Something believable. Maybe I could say that it was all some sort of twisted lie that Mira had created to get Diya to hate me? But could I lie to my best friend? I wasn't a good friend anyway, sleeping with her brother.

A lie would only make it worse.

Chewing on the inside of my cheek, I stared down at my thighs.

But how did she find out so quickly? Did someone record us and send it to her? Maybe … maybe her stepfather decided to rat me out to her.

If that's what happened, then …

My gaze met Calix's unreadable one. A flicker of something—maybe concern, maybe guilt—flashed in his eyes. I wasn't sure what it was, but I knew that he was the reason my best friend might never forgive me.

For a brief moment—to protect myself—the thought passed in my mind to tell him about his sister and his stepfather. But it quickly passed. Even if he did tell Diya, I couldn't tell Calix about their relationship. I wasn't that two-faced.

Who knew what Diya thought of me now though?

"You sure you're good?" Frasier asked, more quietly this time.

But it didn't matter because Cairo had already turned off the movie, and they all were staring at me intently, even Rush.

Frasier squeezed my thigh. "You're shaking."

"I'm fine," I whispered, heart pounding inside my chest.

The phone buzzed again.

Diya: It's important.

Oh God! No exclamation point. Just a straight period. Someone, kill me!

I stared at the screen, my mind racing.

Why did I think that I could hide this?! It wasn't supposed to happen this way. She wasn't supposed to find out. We were supposed to hook up once, maybe twice, and that would be that.

But no. I had to catch feelings.

Not only for Calix, but for all of these stupid guys.

My Read receipts were on for her, which meant that she could tell when I read her messages. I needed to come up with something quick, a distraction to give me a bit more time. Maybe I could feed into her thoughts about Cairo and me.

Me: I'm at Cairo's. What's up?

When my phone buzzed again, I quite literally jumped up from my seat.

"God, you're so fucking dramatic," Arch growled. "Turn the movie back on."

"Give me the phone," Frasier said. "Want me to respond to her?"

"No, no," I said, shaking my head and deciding to ignore my stepbrother. "I'm fine."

Another message.

Diya: When you're done, come over.

Fuck, this was serious. My hands were clammy, and I desperately tried to figure out what I should do. Should I go now? Should I text back and ask what it was about? Or should I just wait and hope for the best? Ignore her maybe?

My gaze met Calix's again, and he held out his hand for the phone. But I turned it over in my lap. What would I say if she confronted me? Apologize for fucking her brother? I didn't regret it. I loved—*love?!*—the way he made me feel, the connection we had.

No, no, no, no. It couldn't be love.

Another buzz.

Diya: Don't ignore me, Astrid. Just come over when you're done.

Calix took the phone out of my hand, and I jumped up to get it back. I didn't want him texting her and revealing anything. He knew how much keeping this a secret meant to me, and if she didn't know yet and he told her … I'd be screwed!

"No! Don't respond to her. Please!"

After depositing the phone into his back pocket, he sat back down on his seat. "I won't."

"Then give me my phone back."

"No."

"But—"

"But …" Calix started, peering over at me, his unreadable expression turning into a smirk. "We own you now, Hellcat.

Wasn't that obvious from what we did to you in the bar? You'll do what we say, and right now, we're watching a movie. So, keep your pretty ass seated in that chair and relax."

A wave of heat rushed through my body. Something about his tone …

"Do you understand me?" Calix asked as the others looked on in agreement.

I pressed my lips together and sat. "Yes."

Once the guys shared a look, Cairo grabbed the remote. Just before he could turn the movie on again, someone knocked on the door, and his maids walked into the room.

"All of your favorites. Even for you, Miss Astrid."

They set a platter of food down for the boys, then brought me my own little tray, filled with all of my favorite foods.

How did they know all my favorite foods? Did Cairo tell them? My eyes widened slightly, and I glanced at Cairo, who paused for a moment. *How did he know?*

He almost looked as confused as I did.

My gaze traveled to the others. When my gaze met Arch's, he snapped his head back toward the screen.

"Eat up!" one of the girls murmured. "We'll check in on you in a bit to see if you need more."

CHAPTER FORTY-ONE

ARCH

AT THE STOPLIGHT, I tightened my hand around the steering wheel and peered over at Astrid. Her arms were crossed over her chest, her knees bouncing, and her gaze was focused on the window on the passenger side.

She hadn't wanted to go to Diya's house, like she had apparently promised her after we finished up the movie. So, now, I was stuck taking her annoying ass home.

"Did you tell Cairo's maids what I liked to eat?" she asked.

"Why the fuck would I do that?" I growled, clutching the steering wheel.

"Because Cairo didn't."

"Maybe you're just predictable."

"Predictable?" she repeated. "Maybe you just like me."

"Like you?" I scoffed. "You fucking wish."

"Well, you're the only one in The Crew who knows what I like to eat."

"You're crazy."

"I'm not."

"Yes, you are."

There was a long pause.

"Why couldn't Calix take me home?" she muttered. "I hate you."

"Because he doesn't like you as much as you think he does."

"And you do?"

"Fuck no," I growled. "We live in the same house, so I'm stuck with you. Besides, if you wanted Calix to take you home, then you should've gone in his car to his house, where your *supposed* best friend is waiting for you."

"And let her know that he and I are dating?! Hell no."

"You and Calix are not dating," I said through clenched teeth, knuckles whitening. "He just wants to fuck you. That's all you're worth to any of The Crew. Just some easy piece of meat that we can all use."

Astrid snapped her gaze over to mine, eyes wild. I bit back a smirk, knowing that my words had gotten underneath her skin. She flared her nostrils, and I pressed on the gas to continue driving toward our house.

"I am not," she snarled.

"Sure."

She shoved me hard on the shoulder. "I am not. Take it back."

"What? You want me to lie to you?"

After glaring at my profile for another moment, she turned her stare to the windshield. "You're a piece of shit. Just because *you* want to fuck me doesn't mean that that's what the other guys only want."

"Get your head out of your ass. I don't want to fuck you."

"Suuuuure," she said, spitting my words back at me. "Seemed like you did earlier."

"You have nice tits. That's all."

"Wish I could say the same about your dick."

I flared my nostrils and slammed on the brakes, glaring at her. "The fuck did you say?"

"You heard me."

"Repeat it."

She smirked at me. "No."

"Repeat it, Hellcat. I dare you."

Tongue running across the front of her teeth, she faced me again. "Wish I could say—"

Before she could finish her sentence, I curled my hand around the front of her throat and pinned her to the passenger seat. "Be careful what you say next or else I'll make sure I get you on record, begging for my cock inside your throat."

Astrid pressed her legs together.

"Is that what you want, Hellcat?" I asked, drawing my thumb down her neck. My dick hardened inside my jeans. I strummed my fingers against her skin. "You want your stepbrother to ruin you for anyone else?"

"Fuck," she said, glaring at me, "you."

"You must want that so badly, huh? You keep repeating it as if you're daring me to."

Instead of responding, she narrowed her eyes at me.

That brat.

"You can be a brat with Cairo all you want," I said. "He probably lets you walk all over him. But with me, that mouth and *those* eyes are going to get you thrown out of my car, on the side of the road, so I can shove my cock down your throat and make you apologize for it."

"Mmhmm," she hummed. "I'm sure that you're going to—"

I pulled over to the side of the road, got out of the car, stormed around it to her side, and yanked her door open. Tonight, she'd learn not to test my patience. And I would rejoice in every moment of making her my dirty, filthy little whore.

CHAPTER FORTY-TWO

ASTRID

"YOU'RE NOT GOING to do shi—"

Before I could finish my sentence, Arch grabbed a fistful of my hair, pulled me out of the car, and shoved me onto my knees. Cars whizzed past us on the main road, and I felt like the dirtiest, most disgusting whore ever.

And—*God*—did I love it.

When Arch pulled back on my hair, I glared up at him, nostrils flaring. "You're a piece—"

He spit on my face, and warmth exploded through my pussy. I pressed my thighs together and bit back a whimper as he rubbed his spit into my face. Then he shoved four fingers into my mouth. I bit down on his fingers.

After hissing in pain, he smacked my cheek and pushed his fingers into my mouth again, as if I wouldn't do the same fucking thing to him. I bit down again on his fingers, earning myself another smack. This one harder.

"Keep it open," he snarled.

"Or what?" I gargled on his fingers, spit rolling down my chin.

He smacked me again. "Or I'll make sure it stays open myself."

I spit up at him, "How are you going to do that? Don't have anyone to help you keep it—"

Arch pulled me to my feet and ripped off my bottoms and my top, so I stood completely naked near the passenger side of the car. Before I knew it, he had me bent at the hip, my tits pressing against the window.

"You want to be a fucking bitch?" he growled. "I'll keep treating you like one."

My pussy was salivating, my legs already weak. Arch lined himself up at my entrance, and I tightened in anticipation. I curled my toes and arched my back, knees gently bent, my panties scrunched at my ankles.

He thrust into me. "A breedable fucking bitch."

A soft whimper left my mouth, and my fingertips whitened against the glass.

Every thrust became rougher, his dick somehow getting deeper. Whines and whimpers tumbled out of my mouth, my tits bouncing wildly against the window. He gripped my hips tightly, pounding into my cunt.

"Apologize," he growled.

What does he want me to apologize for again? Being cute?

"No," I said in a breathy whisper.

Arch stopped completely, the tip of his dick at my entrance. My eyes widened, and I whipped my head around.

Why did he stop?! My pussy pulsed wildly, desperate for him to be inside me again, filling me over and over and over.

His grip on my hips tightened. "Apologize."

"N—" I began, but realized that he really wasn't going to push himself inside me until I apologized to him. "I … I'm sorry. Please, put it back inside me." I tightened harder. "Please, Arch. I'm sorry."

"That's no way to apologize," he said. "You know what you have to say."

"Arch," I whimpered, "please."

"Say it, Hellcat."

"Breed me," I whispered.

"I want to hear you."

"Breed me."

"Loud and fucking proud for your stepbrother."

"Breed me!" I cried, pushing my hips back toward his.

Arch slammed his dick deep inside me, and I moaned out in pleasure. He pounded into me wildly.

With one hand on my lower jaw, forcing it open, Arch placed his other hand on top of my head, his fingers peeling my eyes open for him. He thrust himself into me and up against the car. "Keep those pretty eyes open for me."

The pressure rose higher and higher inside my pussy, pushing me closer to the edge.

"You see how your mouth should look around me?" he growled, shoving my face into the side-view mirror. "Open and obedient."

Heat exploded through my body, and I cried out in pleasure. I gripped on to his forearm to hold me up as wave after wave of ecstasy rushed through my body while I stood on the side of the road, in the middle of Redwood, as my stepbrother's cum shot into me.

CHAPTER FORTY-THREE

ASTRID

SITTING IN THE CAR, I gripped the steering wheel so tightly that my knuckles whitened as I stared at Diya's house. Usually, as soon as I pulled up to her place, I jumped out of the car and headed to the front door immediately. But tonight, *oh boy*, that was not happening.

Dim moonlight illuminated the brick exterior near the front door. My heart pounded.

I'd been sitting on the side of the road for at least ten minutes, hoping that Diya wouldn't notice and run out to get me. I needed to build as much courage as I could in case this really was the end of our friendship. My fault, of course.

My gaze dropped to my phone sitting in my lap, Diya's texts playing on replay.

Diya: We need to talk.

God, I wanted to die right now.

Knee bouncing, I grabbed my keys from the ignition and stuffed them into my purse. Fuck it. No more waiting. I had to rip this Band-Aid off and get this over with right now. If I waited any longer, I'd drive back home and—

Before I could finish my thought, the front door opened, and Calix walked out, his broad shoulders relaxed and his hands stuffed into the pockets of his jean jacket. Where was he going? He hadn't told me that he had anywhere to go tonight.

Maybe he was going to see someone else … Mira perhaps?

The thought hit me hard, both sharp and unwelcome.

"No," I murmured to myself. "You're not following him."

I was just looking for ways to get out of talking to Diya.

I stayed in my car as Calix slipped into his and drove off, his taillights disappearing down the street. After pushing my feelings away, I exited my car and headed up the driveway, then up the front walkway to the door.

My fingers hovered over the doorbell.

Fuck. Fuck. Fuck. Fuck. Fuck. Fuck. Fuck.

When I finally muttered, "Fuck," aloud, startling my-damn-self, I pressed the button and listened to the chime echo inside the house. One moment passed, then another. Then the door swung open, and I nearly melted into the concrete.

This was—

Diya's stepdad stood at the door. My eyes widened slightly, and then I narrowed my eyes at his friendly smile.

I know he ain't smiling at me like that if he told Diya all my secrets!

We were going to have some major problems …

"Astrid," he said, "Calix just left."

Oh, I know he didn't just say that!

I narrowed my eyes even more, nearly squinting at him. "I'm here to see Diya."

After raising his brows slightly, he moved aside. "Of course. Come in."

Once I stepped into the house, he shut the door softly behind me. I peered up the stairs, my stomach in knots. If he was making jokes like that with Diya at home, knowing that I had wanted him to keep it a secret, I could only imagine what Diya knew.

I twirled around to face him and dropped my voice. "Does Diya know?"

"Know what?" he asked, a small smirk curling onto his lips.

Before I could ball his collar into my fists and shove him against the wall, I clasped my hands behind my back. I couldn't forget that this man was my teacher too. If I hit him, he could utterly ruin my perfect grades.

"If she knows," he started, "it's not because of me."

That didn't answer my question! God, I'm so dead.

"Is she upstairs?" I asked, heart pounding so hard that I could feel it in my throat.

"Is that Astrid?!" Diya shouted from upstairs, her quick footsteps following. A moment later, she appeared at the top of the steps and ran down them. "It's about damn time that you got here."

Without giving me a chance to respond, she grabbed my wrist and pulled me up the stairs and down the hallway. When we finally reached her room, she pushed me inside and shut the door behind us.

"What took you so long?" she asked. "I needed you."

"Are you mad?" I asked quietly.

"For you being late?! Yes!"

I stared at her for a couple of moments, slowly realizing that she didn't know. Thank God that she didn't know! Oh Lord, I was safe from our friendship exploding ... at least for now. I placed a hand over my head and collapsed onto her bed.

"Astrid!" Diya said, jumping onto the bed with me. "This is no laughing matter!"

After suppressing my nervous giggles, I sat up. "What is it? Spill."

Diya glanced at the door, then back at me. She pulled something from her back pocket and placed it in my hands. My eyes widened as I stared down at the pregnancy test with *Positive* written across the screen.

CHAPTER FORTY-FOUR

ASTRID

"YOU'RE FUCKING with me right now," I whispered, staring down at the test.

Diya sat on her knees and chewed on her inner cheek. "Astrid, I don't know what to do."

I raised my gaze to her. "And you thought I would?!"

After shrugging her shoulders, she stared at me for a few moments, then threw her head into her hands. She mumbled something, but I couldn't quite make it out until she finally jumped up and began pacing. "I don't know how it happened."

"Girl, be so fucking for real right now."

"All right, I know how it happened, but we were so careful," she said.

I narrowed my eyes at my bestie. "Mmhmm. Careful as in …"

"As in … you know …" She shrugged again. "Sometimes pulling out."

"Sometimes?!"

"Maybe once …"

"Once?! Diya!"

"What am I supposed to do?! He's so fucking sexy, and I don't know how to tell him."

"He doesn't know?!" I whisper-yelled. "He's your stepdad!"

"I know. I know." She placed her hands over her face. "I know!"

"I don't think you know."

"I do, but he has such a big dick …"

"Oh my God," I said, as if I hadn't convinced myself that sleeping with Diya's brother wasn't a problem because he had a big dick, too, and how could anyone ever say no when they were getting dicked down so, so good?

"It's bad, isn't it?" she asked.

"Bad?!"

I didn't know what to say, except to repeat her words. Diya was *not* the type to get pregnant young. Not saying that she'd be a bad mother, but she had so many aspirations to move far, far away, and she had so many mommy issues.

"Oh God," she whispered, pacing the room and running a hand through her hair. "Oh God, when Calix finds out, he is going to kill both of us. What am I supposed to do?! How am I supposed to tell either of them?"

"Does Mr. Stepdaddy want kids?" I asked.

"Yes. No. I don't know."

"Have you talked about it?"

"No, but … don't judge me, okay?" She peered over. "He has a breeding kink."

"Girl, don't we all at this point?" *Must run in the family.* "Let me guess. You have one too."

Diya got all red and covered her face with her hands. "No! Maybe. What do I do?!"

"Do you want to keep it?"

Diya's face dropped. "I don't know."

"There are options, you know. Adoption or abortion."

Her lips curled into a frown. "I don't know. I don't want to do either of those, but I … I can't see myself raising a baby now. What if people start asking who the father is? How am I going to say my teacher?"

"Ask Sakura Sato."

"But she's, like, so popular."

"She is not."

"She is now."

"She'll still talk to you."

"No, she won't."

After handing back her pee stick, I pulled out my phone and found Sakura's contact. Last year, we'd had to do a project together for Civics, but I hadn't talked to her since. She had always been quiet and kept to herself.

"What are you doing?! Don't tell her!"

"I'm not going to tell her that you're pregnant. I'll say that I am."

"Astrid, you don't have to—"

"Oh my God, girl. Shut it and let me work my magic."

Me: Hey, Sakura! Sorry for messaging you so late. I kinda … ran into a predicament and was wondering if you could give me some advice. This teacher and I … well, I'm sure you could guess what happened. Do you have time to meet up tomorrow for coffee?

Diya and I stared at the phone for what seemed like forever until Sakura began to type.

Sakura: Hi! Yes. 4 p.m.?

Me: Sounds great! See you then. :D

"See? Easy-peasy. Besides, I don't think you have anything to worry about. You won't even be showing by the end of the year," I said, then scrunched my eyebrows together. "Wait, how far along are you? How long have you been sleeping with him?"

Diya raised her gaze to me and grimaced.

"Oh God," I murmured.

"It started … a few months ago."

"A few months?! And you didn't tell me officially until—you know what? It doesn't matter. We have a coffee date with Sakura tomorrow." I jumped off her bed, pulled down the blankets, and pointed. "Until then, get some rest."

CHAPTER FORTY-FIVE

ASTRID

"I'M SO NERVOUS," Diya whispered to me, her arm locked around mine as we walked into the café ten minutes before four. She dropped her arm and grabbed my hand instead, her opposite hand on her belly, almost instinctively. "Do you think she'll judge me?"

"No, you shouldn't worry."

"But … it's just …"

I faced her and placed my hands on her shoulders. "Why don't you grab us a table? I know that you're nervous. It's natural because this is all so new. I'll get you some tea. Go sit and relax a bit, so Sakura won't know that you're the one pregnant."

Diya grimaced, but nodded and found a table near the window.

Once she sat, I walked to the cashier and ordered two hot teas. My phone buzzed in my pocket, and I glimpsed quickly at it, my stomach in knots. Two missed texts from Calix and one missed call from an unknown number.

I had been avoiding Calix like the plague today because I didn't know what to say to him. He had noticed that his sister was acting weird and even texted me about it, but I couldn't tell him this. He would actually kill his stepfather.

"Two green teas!" the barista shouted.

After scooping them up, I headed to our table and sat next to Diya.

"What do you think she'll say?" Diya asked.

"I don't know."

"It's after four," Diya said. "You think she's actually coming?"

It was five after four in the afternoon, and Sakura wasn't here yet.

"She's probably running a bit late."

I sipped on my drink and stared out the large window, watching Mr. Avery pull up in his car, parking right near the front. He helped Sakura out of the car, and she waved him off as if she didn't want him to come in with her.

Then Sakura hurried into the café, her hair a mess on her forehead and her belly bump definitely noticeable. From what I had gathered from the rumors, she had been pregnant since September or October, which meant that she was several months pregnant now.

"Sorry that I'm late! I had a doctor's appointment," she said.

"It's okay," I said with a small smile. "Thanks for coming."

"Of course." She sat down across from us. "Anytime."

"Do you want anything? Coffee? Tea? I can get you something," Diya said.

She shook her head. "No, no … I'm good."

"Are you sure?" I asked. "It's no problem."

"If I drink anything, I'm going to have to pee again," Sakura said.

Once Sakura settled into her seat and pulled off her coat, she placed her forearms on the table and leaned forward. "So, tell me all about it. Who is it? What happened? How far along are you? Anything you want to know?"

Diya and I glanced at each other for a few moments, and then I cleared my throat and peered at Sakura, unsure about how much Diya wanted me to say.

"It's … a bit complicated. I don't know if he wants me to tell anyone that he's the father yet."

"Oh, that's totally fine," she said. "I shouldn't have asked. I know it's a touchy subject."

Another small silence fell upon us, and then I sat up taller because Diya really didn't want any part in this. She just wanted to listen, which was fine because we needed to come up with some type of solution before her brother found out.

Sakura reached across the table and grabbed my hand. "I know it's hard."

"It is," I whispered.

"You don't have to tell me, but you've told him, yes?"

I chewed on the inside of my cheek. "Well … not yet."

"You should."

"What if I don't know how he'll react?"

"Do you want to keep it?" Sakura said.

"I don't know. Did you want to keep it?"

After a slight pause, Sakura smiled softly and stared out the window at Mr. Avery, who sat in his car, waiting for Sakura. From what I had been told, he had been particularly protective of her lately and shielded her from a lot of the drama throughout her pregnancy so far at Redwood.

"I did," she said. "I didn't think I would want to, but … I love him."

Diya glanced down at her lap, her gaze softening and a smile crossing her face. I smiled to myself and nodded as if in agreement, though I couldn't relate at all to this. If any of the guys got me pregnant during high school, I didn't know what I would do.

But maybe I should keep a better eye on that with all the fucking we had been doing …

"You knew when you found out if you wanted to keep it?" Diya asked.

"Sorta," she murmured. "But I was really scared."

"Aren't we all?" I said.

"How did Mr. Avery respond when he found out?"

"Overall, he was really"—another pause—"really, really happy."

With a redness to her cheeks, Diya smiled. "That's good."

Sakura glanced between us, then turned toward Diya. "I'm not going to lie to you. It's going to be really hard, especially in the beginning and once everyone at Redwood finds out. We're almost in the middle of second semester, so it might not be too bad. You may be able to hide it."

"Oh," Diya said, stiffening and peering at me. "It's Astrid ..."

After moving closer, Sakura lowered her voice. "Yes, of course. Astrid's pregnant."

Except the look in her eyes made it obvious that she knew who really was the pregnant one out of the two of us. She wasn't going to be named the valedictorian for nothing. Sakura was smart and could pick up on the smallest of things.

"If she needs anything throughout the pregnancy, I'm always here," Sakura said to Diya.

Diya nodded softly, tears welling in her eyes. "Thank you."

CHAPTER FORTY-SIX

CALIX

REDWOOD ACADEMY BUZZED WITH CONVERSATION, slamming lockers, and the occasional teacher screaming at a student at seven fucking thirty in the morning. I grumbled to myself and headed to my locker, half listening to Arch bitch about something.

My gaze scanned the crowd for Astrid. She had been acting weird these past few days.

First, it had been sending me half-assed messages. Then she started ignoring me completely. My sister had barely said anything to me whenever I asked about Astrid, keeping her mouth shut and acting like she didn't know what I was talking about.

I balled my hand into a fist. I didn't like it one bit.

Rush leaned against the lockers beside mine, arms crossed. Cairo stood beside him, backpack hunched up onto his back and his head buried into a textbook, studying before his exam in Physics today.

"Hey," I said, interrupting Arch. "Has Astrid said anything to you? She's been … weird."

Cairo looked up from his book at the mention of Astrid.

"Gonna have to be more specific. She's always fucking weird."

Trying to seem less affected than I actually was, I shrugged. "I don't know. She's been ignoring me these past couple of days. I thought, maybe, something had happened at home with your parents or something …"

Rush peered over. "She messaged me last night."

"She did?" I asked.

"Yeah, wanted to meet up later today."

"Bullshit," Arch said. "She doesn't want to hang with you."

"Swear," Rush said.

"Well, ask her what's up," I said, attempting to not be a dickhead to him.

Yet my jealousy was bubbling up in my stomach. For Astrid, I would fight, but Rush could fucking obliterate me with a single punch. Still, my fist was twitching in envy. Rush and Astrid weren't even close. Why did she want to hang out with him?

What's her problem?

"I told her no." Rush chuckled. "Man, she's hot when she's mad."

"Why the fuck is she ignoring me?" I muttered.

"Maybe she's finally realizing how boring you are," Frasier said with a smirk, shoving his phone into his pocket. "I mean, come on. Your dick can only get you so far, Calix. She needs some adventure in her life."

"Right," I growled. "Because you're so adventurous."

His shit-eating grin widened more. "I'm just saying, maybe she's thinking about me."

Rush shoved him lightly. "Or maybe she's sick of both of you."

After a tense silence between all the guys except Cairo, Cairo cleared his throat. "So, what's the deal with your race this weekend, Rush? Is it actually on, or did they cancel this one because of the weather?"

"Depends if you're actually planning on showing up to this one, C," Rush said.

"I don't have an exam next week, so I'll be there if they have it and as long as you plan on winning."

"Oh, I'm winning," Rush said. "Brewer can suck my dick."

"Confident as ever," Arch murmured. "If that asshole wants to start shit again, I'm ready."

I shoved my backpack into my locker and pulled out some books, glancing down the hallway and catching a glimpse at a couple of Astrid and Diya's friends. They giggled with each other, but the girls were nowhere to be seen.

What the hell?

Arch leaned against the locker beside mine. "You good?"

"Seriously, nothing's been off with Astrid?"

He shrugged. "Not really. She's been … quieter than usual, I guess. Mood swing?"

Mood swing? Right.

"Maybe she's overwhelmed with school," Cairo offered, shutting his book and letting it fall by his side, one hand on his glasses to adjust them. "She hasn't said much to me lately, but she seemed stressed this morning."

Everyone turned to him.

"You saw her this morning?" Frasier asked.

Cairo shrugged and peered down the hallway. "Class is starting soon. I have to—" Before he could get anywhere, Frasier grabbed his shoulder and stopped him. Cairo grimaced and scratched the back of his head. "We usually grab … coffee before class."

"But you saw her this morning?" I responded.

"Maybe … it was just that—"

A group of cheerleaders walked by, giggling loudly with each other, their voices drowning out Cairo's softer one.

"Did you hear about Astrid?" one of them said, her voice sharp with excitement.

"Yeah," another girl said. "I heard she's pregnant."

CHAPTER FORTY-SEVEN

ASTRID

"OH MY GOD," Diya said, staring down at her phone from the driver's seat.

I hummed to myself and sat in the passenger seat of her car, scrolling through social media before school. Calix had messaged me about a billion times since last night, wondering why I wasn't responding to him, if it was something that he had done …

While I'd tried to reassure him that it was nothing, I had racked my brain for so many reasons why I could be acting this way. But the truth was that my best friend and his sister was pregnant by his stepdaddy, and he wasn't going to like that.

Diya froze beside me. "Astrid, you're not going to believe this."

"What happened?" I asked, ready to believe almost anything that happened in this town now.

This past year had been nothing but drama, drama, drama, drama, and now with my best friend pregnant … it was only going to get crazier.

A direct message popped up on the app.

Calix: Where are you??

After blowing out a sigh, soft enough so Diya didn't question it, I ignored the message on my screen and exited all of my social media. *God, it has been so hard, ignoring him. I need to come up with a good excuse soon.*

Calix wasn't going to wait much longer, not after adding two question marks.

The phone buzzed again, and I clutched my hand around it. *He isn't going to let this go—*

Arch: It'd better be mine.

My brow furrowed, and I clicked on his message to see nothing more. No texting bubbles. No other messages. Just one text that didn't make any fucking sense. But, hey, it *was* Arch.

When my phone buzzed for a third time, I immediately tapped open the message.

Cairo: I'll make sure you can make up your Physics exam. Stay home. I'll see you soon.

Then another.

Frasier: Tell me what you need, and I'll pick it up after school for you, baby. 👶

I scrunched my nose. *What's with the emoji? And why are they all acting weird?*

"I'm so sorry, Astrid," Diya said, eyes filling with tears.

Oh gosh, the hormones are already kicking in. I don't think I'm ready for it.

Once I set my phone on the dashboard, I pulled Diya into a hug. "Shh, shh, shh. It's okay, Diya. You don't have anything to apologize for. I know that this week has been especially hard for you. Don't worry. I will—"

"All of Redwood thinks you're pregnant," she said.

I stiffened. "What?"

"All of Redwood thinks you're pregnant."

"What do you mean, they think I'm pregnant?"

She pulled back slightly and showed me her phone, where

Calix had texted Diya less than two minutes ago, asking where I was and if she had known that I was pregnant. I snatched the phone from her hand and immediately messaged him back.

Diya: What? Where did you hear that???

Texting bubbles appeared almost instantly, followed by another message.

Calix: Some girls were talking about it in the hall.

Calix: Where is she?

My heart dropped, and I slowly handed Diya's phone back and stared out the windshield. How had they found out about it so quickly? We had only told Sakura last night, and I hadn't thought she'd tell anyone.

Maybe she'd mentioned it to one of her guy friends, and they'd mentioned it to someone else? But … no. I still couldn't see any of them spreading drama, not when Sakura herself was pregnant. They wouldn't do that to someone.

"I'm sorry," Diya cried, head in her hands. "I'm sorry. I should tell everyone that it's me."

"No," I said, shaking my head. "No. No. No. No. It's okay."

If I had to protect my best friend from the bullying by taking it myself, then I would. I wasn't actually pregnant, not *really* hormonal, only when I needed some dick. I could endure the abuse for the first month or so.

But what about the guys? I'd have to tell them, right?

I scrolled back through the messages on my phone.

Calix: Where are you??

Arch: It'd better be mine.

Cairo: I'll make sure you can make up your Physics exam. Stay home. I'll see you soon.

Frasier: Tell me what you need, and I'll pick it up after school for you, baby. 👶

Heat rushed through my body, and I pressed my thighs together. It probably *wasn't* a good time to be turned on as my best friend cried in the seat beside me, but tell me why they all seemed to be … okay about it? Excited almost?

Calix was searching for me. Arch wanted the kid to be his. Cairo was being the cute, loving guy that he always had been. Frasier was going to get me anything I needed. And Rush …

My gaze dropped, scanning to see if I had missed a message from him.

I guessed Rush really didn't care.

He didn't want to hang out after school. Barely spoke to me. Didn't message me.

"I'm sorry, Astrid." Diya sobbed.

"Diya, I already said not to worry. We'll just play this off. It'll be cool."

"Cool?!"

"You know how much Redwood Academy loves drama," I said. "Let's give it to them."

While she was in the middle of crying, she cracked a small smile. "How?"

"You wipe these tears," I said, pushing them away with my thumbs, "and get to first period. I'll stay home today to really stir everything up. People won't be able to stop talking about why I'm not in class."

"B-but why?" she asked.

I tucked some hair behind her ear. "Because I love you and I care about you."

"People will wonder whose it is," she said.

"Tell them that it's Principal Vaughn's … before Poison chopped his head off."

That'll really make everyone go nuts!

"B-but—"

I hopped out of the car, ran over to her side, and yanked her out, pushing her off toward her first period. I might've had a Physics exam today, but Cairo had me covered. This would surely spice up second semester, even more so than fucking five best friends.

Once she disappeared into the building, I headed across the parking lot toward my car.

A car sped up beside me, and Rush rolled down the passenger window.

What is he doing here? Last time I talked to him, he didn't want to hang.

"Rush?" I whispered, heart racing inside my chest.

"Get in, Astrid. We're going for a ride."

CHAPTER FORTY-EIGHT

RUSH

"WHAT DO you want to talk about?" Astrid asked from my passenger seat, playing with the ends of her skirt.

To my surprise, she had willingly gotten into my car without much asking back at school.

I tightened my hand around the steering wheel to keep myself composed.

We had left Redwood about ten minutes ago, and neither of us had spoken a word to each other. But I couldn't handle the thought of her actually being pregnant with one of the other guy's kids. I hadn't even fucked her yet.

That was my fault for not claiming her from the beginning.

The first goddamn time she had begged for me, I should've filled her with my cum until there wasn't a thought about whose child she had growing inside her belly right now. Everyone would know that it was mine.

"Don't play games with me," I growled.

"How am I playing games?"

After driving up onto one of the illegal race tracks, I parked and turned toward her, still clutching the steering wheel with all my might, my jaw clenched hard. "Who started that rumor about you being pregnant?"

A small smirk crossed her face. "It's not a rumor."

"Bullshit. You're not pregnant."

"What makes you think that?"

If she was … and I hadn't fucked her yet …

"Who started the fucking rumor?" I snarled, quickly losing my temper.

"It's not a rumor."

I released the steering wheel from my death grip and pulled her into my lap, wrapping my hand around her throat, my lips grazing against her ear. "I'm going to give you one last chance. Is that the lie you're sticking to?"

She pulled her thighs together as best she could, swallowed, then nodded. "Yep."

With one hand still around her throat, I shoved my other up her skirt and swooped her panties to the side, immediately finding her clit. She jerked up, her cheeks flushing red and her smirk widening.

"It's true, Rush," she taunted. "You jeal—"

After tightening my grip around her throat, I rubbed her desperate, lying little cunt faster. Her legs began shaking all around me as she tried to pull them together, but I kept them forced apart, wanting to torture her.

"Tell me it's not true," I growled.

She grasped my shoulders tightly, a moan leaving her lips. "No."

I moved my fingers faster over her clit, grinding my bulge up into her. "I want the truth."

Her lips parted the way they did right before she was about to come, and I pulled my fingers away from her. She furrowed her brow and tried to get herself off on my bulge, bucking her hips back and forth.

But I lifted her up a few inches with the hand I had fastened around her throat.

"Rush," she cried. "Please!"

"Tell me what I want to hear."

"Please, let me come!"

When I knew she had dropped down from her orgasm, I placed my fingers back on her clit to build her up again.

"You know what you have to say to come. Don't think for a second that I'm going to let you, just from you begging and pleading with me."

She whined and grabbed my wrist. "Rush, please ..."

I clenched my jaw and continued despite her attempts for me to stop.

"I'm pregnant, and you're not the—"

Just as she was about to come again, I pulled my hand away.

"No," she cried, attempting to yank my hand back. "Please. Please. Please. Please!"

For a second time, she dropped down from her orgasm, and I replaced my fingers.

Her legs were trembling, her cheeks flushed, her eyes hazy and desperate. "Please ..."

"The truth," I growled. "Give me the—"

"I-I'm not pregnant!" she cried, bucking her hips back and forth. "Please, let me come!"

My lips curled into a smirk, and my dick hardened even more. I moved my fingers away from her clit and unbuckled my belt. "Good, but by the time I bring you back to school, we'll make sure that you are."

CHAPTER FORTY-NINE

ASTRID

ONE MOMENT, Rush was teasing and taunting me with his fingers. The next, his belt was unbuckled, and he was pressing his head against my entrance. I whimpered and spread my pussy lips apart, giving him better access.

"Please ..." I whispered. "Please, give it ..."

Rush shoved his fat cock inside me, and I cried out in pleasure. My fingernails dug into his taut shoulders, and I tugged on his sweatshirt, desperately being filled with all of him. He thrust deeper and deeper and deeper inside me until his balls were pressed against my hole.

"Oh my God!" I cried, setting the tops of my feet against his thighs to bounce.

I moved up and down on his dick, my tits in his face.

I hadn't wanted to tell Rush. I didn't want to tell anyone at all. Diya wanted me to keep it a secret, and the more people who knew that I wasn't really pregnant, the more people would put two and two together and realize that it was Diya.

But how could I resist the man who had been teasing me for weeks now?

Rush grabbed a fistful of my hair and tugged back on it, burying his face into the crook of my neck. He ran his mouth across my skin, his slight stubble tickling me. Heat coursed through my body.

I bounced up and down on his cock, meeting his thrusts. My head lolled back so I stared at the ceiling of his car. Up and down. Empty and full. Over and over. I curled my toes, the pressure building up higher inside me.

"Fuck, your pussy is so tight," he growled.

"Tightest pussy you've ever had, isn't it?" I asked.

I didn't know what had come over me, but somehow, somewhere, I had gathered this confidence. Rush had probably been inside of many women before, but I wanted to be the best one.

"Only pussy I've ever had," he grunted.

My eyes grew wide, and I clenched. Hard.

The only pussy he's ever had? Does that mean ...

"The first pussy I get to feel wrapped around my cock and the first pussy I get to fill to the brim with my cum, so it's dripping down your thighs all the way back to school, and we can show the rest of Redwood who you belong to."

Fuck! How does that make him even hotter?!

He ran his mouth all over my body, down my chest, from one breast to the other, sucking on my nipples, biting them, tugging on them. "Tell me you want it, Hellcat. Tell me you fucking want every last drop of cum in my balls."

"I don't want it," I cried. "I *need* it! I need your cum. Please, give it to me!"

A couple more hard, deep thrusts, and then Rush stilled inside my pussy. Pleasure exploded through me, my body's instinctual reaction at finally being filled with his cum—something that I had been waiting for, for so goddamn long.

I tried to push my thighs together to displace all the pleasure, but Rush kept himself nestled inside my tight pussy, never letting me pull him out more than a couple of millimeters. He lifted his hips to get even deeper.

"Fuck," he grunted. "You feel so good."

"More," I pleaded. "Fuck me again. Give me more of your cum."

"You want more of me?" he asked against my lips.

"Please …"

Rush pushed the door open, lifted me with his cock still deep inside me, and stepped out of the car. I wrapped my legs around his waist, not wanting him to pull out of me. His cum was dripping around his cock and out of my pussy, the wetness rolling down my thighs.

After he set me on top of his car, I leaned back against my forearms. Grazing his hands down my thighs, he took my knees and parted them, his mouth coming down on my neck again, this time sucking harder. Each kiss, he sucked on my skin, moving further and further down my body and definitely leaving marks each time.

He reached over his head and tugged off his shirt, his body huge underneath the sunlight. I clenched around him even tighter, so fucking lucky to have a man like him inside me, to be his first, to take his cum.

"Watch me fuck your swollen little cunt," he growled, seizing my hips.

When he pulled out of me and pushed himself back into me, I moaned. The mere sight of him pushing his cum deeper into my pussy did terrible, terrible things to me. I dug my fingertips against his car until they turned white, letting him fill me up.

Over.

And over.

And over.

And over.

Back and forth. In and out. Empty and full.

"God, you're so fucking sexy," he growled. "These hips." He moved his hands further down my legs. "These thighs." He continued until he was gripping my ankles, holding them in the air and apart, his gaze on my cunt. "The way you take my cock so well."

"If any of the guys saw the way you're using me right now, they'd be so jealous."

My words made him even more feral, and he pounded into me faster, his muscles straining underneath the light. He used his grip on my ankles to thrust in and out of my cunt, faster and faster and faster, and then he stopped.

Pleasure rushed through my pussy, and I cried out, coming once more.

After a few last pumps, he pulled out, breathing heavily.

"Take a picture," I murmured, lying back on the hood of his car with his cum leaking out of my pussy. "Keep it with you in your car when you race."

CHAPTER FIFTY

ASTRID

WHEN WE RETURNED to Redwood Academy, it was lunchtime, and I really, really, really wasn't sure how I was feeling about the whole rumor thing.

I had told Diya that we could go along with it because I didn't want her stressing, but now *I* was because as soon as Rush opened the door for me to enter the school, everyone—and I mean, everyone—was staring. Even the teachers.

Vaughn's name was being thrown around behind hands. The noses were scrunching. And the side-eyes were siding.

"Who started the rumor?" Rush asked calmly, though I could tell that he was on the verge of exploding.

"Don't worry about it."

"They're saying it's Vaughn's," he said as if he still didn't believe that I wasn't pregnant. Or maybe this was just him being overprotective. "Did he rape you last semester?"

"No!" I exclaimed, glancing around nervously and hoping that he'd keep his voice down. As we approached the cafeteria, I didn't want anyone to catch wind and start any more untrue rumors. "Look, I'm not the one actually pregnant."

"Not yet," he said under his breath, and I elbowed him in the ribs. "But someone is?"

I gulped. "Yes, but you can't say anything to the other guys. I don't want them to find out." *Especially Calix.*

"Is it Diya?" he asked.

My eyes widened, and I stopped. "How'd you know?"

"Because Calix was bitching all morning about how you have been ignoring him. You fucked Cairo this morning in the Dunkin' parking lot. Were asking me about—"

"How did you know that I was with Cairo this morning?"

"Because I saw you."

"You're stalking me?"

A low chuckle left his mouth, but he didn't answer. He continued heading toward the cafeteria.

"Rush?!" I said, hurrying after him.

"What?"

"Forget it. You can't say anything to Calix, okay?"

"And if I do?"

"Then I won't fuck you for the rest of your life."

Another low chuckle left his mouth. "Are you sure about that? Don't make promises that you can't keep."

I flared my nostrils. "He will kill her if—"

"I won't tell him or any of the other guys."

We stepped into the cafeteria, and everyone looked at me, suddenly quieting down. I felt like I was in one of those cheesy high-school dramas.

Rush leaned closer to me. "But whose is it?"

"Didn't pin you as one for drama," I hummed quietly, hoping nobody would hear.

I headed for the girls' table. It was bad enough about the rumor, even worse that I was walking into the room with Rush—someone who barely talked to anyone.

My gaze landed on The Crew, who was sitting next to my friend group, Calix right beside Diya. All their eyes were on me and Rush, the guys looking especially pissed. Not at me. But at their best friend.

I sat on the other side of Diya, heart pounding out of my chest. "Did we figure out how everyone found out?!" I whisper-yelled at her.

"Sakura said that she didn't tell. It must've been someone who overheard us at the coffee shop yesterday."

Fuck.

Ruby smirked at me from across the table. "It's definitely not Vaughn's, is it? Who have you really been fucking, Astrid?"

Oh, this ho knows exactly who I've been fucking!

Rush took the only open seat beside her, his gaze on me, which made Calix even angrier. Arch chuckled as if he knew exactly what had happened and why we had walked into together.

Frasier was seated next to Cairo, who passed me a note. I unfolded it.

Don't worry. Physics is covered.

When I peered back up, he offered me a warm smile. Butterflies fluttered through my chest at his thoughtfulness. I'd have to repay him later.

What surprised me the most wasn't that the rumor had spread so rapidly around Redwood. It was that I'd literally fucked all these guys in very public spaces now, and nobody else seemed to know about that! If the student body wanted something to gossip about, Astrid getting railed by five guys at once was probably the thing they should've clung on to.

Someone cleared their throat to my left, and I looked over to see that Calix had moved his sister to his seat and taken hers, his hand now on my elbow.

"We need to talk," he said. "You've been ignoring me all morning, and now this?"

"Actually, I have …" I started looking for any type of excuse. "I need …" *What can I say to him?!* "We can—"

"I need to speak with her first," Diya and Calix's stepfather said, standing beside one of the deans. His arms were crossed over his chest, and he was staring down his nose at me. "You can gossip with her later, Calix. Astrid, in my classroom. Now."

CHAPTER FIFTY-ONE

ASTRID

"OKAY," I said, voice hoarse.

Calix grabbed my hand, but I yanked myself out of his hold. God, I hated being so mean to him, but this was not good! As far as I knew, Diya's stepfather did not know about the baby he'd put into Diya's stomach. What was I going to say?!

When I stood, the entire student body looked in my direction. Why was my life like a sitcom that wasn't funny anymore?! I felt like I was jumping from one scandal to another, and I didn't actually even have any scandals!

I grabbed my bag and headed out of the lunchroom, following him.

Of course, this looked like the baby was actually his. Not Vaughn's.

"I'll come with you," Diya said, hopping up behind me.

"I just need to speak with Astrid," he said sternly.

My eyes widened, and I scurried as quickly as I could to the hallway.

Out of all the teachers who could call me into their classroom during lunch, why the hell did it have to be him?! Why couldn't it be my Physics professor, asking why I missed the exam?!

We walked to his classroom in complete silence. Each step felt heavier than the last, and my palms were beginning to sweat. A lot. Now I had to come up with an excuse for him too—something that Calix would believe.

Once we reached the room, he held the door open for me to walk in. I lingered by the door, my hands fastened around the straps of my bag. My mind was spinning with every possible excuse that I could give him.

"Take a seat," he said, shutting *and locking* the door behind me.

"Fuck," I murmured under my breath.

After I dumped my backpack onto the floor, I sat and knocked lightly on the wooden desk with my knuckles.

He pulled up a chair and sat right in front of me, crossing his arms over his chest and clearing his throat. "So?"

"So ..."

"I heard the rumor."

"Who hasn't?"

He pressed his lips into a tight line. "Is it true?"

I blinked a couple of times. "I ... it's ..."

While he didn't react immediately, he narrowed his eyes. "Is it Calix's?"

My mouth dried, heart hammering inside my chest. "Wh-what?"

"Calix. Is it his?"

When I opened my mouth, no words came out. I intertwined my sweaty fingers and looked anywhere but at him. Rush already knew that I wasn't actually pregnant, and I couldn't let Diya's stepdad know either. It was his, for fuck's sake!

"Maybe," I said, voice wavering.

The silence stretched, and then his expression shifted. "Are you actually pregnant?"

"Yes," I lied quickly so he wouldn't think I was hiding something. "I am."

I eyed him, unsure how or why he looked too controlled yet also concerned at the same time, as if he didn't want to believe me —or maybe he didn't.

He nodded slowly and pursed his lips. "And you're saying it *might* be Calix's?"

"Maybe. I'm not sure."

"You've been getting around with The Crew."

I swallowed hard. "How'd you know?"

"The same way I know that you're not actually pregnant," he said. "Diya."

"Diya?" I repeated to buy myself some time. "Diya told you? About what?"

"About you seeing The Crew."

"What about seeing Calix?"

"She doesn't know about that."

I blew out a breath. "Good."

But that doesn't erase the fact that he knows I'm not actually pregnant!

"Diya has been withdrawn lately, and now I hear this rumor about you," he said.

My throat tightened, and I tried to keep my expression neutral. Was he really that observant, that calculated?! I wiped my palms onto my thighs and looked away from him, heart racing inside my chest.

"I don't know what you're talking about."

He hummed in response.

"Really," I said, grabbing my backpack. "I don't."

After a moment, he stood and moved his chair back to its original position, giving me space between him and the door. "You can go."

Fuck! Fuck. Fuck. Fuck. Fuck. Fuck!

Deciding not to stay because I couldn't convince him otherwise, I shot up from my seat and headed straight for the door. I stepped into the hallway, and the door clicked shut behind me.

Diya is going to hate me!

CHAPTER FIFTY-TWO

CALIX

AS SOON AS the last bell rang, the hallways exploded with students racing out of classrooms to get home. But I wasn't in a rush to leave. I was in a rush to get to Astrid's classroom before she had a chance to leave.

I shoved people out of the way, passing by her locker and not finding anyone. After continuing through the chaos, I popped my head into the classroom where her last class was supposed to be, only to find a couple of students chatting in the back.

"Fuck," I murmured under my breath.

Something wasn't right, and I was going to figure it out, one way or another. Was she really pregnant? And by who? I didn't believe that it was Vaughn. No fucking way. Diya would've told me last semester. Was it my stepfather, that bastard?!

Once I ran down the stairs to the first floor, I spotted Astrid just as she slipped out of the back entrance, her bag slung over her shoulder, her hair in her face, like she didn't want to be seen. My stomach twisted.

She walked quickly toward her car parked in the student lot. I kept some distance so she wouldn't notice me. If I had to stalk her to figure out what was going on, then I guessed I had to resort to stalking. She wasn't going to willingly tell me.

When she climbed into her car and pulled out of the lot, I made a break for my car and hopped right in to follow after her. With the mess of students leaving Redwood Academy for the day, it was easy to conceal my car for a bit.

I stayed two cars behind, keeping my gaze focused on hers. She took a turn onto Main Street, heading straight for the beach. The cars ahead peeled away, forcing me to slow down enough so she wouldn't recognize my car right on her ass.

A couple of moments later, she pulled into a small lot at the beach and parked beside Diya's car and another that I didn't recognize. After she started up the dune toward the beach, I parked in the opposite lot, ran across the street, and followed after her.

In the early spring, there weren't many people on the beach. So, I stayed a ways away and watched from afar, hiding behind the dune so they wouldn't see me. Astrid stopped when she reached Diya and … Sakura Sato.

Sakura Sato was the valedictorian of our class and … pregnant by her teacher.

My stomach dropped, and I balled my hands into tight fists. This only confirmed more and more of my suspicion that my own fucking stepfather had fucked my girl. Astrid was here to ask Sakura about how to handle the drama when it broke, and Diya was here for support.

While I couldn't hear what they were saying, Diya suddenly broke down crying, her shoulders shaking as Astrid pulled her into a hug. Astrid rubbed her shoulders, back and forth, and frowned at Sakura.

I narrowed my eyes. Why was Diya crying?

She rarely cried, only when it was serious, only when …

My eyes widened as the pieces suddenly began to click altogether. What if the rumor wasn't about Astrid at all? What if Diya was the one who was pregnant? What if Astrid was covering for her, taking the heat at school to protect her?

It'd explain Astrid's strange behavior, the way she'd been avoiding me, Diya crying.

Fury bubbled up inside me. If Diya was pregnant, who the hell was the father? Who had done this to her? All she did was go out with Astrid and stay home. The thought of some guy using her and leaving her to deal with this alone made my fucking blood boil.

Diya was my sister—my family—and I wasn't about to let anyone hurt her.

I clenched my jaw so tightly that I chipped my tooth. Sakura stood near them, saying something that I couldn't quite make out. Whatever it was didn't help because Diya continued to sob, only louder.

Knuckles whitening, I forced myself to turn around and stormed toward my car. I wanted to run down there and demand answers, to force her to tell me who had gotten her pregnant so I could kick his ass, but I couldn't.

She wouldn't tell me. She'd only hide it from me more.

So, I slipped into my car and slammed the door shut, glaring through the windshield and hurling my fist into the steering wheel.

Fuck! What was I going to do? Get it out of Astrid? Would she even fucking tell me at this point?

A sharp knock on my window snapped me out of my thoughts.

I whipped my head around, expecting to see an angry Astrid, only to come face-to-face with the one fucking bitch that I never wanted to see in my life again—my ex and Astrid's ex–best friend. Mira.

CHAPTER FIFTY-THREE

ASTRID

A SOFT ORANGE sky decorated the horizon, glowing against the ocean. Waves crashed against the sand, the salty particles dancing in the air. I gazed at the seaweed ebbing and flowing in the water.

My chest was tight. Diya had left a few moments ago, her tears spilling down her cheeks. She had asked to be alone, which really meant that she was going back to her stepfather so he'd comfort her. But he knew, and I hadn't found a good time to tell her.

I exhaled and ran a hand through my hair. "How long will it take for the rumors to die?"

Sakura frowned and followed my gaze. "I don't know. I'm so sorry."

"It's not your fault."

"We should've been quieter when we talked at the café. People are always listening."

"Some people have nothing better to do than start drama," I hummed.

If I had learned anything at Redwood Academy, it was that people's lives were just so shitty that the best thing they had going for them was hurting other people. Nice people, people who had good lives, *rich* lives—and not in terms of actual money —didn't hurt people like this.

After stuffing her hands into her pockets, she turned toward the dunes. "I should go."

I walked with her toward the parking lot. "You think she'll be okay?"

We stepped off the sand and onto the cracked concrete.

"I don't know."

My lips curled into a frown. "She's scared, and I don't blame her."

Sakura gently squeezed my elbow. "You're a good friend for taking the heat."

"Thanks," I whispered. "I appreciate it."

Once she slipped into her car, I walked to mine and grabbed the door handle. I didn't know why, but I scanned the lot, and my gaze landed across the street on a pair of cars parked right next to each other.

I furrowed my brow. *What the hell? Is that …*

Calix.

My fingers danced against the door handle, and then I dropped it. *What's he doing here? Did he follow us down to the beach? If I were him, that's what I would do, especially if someone had been ignoring me the way I had been with him.*

When Sakura sped out of the lot, I crossed the street to confront him. I didn't know what I was going to say, but I had to finally talk to him because I didn't want him stalking me and finding out what really was going on. Not until Diya was ready.

Yet the closer I got, the … the more something felt off.

Who is he with?

Once I reached the driver's window, I froze in my tracks. Inside the car, Calix was sitting in the driver's seat, completely oblivious to me standing right beside the car, staring at … his ex-girlfriend and my ex–best friend, Mira.

Her gaze lifted from him to me, her smirk widening.

For a moment, I just stared at the scene in front of me, not knowing how to feel. But then something clicked inside me, and I threw the driver's door open, swallowing the bile in my throat. My chest tightened.

What the hell is he doing here? And with her, of all people?

Calix flinched, his head snapping toward me. "Astrid, I—"

"Well, well, if it isn't Astrid," she murmured. "How's the pregnancy?"

I balled my hands into tight fists. "It's good. How's yours?"

"I'm not pregnant," she said, placing her hand on Calix's thigh. "Not yet."

Fury bubbled inside me, and I drew my tongue across my teeth, beckoning myself to not say anything mean, but I couldn't handle it anymore. She had been nothing but rude to Diya and me since she had dated Calix.

"Sure looks like it," I growled.

"Don't be a fucking bitch."

"Astrid," Calix said, shoving Mira's hand off his thigh, "it's not what—"

"Mmhmm," I hummed. "Sure."

"I swear to God," Calix said. "You don't believe me?"

Mira laughed from the passenger seat. "Relax, Astrid. I just wanted to talk."

I nodded because I didn't believe this bitch for one moment.

"You seem a little worked up though. Jealous?"

"You seem like a dumb little bitch," I said between my teeth. Then I turned toward Calix and glared at him. "I just don't appreciate being lied to."

"I didn't lie to you," Calix said, jumping out of the car. "I didn't know she'd be here."

"So, you followed me here, and she followed you?"

"Yes."

While I wanted to believe him, how could I? She was sitting in his car. If he hadn't wanted her here, why had he invited her inside the car? Why had she felt like she could place her hand on his thigh like that? Not his knee. His thigh.

"Save it," I growled. "I'm done."

Without waiting for him to respond, I marched back to my car. Calix ran after me, calling my name and beckoning me to hear him out. But I had just spent the day being bullied by people at school over a rumor, had to comfort Diya for the past half hour over the pregnancy, now this?! I needed time to myself.

I climbed into the driver's seat, shut the door, and locked the car before he had a chance to stop me. Then I started the engine and peeled out of the lot. My mind was spinning, my emotions a tangled mess.

If Calix wanted to play games, fine. I could play too.

Frasier's place it was.

CHAPTER FIFTY-FOUR

ASTRID

"YOU WALK SO FAST," I murmured, breathing heavily.

Out of all the places that Frasier could've taken me, we ended up in the same place as last time—the middle of the forest. I still couldn't wrap my head around him being a nature, hiking kinda guy, but this man was power-walking through the woods in front of me.

I had pushed Calix out of my mind—or at least, I had tried to.

"Forgot the pregnant lady is out of shape," Frasier said, pausing for me.

"I am not out of shape," I huffed. *And I am not pregnant either.*

The sound of waves crashing against the shore drifted through my ears, and I squinted my eyes, attempting to see through the woods at my darkening surroundings. While it was *supposed* to get darker later, it was still dark so goddamn early.

"Where are we?" I asked.

Frasier captured my hand. "You'll see soon."

I stepped over a tree knot. "You're really into hiking?"

"What? Still can't peg me as the outdoorsy type?"

"I mean"—I smirked—"if you want, I *can* peg you. Just not outdoors."

"Don't tempt me, babe. I'll let you, if that's what *you* want."

Warmth exploded through my body because while it wasn't something that I had ever fantasized about, the way that Frasier was willing to do anything for me just because I wanted him to made me clench.

Too bad Calix can't be the same way. Still not over that ho.

With my hand wrapped tightly around his because the tree roots were becoming the only thing to walk over, I shook my head. "Yeah, sure, let me think about it. Maybe we can record it and share it on social media so the school has something else to gossip about."

"We can do that."

I arched a brow and looked over at him, catching that smug smirk. "Oh, yeah?"

"The whole school getting to see you fuck me?" he murmured. "It's what I dream about."

A laugh left my mouth. "Shut up."

"I'm serious, babe," he said, pausing once we reached the top of the mountain. "Why don't we start by recording tonight and sending it to The Crew to see what they have to say about me fucking our girl?"

"What are we going to do—"

Before I could finish my sentence, my jaw dropped open slightly. I had lived in Redwood all my life, but I had never seen something like this before. The ocean stretched out in front of us for miles and miles, the moonlight shimmering on the water's surface like liquid silver.

Frasier grabbed a blanket out of his backpack and tossed it onto the ground, feet away from the cliff that jutted out toward the sea. Stars twinkled up above in the sky. I walked closer to the cliff, realizing how high we had climbed.

"Wow," I whispered. "It's beautiful."

"Just like you," he said.

I cut my gaze to him and burst out laughing. "Frasier, you are *not* the cheesy type."

"You're right," he said, gesturing to the blanket. "Get down there. Face down. Ass up."

"Don't tempt me, babe," I said, shooting his words back at him.

Once Frasier sat down on the blanket, he stared over the edge of the cliff and out to the ocean. I plopped down next to him and released a long sigh that I had been holding in since I had sped over to his house.

Today had been fucked. Absolutely fucked.

"You good?" he asked softly.

"I don't know."

"Is it Calix?"

"Yes."

"He's been a psycho bitch over you all day."

"Over me?" I scoffed. "Yeah, right. Doesn't seem like it sometimes."

A long silence stretched on between us, and then Frasier brushed his thigh against mine. "You know, I really meant what I texted you earlier. If you need anything, tell me, and I'll handle it for you, if it has to do with Calix or the baby."

In my mind, Frasier had always been the playboy, the flirt, the guy who would never settle down. Yet everything seemed so genuine with him, always. My stomach twisted as I wondered if he was just playing me like Calix had been.

Still, it felt so real.

"Frasier," I murmured, "about the rumor …"

"What about it?"

"You can't tell anyone, but … I'm not actually pregnant."

Frasier paused for a moment, then shook his head. "Damn it."

My eyes widened, as I hadn't expected that to come out of his mouth. "What?"

His smug smirk returned. "I knew it."

"How?"

"Come on, baby," he said, drawing out the words. "You would've told me first."

I rolled my eyes. "No, I wouldn't have."

"Don't lie to yourself."

He moved closer, his warm breath fanning my face. I shivered at how close we were.

He tucked some hair behind my ear, his fingers just grazing against my cheek. "You love me."

I sucked in a breath. "I'm not lying."

His gaze dropped to my lips. "But you love me?"

My heart was pounding inside my chest. "Wh-what?"

"Do you love me, Astrid?" he asked, his intense eyes on mine.

"Do I ... do I love you?" I repeated.

How ... can ... What do I say to that?

He drew his nose up mine. "Do. You. Love. Me?"

My gaze traveled from one of his eyes to the other. "I ... it ... you ..."

"It's a yes or no answer," he murmured, lips millimeters from mine. "Do you love me, Astrid?"

"Yes," I whispered, crashing my lips against his. "Yes, I love you."

CHAPTER FIFTY-FIVE

FRASIER

ASTRID LOVED ME.

I kissed her back, my hands all over her body. Though I had persuaded her to admit her feelings toward me, I hadn't thought she'd actually say it. I hadn't thought anyone would actually say it to me.

"I love you, Frasier," she murmured against my lips again. She wrapped her arms around my shoulders and pulled me closer to her, gently tugging on my hair as my tongue slipped into her mouth. "You don't know how much."

She wasn't the type of girl who fell for guys like me.

And yet, here we were, sitting on a cliff overlooking Redwood. Her face had been glowing from the moonlight since we had made it up here, and I … I hadn't even expected to ask her if she loved me. It'd just come out.

But she looked too goddamn fucking beautiful.

After I moved closer to her, she leaned back until she was lying on the blanket. I sank between her thighs, forearms on either side of her head, deepening the kiss. Still, I couldn't wrap my head around this.

Astrid loved me.

Me!

The guy who couldn't keep a relationship longer than a month, the guy who never let anyone get too close, the guy who dated a girl for a day and then pushed her away because after what Dad went through with my mother, I didn't like commitment.

Except … I loved Astrid too.

I hadn't realized it until tonight, but I was obsessed with her. The thought of her being pregnant with anyone else's baby had driven me insane, despite how much I tried to keep my cool today. Still, if she had really been pregnant, then I would've actually wanted to take care of the child with her.

When I finally broke the kiss, I stared down and pushed some hair off her face.

"I love you too," I said, the words tumbling out before I could stop them.

Her eyes widened. "You … you do?"

"Yes," I murmured against her lips. "I love you."

Expression softening, she smiled. "You're not just saying that?"

"No, I mean it. I want you to be mine. For real."

Eyes shutting softly, she smiled even harder and grasped my face to bring me back to her. I placed my lips against hers, and she slid her hands down to my chest. Once I moved my hands to her waist, I deepened the kiss.

"Frasier," she murmured, her voice low and breathless as her lips trailed along my jaw.

My body shuddered, and I pushed her skirt to the side, sliding two fingers into her. She arched her back, pressing her body against mine and making me even harder. I set my thumb against her swollen clit.

"I want you inside me," she breathed out onto my lips. "Please, Frasier."

I curled my fingers inside her, catching her G-spot.

"Please," she cried, digging her fingers around my shoulders. "I need it."

"Say it again."

"I want you inside of me," she cried.

"Not that."

She sucked my bottom lip between her teeth. "I love you."

I curled my fingers and hit her G-spot again. "Again."

"I love you."

And again, I massaged the bundle of nerves deep inside her. Over and over. Until her legs trembled uncontrollably around me. She gripped onto me tighter, her head lolling back and her mouth dropping open.

Once she came down from her orgasm, I pulled my fingers from her pussy and sucked them into my mouth, tasting her on them. Then I undid my pants and pulled out my throbbing cock, desperate to finish inside her.

After peppering wet kisses down her neck, I groped her breasts, trailed my lips lower down her chest, and sucked one of her nipples into my mouth, biting down softly. Then I lined up and slid my cock deep into her pussy.

"Oh my God!" she cried, clenching around me. "More! Faster!"

I pulled her toward me with each thrust, pumping harder and faster. "You're mine."

"I'm yours," she breathed. "I'm yours. I'm yours!"

Resting my forehead onto hers, I thrust all the way into her pussy and stilled as her cunt tightened around me. A low grunt left my mouth, and she clenched even harder, milking every last drop of cum out of my balls.

"God, I fucking love you," I murmured, placing my lips back onto hers.

CHAPTER FIFTY-SIX

ASTRID

"YOU WANT ME TO COME IN?" Frasier asked, leaning his forearm against the front door and wiggling his eyebrows at me. Moonlight bounced off his face, illuminating his skin. "We can make more babies."

"More?!" I giggled quietly. "I don't think so."

His gaze dropped down to my lips as I laughed, and my cheeks warmed. I didn't know why I was suddenly so … embarrassed around him. Ever since we had pulled on all our clothes, I had been more self-conscious than ever.

Maybe it was because I'd never felt like this about anyone before. And when I say that I felt this way, I meant about … more than just Frasier. Sure, Frasier was the first guy that I'd admitted it to, but the other guys in The Crew …

Especially Calix …

I quickly pushed him out of my mind because I didn't want to think about him and Mira. Then I wrapped my arms around Frasier's waist and pecked him on the lips. "I'll see you tomorrow at school."

"I'll pick you up," he said.

"No," I responded too quickly. "I mean, no, that's fine. I'll meet you at school."

After arching a brow, he returned the kiss and headed back to his car.

Whew, that was a close one. I didn't think he knew yet about my mornings with Cairo, and I didn't want to have that taken away.

Was it wrong to be with all these guys at once? Yes. One hundred percent.

But they seemed—*dare I say*—fine with it. At least, most times.

Before Frasier sped off, I slipped into the house and dropped my keys on the side table. All the lights were off, which meant that Dad and my stepmom were fast asleep. Shadows stretched across the stairs.

I kept my footsteps light, attempting to get to my room before anyone could ask any—

"Where the hell have you been?" someone said behind me.

I leaped up, my heart nearly exploding out of my chest, and twirled around to see Arch standing in the living room, in the dark, near the front window, as if he had been waiting for me to come home.

My stomach twisted, and I took a step backward. "None of your business."

He pushed himself off the wall and stalked closer. "It's late."

Another step back. "Mmhmm."

"What were you doing with Frasier?"

I craned my head up to keep eye contact as he approached. "What, are you jealous?"

"No."

"Sure sounds like it."

Arch let out a humorless chuckle and stepped closer, his body posturing over mine. "Don't act all bratty with me right now, Hellcat. I'm not in the fucking mood for it. What were you doing out with him?"

I crossed my arms. "Fucking him."

"Don't you have more important things to do?" he growled.

"Like maybe setting everyone at school straight for spreading the rumor that you're pregnant with Principal Vaughn's kid? Sounds more important than fucking the man-whore."

I flared my nostrils. "Guess we have different priorities."

"Are you fucking stupid, letting that rumor run wild?"

"It's not a rumor."

He moved even closer to me, bumping me back into our parents' bedroom door. "Principal Vaughn didn't get you pregnant. You weren't part of some underage sex ring. You barely leave the fucking house."

I stood my ground because two out of the five guys now knew about me not being pregnant, and I couldn't let Arch, out of all of them, know. He'd surely tell everyone the truth to ruin my life.

"It's not a rumor," I said again, his body flush against mine.

Arch snapped a hand around the front of my throat and pinned me to the door. "Bullshit." He grazed his nose against my ear, his warm breath fanning my skin. "You really want to get pregnant that badly, don't you?"

"I don't know what you're talking about."

"Oh, you don't?"

"No."

"I don't know why you want the entire school to think you're pregnant when you're not," he growled. "But you're doing everything in your power to actually get pregnant, huh? Your early mornings with Cairo, sneaking away with Frasier to the woods, Calix in his bedroom in the same house where your best friend lives. Rush now too."

"Have you been stalking me?!" I whisper-yelled at him.

But, damn, did the thought get me wet.

"Now, it's my turn," he murmured, fingers pressing against my clit through my bottoms. "Let's get you pregnant right in front of our parents' bedroom."

CHAPTER FIFTY-SEVEN

ASTRID

HEART POUNDING INSIDE MY CHEST, I grasped Arch's wrist in hopes that he'd stop because if either of our parents woke up and saw us like this … that'd be even worse than them thinking I was pregnant! Yet Arch just pushed me further against their door.

He closed the gap between us, his lips crashing onto my mouth, his tongue slipping between my lips, and his fingers still rubbing small circles around my clit. I curled my toes and whimpered into his mouth.

"Arch, we … we can't here," I whispered.

Pressure built up higher and higher inside my core. I pressed my legs around his hand to displace all the pleasure. He moved his lips from my lips to my jaw, then further down to the column of my neck.

Fuck. Fuck. Fuck. Fuck. Fuck. Fuck!

"Spread your legs," he murmured against my ear. "Before I spread them for you."

I moved my legs apart because if I forced Arch to do it, then I knew I wouldn't like the consequences. He'd be loud, wake our parents, and I wouldn't even put it past the maniac to fuck me in front of them too.

With his hand around my throat, he strummed his fingers against my neck and growled lowly. Heat raced through my body to my cunt, and I began bucking my hips back and forth against his fingers, pushing myself higher.

After leaving sloppy, rough kisses on my neck, he made his way back up to my lips and puckered them for me with his hands. I stared at him through wide eyes, my brow furrowed and the pressure about to tip me over the edge.

"Don't fucking come," he growled against my lips. "Not until I'm inside you."

"Please …" I whimpered.

"No."

I grabbed the front of his pants and pulled his huge cock out of them, desperately stroking it. Pre-cum dribbled out of his head, and I swiped my thumb across it to wet it before he shoved it inside me.

"Please. Please. Please. Please," I whined softly against his mouth.

Arch smacked me on the cheek, and I stroked him faster. His fingers continued in circles around my clit, and I sucked his lower lip into my mouth, the pressure about to explode inside me. I spread my legs and lined him up against my entrance.

"Put it inside me, Arch, please …"

Arch smacked me on the cheek again, causing heat to course through me.

"Arch …"

"Louder."

"B-but …"

Smack. "Louder."

"Please, put it inside me," I cried. "Please."

"Good *fucking* girl," he said, slamming inside me.

Ecstasy exploded through my core, and I grasped on to him, my pussy pulsing all over his huge cock. He wrapped his hand around my neck again and pinned me against their door, pushing me into it over and over.

It creaked every single time, and suddenly, the hallway felt so small, like every little noise was echoing through the house and into their bedroom. He placed his other hand over my mouth, his forehead against mine and his gaze on me, as if he was daring me to make a sound.

"More," I mumbled against his hand. "More, please. More."

He slammed into me harder and harder, getting as deep as he could get, until his balls were pressing against my entrance. I whimpered against his hand, tears welling in my eyes from the pressure of trying to keep quiet when all I wanted to do was scream out in pleasure.

"Fuck," he groaned against me, his eyes slowly rolling back inside his head. He slammed into me a couple of more times, his breathing hitching. "Your pussy is so fucking tight and wet tonight. So fucking wet."

"Please," I whimpered. "Come inside me. Please, come inside me."

"What do you want?"

"For you to get me pregnant. For you to breed me. Please, breed me."

Another low growl left his mouth. "Astrid, you're a bad fucking girl, aren't you?"

"Please," I whimpered. "I want my stepbrother to breed me!"

He shoved his fat cock as deep as he could inside me, then stilled. Pleasure exploded through my body, and my legs gave out so only he was holding me up. I grasped on to his shoulders and whimpered.

While I wasn't pregnant and I didn't want to be, if I kept this up with these guys … then I surely would be soon. I needed to be careful, but I didn't think any of The Crew would let me be. They wanted me pregnant. They wanted their babies inside me.

CHAPTER FIFTY-EIGHT

ARCH

SUNLIGHT POURED through the windows into the room. I turned onto my side and tugged Astrid closer, breathing in the scent of her strawberry shampoo. Mom and Astrid's dad talked quietly in the kitchen, their voices drifting underneath the door.

I blinked my eyes open slowly, catching the golden glow against Astrid's face.

Her head rested on my biceps, face relaxed, lips slightly parted. She looked ... peaceful.

My chest warmed, and for a moment, I forgot the rules that I had set for myself. While I didn't want her with any of the other guys in The Crew, while I wanted her pregnant even ... I had promised myself that I wouldn't cross one particular line.

Catching feelings.

Fingers twitching to brush a strand of hair out of her face, I stopped myself, my hand hovering in the air before I clenched it into a fist.

What the hell are you doing, Arch? I stiffened, the warmth of the moment quickly replaced by anger.

What am I doing here? I should've slept in my own bed.

After carefully sliding my arm out from underneath her head, I shifted away. The bed creaked under my weight, and I froze, hoping that she wouldn't wake up. I didn't want to see her all sleepy again, curling up next to me like she wanted … like *I* wanted … something more.

Fuck that.

She stirred, her brows knitting, but then she turned onto her side.

I released a quiet breath and sat on the edge of the bed, tugging on my pants. I shouldn't have fucking allowed myself to sleep with her last night.

Fucking? That was fine.

This? Fuck no. Never.

But I couldn't help myself.

Not when I had seen her walk in after her date with Frasier.

Not when I pushed her up against our parents' bedroom door.

Not when I took her to bed and lay down beside her.

She hadn't asked me. She hadn't fucking asked me, and I had done it anyway.

I clenched my fists, my nails digging into my palms as I tried to bury my feelings. I couldn't afford to feel this way about anyone and especially not her. Everyone in The Crew was obsessed with her, and … *fuck,* I was too.

Memories of that fucker I used to call Dad seeped into my mind. The way he'd looked at Mom, the way his affection always turned to anger, the way he'd twisted into an ugly monster behind closed doors.

I refused to be like him.

I refused to even allow myself to *get* into a relationship so I couldn't be like him.

Once I grabbed a hoodie that Astrid had stolen from me a couple of weeks ago, I tugged it over my head. My breathing hitched, and I stood, desperate to get out of this room that felt like it was closing in on me.

I shouldn't be here. I shouldn't be here. I shouldn't be here.

"Arch?" Astrid whispered right before I grabbed the door handle.

"Go back to sleep," I growled, voice void of emotion.

She frowned and propped herself up onto her elbows. "What's wrong?"

"Nothing."

I didn't know why I hadn't grabbed the door handle and stormed out of the room, but I stayed planted to the spot as Astrid slipped out of the bed and walked over to me. I turned my head away, not allowing myself to look at her.

"Don't be a dick. Tell me what's wrong."

"There's nothing wrong."

"Then why are you in my bedroom?"

"Because we fell asleep together last night."

Astrid stayed quiet for a long time, but I could feel her eyes on me. Then, suddenly, she curled her arm around mine and pulled me closer with it. In my peripheral vision, I saw the smallest smile on her face, cheeks rounding.

"I know," she whispered.

She knew, and she still asked me?

"Is that why you're leaving?" she asked. "You're scared?"

I yanked myself out of her grasp. "Scared of what? You?"

"Not of me," she said, readjusting herself. She scanned my face for a few moments, her gaze drifting from my eyes to my lips and then back up, her breath hitching for a moment. "I mean … of … this?"

"Of what?" I asked again.

"Of us."

"Don't be fucking stupid, Astrid," I growled, throwing the door open. "There is no us."

CHAPTER FIFTY-NINE

ASTRID

"FUCK!" I cried, tugging on Cairo's hair and keeping him close to my pussy, his tongue drawing circles around my sensitive clit. Pleasure exploded through my body, my legs shaking uncontrollably. "Don't s-s-s-stop!"

Cairo stared up at me through his glasses, his hands gripping my thigh.

God, how does he know exactly how to touch me?!

"We have to stop doing this at Dunkin'," he grunted. "Next time is at my house."

My head lolled back as I just thought about what he'd do to me there, and I bucked my hips back and forth, riding out my orgasm all over his face. Wave after wave of ecstasy flowed through me.

With my chest rising and falling in quick motions, I leaned back against Cairo's passenger seat and pushed some hair out of my face. The Dunkin' parking lot was quiet this morning, the occasional car pulling through the drive-through. Nobody from Redwood, thankfully.

"What's wrong?" Cairo asked, sitting back and readjusting his glasses.

The scent of coffee and doughnuts drifted through the air, and I ran a hand through my hair.

"Nothing," I murmured, still trying to catch my breath.

He leaned toward me slightly. "Is it the baby?"

"Yeah … the baby …"

A long silence drifted through the car, and then he cleared his throat. "Are you sad about not actually having one, or is it something else?" He placed a hand on my thigh and squeezed lightly. "It's okay. You can—"

I furrowed my brow. "Wait, how'd you know that?"

Cairo looked just as confused. "Arch told me."

I rolled my eyes. "Of course he told you."

"He didn't tell Calix, if you're worried about him," Cairo said.

Well, well, well, Arch not being a dick for once? Color me shocked.

The way Arch had looked at me before leaving my room earlier was like he couldn't get away fast enough, like there was something between us that he felt too. I closed my eyes and pushed the memory away.

"What did he actually say?" I asked, raising a brow.

Cairo pulled out his phone and handed it to me. Arch had made a group chat between all the guys in The Crew except for Calix, intentionally leaving him out for some odd reason. Surprising because he didn't have a filter.

Arch: Don't worry about Hellcat not being pregnant.

Arch: I took care of that last night.

That motherfuck—

Frasier: Beat you to it.

Rush: Ha, sure.

Warmth spread throughout my body, my cheeks flushing. I bit back a chuckle.

Before I could respond, my phone buzzed on the console between us.

Frasier: Morning, babe. <3

Cairo raised an eyebrow, though I couldn't tell his emotions. "Frasier, huh?"

"Don't start," I muttered, feeling my cheeks heat even more.

"You're blushing," he noted, hand tightening around the steering wheel. "For him?"

I hesitated as the weight of the past twenty-four hours came crashing down on my shoulders. Between the rumor, fucking Rush, Calix and Mira, Frasier telling me that he loved me, and then how Arch had reacted this morning … I was confused.

And in desperate need to tell someone.

"Frasier told me that he loved me last night," I blurted out.

Cairo's soft smile faded and was replaced by something … darker. "Oh, yeah?"

"And …" I shrugged, a small smile crawling onto my face. "I don't know."

Cairo leaned back in his seat, jaw tightening. "And you said it back?"

"Maybe. Why?"

"Because … you know Frasier's reputation."

I opened my mouth to respond, but Mira's car caught my attention, rolling past Dunkin' with her windows tinted but the speed slow as fuck, so I knew she was watching me. I didn't know what her problem was.

If she wanted Calix—*my hands tightened into fists*—then she could have him.

I glanced down at my phone, not wanting to respond to Cairo right now because I knew about Frasier's reputation and I still had feelings for him. I had feelings for all of them, yet I couldn't tell them. Sleeping with five different guys was different than loving them.

My phone buzzed again, but this time, it wasn't Frasier. It was Diya.

Diya: Astrid.

Diya: I need you.

Diya: Please, come now.

My stomach dropped.

"What's wrong?" Cairo asked, sitting up straighter.

"It's Diya," I said, already opening the car door and running to my car. "Something's wrong."

CHAPTER SIXTY

ASTRID

AFTER FUMBLING WITH MY PHONE, I slipped into my car and tried to turn it on, but my keys were nowhere to be found. I checked my pockets, then the passenger seat, then my pockets again, only to come up empty-handed.

Where the hell are they?

"Astrid!" Cairo shouted from his car.

I glanced over to see him dangling my keys, then jumped out to grab them.

"Do you want me to drive you?" he asked. "You look ..."

"Like I'm going to have a panic attack?" I asked, slipping back into his car. "Yes, I am, and, yes, I'd like for you to drive me, if you don't mind missing first period. I don't know why, but I have this really bad feeling in my stomach."

Something wasn't right. I just knew it.

My phone sat on my bouncing thigh, Diya's messages on the screen.

Diya: Astrid.

Diya: I need you.

Diya: Please, come now.

Something about those words sent a chill up my spine. He sped out of the Dunkin' parking lot and headed straight for Redwood Academy, driving through the parking lot to see if Diya was here.

But she wasn't, and neither was Calix.

"Fuck," I murmured. "He found out."

"Who? Calix? About what?"

"About Diya being pregnant."

"Diya's pregnant?" Cairo asked.

Guess he doesn't know as much as I thought ...

"Yes, but you can't tell anyone, okay? She'll kill me ..." *If Calix hasn't killed her yet.*

"Who's the father?" Cairo asked. When I didn't respond, Cairo glanced over at me for a brief moment, pulling to a stop at the Stop sign. He began driving once more, his eyes turning from confusion into shock. "You've got to be kidding."

"You can't tell anyone!" I said, turning toward him and grabbing his hand. "Please."

"I won't, but their stepdad?"

"I know," I whispered, spotting their house in the distance. "I know. I know."

Once Cairo parked out front, I leaped out of the car and headed with him up the front walkway to the door that was wide open. Calix was shouting inside, his voice echoing out the front door. And it sounded like ... crashing and screaming.

"Calix, stop!" Diya shouted.

I hurried into the house, my heart pounding so hard that I could feel it in my throat. My stomach twisted into ugly knots. I ran up the stairs, my mind racing with possibilities as to what was happening—none of them good.

When I reached Diya's room, she was standing on her bed, with her stepfather on one side and Calix on the other. Calix was screaming, shouting at his stepfather, not having noticed me yet. And the poor man already had a black eye forming from Calix.

"Diya!" I shouted, pushing past Calix to pull her off the bed. "Get down."

"Thank God you're here," she cried. "Calix found out. He found out!"

Before she could get caught in the middle of Calix unleashing on her boyfriend—*Can I even call him that?*—I tugged her into the hallway and away from the drama. I ushered her over to Cairo, who stared at me through wide eyes, as if he didn't know what to do.

"Stop him, Astrid." She sniffled. "Please. I don't want anyone getting hurt."

"Astrid, what do you want me to—" Cairo started, but I ran back into the room.

Calix had crossed the bedroom, shoving his fist into his stepfather's face. I wrapped my arm around his waist and yanked him back as hard as I could, giving myself enough space to slip between them.

"Calix, stop!" I shouted, waving my hands back and forth so he'd see me.

"I'm going to fucking kill you," Calix snarled at him, coming back with another swing.

But when he saw me, he stopped his punch and pulled it back, staring down at me through fury-filled eyes. They softened, and then he turned around and stormed straight out of the room. A moment later, the front door slammed closed.

"Where'd he go?" I asked, running into the hallway.

Cairo had his arm awkwardly around Diya, who was sobbing uncontrollably. "I don't know."

I hurried down the hallway, then the steps. "Well, I'm going to find him."

CHAPTER SIXTY-ONE

CALIX

MY KNUCKLES WERE RAW, split open, and bleeding.

I laid my foot on the accelerator and continued forward, unsure where the hell I was going, but knowing that I needed to get as far away from there as possible. I didn't want to see Diya and especially not Astrid. Not like this.

The streetlights and rage blurred into a haze around me, my breaths coming in sharp gasps. I clenched my hand around the steering wheel. I wanted to kill him. No, I *was* going to kill him for what he had done to my sister.

That dickhead had manipulated her, fucked her, and gotten her pregnant.

After speeding all around Redwood for what felt like several hours but somehow only minutes at the same time, I found myself at the Overlook. Light glimmered off the ocean down below, the mountain of rocks the only thing stopping me from driving into it.

"I hate him," I snarled, parking and hitting the steering wheel. "I hate him!"

What had he done to her? Why did she want to protect him?

The questions raced through my mind, and I sneered at the

windshield, imagining finishing what Astrid had broken up earlier. I wanted him dead. I wanted him to see me when he took his last fucking breath.

How could he do this?! I trusted him.

Someone knocked on my window, but I just gripped the steering wheel tighter.

I didn't want to fucking talk, and she knew it.

"Calix!" Astrid yelled outside in the cold. "Open up!"

I flared my nostrils and shook my head.

"Please," she said, knocking some more. "Open the door."

"I don't want to talk, Astrid."

"You don't want to talk, but you need to."

A low growl escaped my lips, and I unlocked the door, but didn't open it for her. She yanked the door open, grumbling to herself, and crossed her arms, her eyes fixed on me. I stared back, empty inside.

Between her not talking to me yesterday because she'd thought that Mira and I were actually together to walking in on my sister and my stepfather this morning, I didn't feel fucking anything anymore.

Her gaze flickered down to my knuckles. "You're bleeding."

"I don't care."

Once she exhaled sharply, she stepped closer and brushed her fingers against my wrist. Her skin felt warm against mine, and I loathed the reaction my body had to her. I didn't want to feel anything, especially not this and especially not now.

"You think beating up your stepfather is going to help Diya?" she said.

"Yes."

"Damn it, Calix!" she snapped. "No, it's not. You beating the shit out of him is not going to stop your sister from being pregnant. It's not going to stop your sister's feelings for him. And it's certainly not going to stop them from being together."

"My sister doesn't have feelings for that fucker," I growled, yanking myself away from her. "Besides, I don't give a fuck if it helps. He deserves worse than a couple of fists to his face. I want to fucking kill him, Astrid."

"If you lay another hand on him, Diya will hate you forever." She furrowed her brow. "And what about you?! What happens if he presses charges? What happens if you do that and you get yourself thrown in prison? You're going to throw your entire life away for this?!"

My breathing came out heavy, my chest rising and falling too fast.

"I don't care," I said through clenched teeth.

But I did care.

Not about him. Not about the consequences.

About the way Astrid was looking at me right now, as if … she was afraid of losing me.

She reached up and cupped my face in her hands, forcing me to look at her. "Don't lie."

"I'm not."

"Yes, you are. You think hurting him will make you feel better. But it won't."

I shook my head, my heart hammering inside my chest. "Then what the hell am I supposed to do, Astrid? Just stand by and let him walk free? Let him act like he didn't ruin her life? He's still married to my fucking mom."

I didn't know what the hell I was doing anymore. And Astrid was getting too close, her fingers now stroking my cheeks, making me feel shit I didn't want to. When I looked at her, I felt something other than rage. Something that scared me just as much.

It always had, since the day I had met her when we were just kids.

Before I could stop myself, I leaned forward and kissed her. There were so many things that I wanted to say to her, but I couldn't get them to come out. How could I tell her how I felt when she thought I was cheating on her with Mira? How could I ask her for help with this when she hated me so much that she didn't give me a chance to explain what had happened?

She placed a hand on my chest and gently pushed it away a moment later. "Calix …"

I stared at her for a couple of moments, then turned away and wiped my lips. "Sorry, I—"

She seized my face in her hands once more, climbed into my lap, and kissed me back.

CHAPTER SIXTY-TWO

ASTRID

I DIDN'T HESITATE. I didn't even think.

I climbed up onto Calix's lap, straddled his waist, and kissed him hard on his pretty mouth. He sucked in a sharp breath, but moved his lips against mine, his fingers dancing alongside my hips, as if he had been aching for this.

After dragging my nails down his chest and abdomen, I curled my fingers around the hem of his shirt and began to tug it up, tracing his muscles. I didn't know which one of us needed this more, and honestly, I didn't care.

All I wanted to do was forget about him and Mira. I hated her, but I loved the fact that he had been begging for *me* to talk to him, for *me* to be with him, for *me* to be *his*. Not her. In this little game that Mira wanted to play, I was always winning.

He broke the kiss so I could tug his shirt over his head. Then he grabbed a fistful of my hair and pulled back on it, leaving my neck open and bare. He sank his face into the crook between my shoulder and collarbone, sucking on my skin.

"You're mine," he mumbled, kissing all over. "Mine. Mine. Mine. Mine. Mine. Mine. Mine. Mine. Mine. Mine."

I curled my fingers around his muscular shoulders, my head lolling back and a soft moan leaving my mouth. He groaned against my skin, his hands sliding up my back, yanking me closer until there wasn't a centimeter of space between us.

Once he tugged off my top, I ground against him, my fingers digging into his muscle, the heat beginning to rush through my body. I clenched, desperate and aching for him to be inside me already.

This was wrong. It always had been. But I didn't care.

"Please," I whimpered. "I need it."

I deepened the kiss, fingers tangling in his hair. When he reached down between us to pull himself out of his jeans, my stomach flipped. We had had sex before, many times, but I felt like it was that first night again, back at that party.

"Don't hold back." I hovered above him, letting him line up at my entrance. "Please, do—"

Another moan left my mouth as he pushed himself up into me. My eyes rolled back inside my head, and I brushed my hips against his, desperate to be filled. He groaned into my mouth and gripped my waist tightly.

"Hellcat," he murmured.

I bucked my hips again, slow and deliberate. "Calix ..."

He wrapped me up into his strong embrace and slammed up into me, groaning again into my mouth. I sat back down on his huge cock, letting him get even deeper inside my tight little pussy. He lifted me up once more. Toes curled, I dropped my hips back, another groan leaving both our mouths.

It started slowly; he'd lift me up, and I'd sit back down.

But it quickly turned into him lifting me up and dropping me back down as he pounded into me. Faster and faster and faster and even faster. Until the entire car was shaking. I cried out in pleasure, the pressure rising higher and higher inside me.

"I love you," he mumbled against my lips, slamming up into me. "I love you so much."

My heart raced, and I exploded around him. "I love you too. God, I love you too!"

CHAPTER SIXTY-THREE

CALIX

ASTRID SAT IN MY LAP, breathing heavily while staring at me in surprise. I looked back with the same expression, my brows drawn together slightly. The words still hung in the air between us, thick and heavy.

I love you.

In the heat of the moment, I'd let it slip out. I was so engrossed in every part of her, so obsessed with her, so desperate for her, that I let it out, and I couldn't take it back. But she said it too. She had told me that … that she loved me.

Her gaze dropped to my lips for a brief moment, and then she tucked some hair behind her ear and smiled, moving closer to brush her nose against mine. "I love you, Calix. I love you so much. I'm not going to take it back."

I pressed my forehead against hers, my heart racing inside my chest. My hands were on her waist, drawing her closer. I brushed my lips over hers, everything melting away outside of us. All my pain, all my fears, all my rage … gone.

While I wasn't supposed to say it, she wasn't supposed to say it back.

And now …

"I love you," I murmured against her mouth. "I'm sorry."

"What are you sorry for?"

After pulling back enough to look at her, I cupped her face in my hands. Her cheeks were flushed, her lips were swollen, and her eyes were filled with … with something that I had only seen when she looked at Frasier.

"For everything that's happened these past few days," I whispered.

She blinked at me a couple of times. "It's okay."

"No, it's not."

She furrowed her brow. "I don't know what Mira means to you, but …"

"She means nothing to me." I brushed my thumb alongside her cheekbone, desperate for her to believe it. "You know that I don't say things I don't mean. She means nothing to me. I fucking love you."

"Then why was she in your car?"

"Because she showed up. Not because I wanted her there." I tensed at the thought of her crawling into my car, blackmailing me with a video of the night we had been at the bar with Astrid. "She got into my car because she wanted to talk. She had a recording of us together."

Astrid tensed. "Why didn't you tell me?"

"How could I? You refused to talk to me, Astrid." I shook my head because that wasn't an excuse. I knew the reasons that she'd refused to talk to me. "It doesn't matter. What matters is that I didn't want her showing Diya because I know you don't want her finding out."

Astrid stayed quiet for a long time, then nodded. "What did she want this time?"

"To get under my skin, make me second-guess things. She always plays those games."

She dropped her gaze. "Did you kiss her?"

"No. I don't want her, Astrid. I only dated her to make you

jealous."

"You what?"

"I only dated her to make you jealous," I whispered. "But you were never supposed to find out."

A small smile crawled onto her lips. "Really?" Then she giggled behind her hand.

I chuckled and tucked some hair behind her ear. "Yes, really."

"Okay," she said, nodding along.

"Okay?"

"I believe you, but if she tries anything else, I'm breaking her nose."

"Go for it." Another chuckle left my lips. "But maybe retake those jiujitsu classes or ask Rush how to fight before that. I've seen the way you punch."

Astrid's eyes lit up, and she punched me straight in the shoulder. "Not nice. I punch really hard actually. I could mess her up, if I wanted to."

"Oof," I murmured, rubbing my shoulder so she'd feel better even though it hadn't hurt one bit. "Sure can, Hellcat." I cleared my throat. "Can we talk about my sister for a sec? I … did you know about it?"

She paused, her smile fading. "Yes."

"How long?"

"For a while," she whispered, placing her hands on my chest. "She didn't want you to know because she knew how you'd react. She's going to be okay. Your stepfather didn't take advantage of her, and your mom … I don't know … I can't really get into it."

I blew a breath out of my nose, not wanting to dive any deeper into this mess, but knowing that I needed to get to the bottom of it. I needed to find out the truth. I needed to know what had really happened.

Because Diya was my sister.

And I'd vowed to protect her from anything and everything.

CHAPTER SIXTY-FOUR

ARCH

WITH MY HAND balled into a fist, I leaned against the wall at the very end of the hallway, impatiently waiting for Astrid to get out of class. She had no fucking idea what she was doing to me. I'd spent the entire lunch period pretending like I didn't care about what Calix had told me.

He loved her, and she loved him?

That fucking bastard. *Him* and *Frasier*.

The end-of-day bell rang, and students flooded into the hallways. I flared my nostrils and stared ahead toward her locker. I didn't want to care. I didn't want to feel this tight, burning sensation in my chest.

But there it fucking was.

Suddenly, she and Frasier turned the corner, heading toward her locker. She threw some hair over her shoulder, giggling at something that he'd said. I gritted my teeth, pushed myself off the wall, and closed the distance between all three of us in four strides.

Before I could register what I was doing, I snapped her wrist and tugged.

"Hey! Arch, what are you—"

I yanked her away from Frasier, not stopping, not even letting her finish her question. I dragged her with me, moving fast with my grip tight around her wrist. I needed to get her alone. I couldn't fucking handle this any longer.

"Arch," she hissed. "What the hell are you doing?"

Frasier shouted after me, but didn't decide to follow.

Fucker didn't deserve her. If someone did that to my girl, I'd make them pay.

Even if we were friends.

After pushing open the nearest empty classroom door, I tugged her inside. The door clicked shut behind us, the only sound echoing through her room? Her sharp inhale and quick breathing.

"Are you fucking enjoying this?" I growled.

She furrowed her brow. "Enjoying what? What are you talking about?"

I stepped closer, and she moved back toward a desk.

"You know what."

Her legs hit the seat. "No, actually, I don't."

I placed my hands on the desk behind her, trapping her and leaning down so we were face-to-face. She wasn't going anywhere until I got my answers. And not the ones that she was going to give me. The ones *I* wanted.

"Being passed around between Frasier and Calix like a dirty whore."

Her eyes widened in rage. "Excuse me?!"

"You heard me. You're acting like a dirty whore."

"And what's it to you? I thought that's how you liked me?" She crossed her arms and met my glare with one of her own, that same smoldering intensity in them that I'd felt last night. "I don't belong to anyone, Arch. Not Frasier. Not Calix. And definitely not you."

"Not me?" I said in a dangerously low breath. A dark chuckle left my mouth. "Not me?"

"What? You mad about that?"

"Mad?" I said because she loved to get under my skin, didn't she? "You have no idea."

She glared at me for a couple of minutes longer, then flared her nostrils. "What the hell is your problem? You get angry at me for being out with Frasier, you fuck me in front of our parents' room, you fall asleep with me, and then you run away like a little girl this morning."

I captured her throat in my hand. "You're my fucking problem, Astrid. You've been my fucking problem since our parents married. I haven't been able to get you off my fucking mind, and it's eating me alive."

Just before she was about to give me a sassy response, she widened her eyes and snapped her mouth closed. She opened it again, only to close it, her brow furrowing, as if she didn't know how to respond.

A long moment stretched between us.

"What are you going to do about it?" she whispered. "About the problem?"

"I can't do fucking anything about it."

"Why not?"

"Because you don't want me to, Astrid," I said.

Why would she want someone like me? Calix or Cairo was probably the best choice between all the guys in The Crew. Besides, I didn't want to get caught up in a relationship and end up becoming just like my fucking father.

She sucked in a breath. "You think I don't want you?"

I leaned in, my nose brushing against hers. *Fuck.*

"Astrid," I warned, "don't start something you can't stop."

She curled her fingers around my shoulders. "What if I don't want you to stop this time?"

CHAPTER SIXTY-FIVE

ASTRID

I WANTED Arch to say it.

I wanted him to break. To snap.

He had been so close to admitting that he wanted me—that he loved me—this morning when we were alone in my bedroom. I had been so desperately craving his words all day, to hear them roll off his lips, like they had with Frasier and Calix …

My fingers curled around his shoulders, and I pulled him closer, *desperate.*

"Hmm?" I murmured, brushing my nose against his. "Because I don't want you to stop."

When his breathing hitched, I thought for sure that he'd let it all out, let it go, tell me what I had been *craving* for him to tell me. But I knew … somewhere deep down … that I wasn't going to get it. Not from him. Not now.

He grabbed me tighter, pressing his body against mine, his breathing coming out uneven. I licked my lips, my heart pounding inside my chest as I watched his gaze flick down to my mouth before snapping back up to my eyes.

"Say it," I mumbled. "Come on, Arch. Tell me."

Another silent moment passed.

Then he let out a humorless laugh and shook his head. "You're delusional if you think I'm going to say that to you. You know I don't do that shit with anyone. I'm not like Frasier or Calix, Hellcat. You're going to have to do better than that."

"Better than what?" I whispered. "What do you want to say to me?"

"You know what."

I pushed my body just enough against him. "No, I don't think that I do."

He clenched his jaw, his eyes flickering with hunger.

God, he's so close to saying it, so close to admitting it to me.

But before he could break, before I could push him just a little further, the door slammed open. Arch immediately stepped back and snapped his head toward the door, his entire body tensing, as if he was uncomfortable.

And Arch was *never* uncomfortable.

Rush leaned against the doorframe and crossed his arms over his chest, looking from Arch to me, then back to Arch. Out of all of The Crew, Arch and Rush were probably the closest, and by the look on Rush's face ...

I couldn't tell if it was a knowing expression or something darker.

Something more animalistic.

After releasing a frustrated breath because I had been so freaking close to hearing those words from the one man I'd thought I would *never* hear them from, I cleared my throat and straightened myself out.

My entire body was burning with tension, the space between my legs ... soaked.

Instead of saying a word, Rush stepped farther into the room and locked the door behind himself. When they shared another look, I swallowed hard and found myself pressing against the desk once more.

"In here, all alone with Astrid, and you didn't invite me?" Rush asked.

Arch clenched his jaw. "You didn't seem interested in fucking her."

"Yes, he does," I murmured, remembering the last time we had been together.

A low chuckle left Rush's mouth as he walked toward us with slow, lazy steps, his gaze never leaving mine once. Warmth pooled between my thighs, and my nipples hardened underneath my shirt.

While Arch usually *liked* sharing with Rush, Arch grabbed my waist and pulled me against him before Rush could approach me fully. I stood between two boulders that called themselves men, with Arch angry and Rush amused.

"Damn." Rush chuckled. "I should've come in earlier."

Arch's grip on me tightened, and before I could even process what was happening, Arch tilted my head back so I looked up at him, and he crashed his lips onto mine. It was anything but soft or careful. It was a claim, a punishment.

He was angry.

Possessive.

Obsessed with the thought of me being his. And only his.

I gasped into his mouth, and he grabbed my hips, lifting me back onto the desk and slipping between them. Rush was suddenly on the other side of the desk, his fingers swooping my hair over my shoulder and to my back, giving himself room for his lips on my neck.

"She was mine before anyone noticed her," Arch growled, breaking the kiss.

"But she's not just yours anymore." Another low chuckle left Rush's mouth. "No, she's ours."

CHAPTER SIXTY-SIX

ASTRID

BEFORE I COULD STOP either of them, their lips were all over me—Arch's on my own and Rush's on my neck. I was trapped between them, small moans leaving my mouth as their hands explored my body, and I didn't want to escape.

Hell, I didn't even try.

When Rush's hand disappeared between my thighs, I spread them further apart and moaned into Arch's mouth. Rush smirked against my neck, finding my sensitive clit and playing with it, *teasing* it.

Arch bit down on my lower lip, and I opened my mouth, inviting him in. He slipped his tongue between my lips and ground his bulge against my cunt, his hands groping my ass on the table. When he pulled away, he smacked me on the cheek. Hard.

I clenched and stared back at him, daring him to do it again.

Another long kiss, then another smack.

Another kiss, another smack.

Another kiss, another smack.

Heat swarmed in my core, and I pulled my knees to my chest,

sitting completely on the small desk, desperate for one of them to finally slip inside me. They were so good at fucking me together; both knew exactly how to move, exactly what to say, how to treat me.

"Please," I cried. "I need more!"

Once Arch pulled away again, I expected another slap, but he grabbed my throat and pushed me backward against Rush until I lay back completely on the desk.

Rush unbuckled his belt, and Arch yanked off my bottoms.

Fuck.

Fuck. Fuck. Fuck. Fuck. Fuck. Fuck. Fuck.

With his hand still around the front of my throat, Arch squeezed. "Open up for him."

For someone who wanted me all to himself ... he sure knew how to share.

When I didn't open up right away, Rush dragged the head of his cock and all his salty pre-cum against my bottom lip. Then he smacked it against my face. I moaned, and he took the chance to slide it inside my mouth.

Fuck, he's so big.

He pushed himself all the way inside me, then stilled. My eyes began to water, and I tried to pull back, but he had one hand on the back of my head, holding me in place.

And then Arch lined up at my entrance and shoved himself inside me.

My eyes rolled back, my cheeks warming. I curled my toes.

God!!!

They both pulled out of me at the same time, then thrust back in. Over and over. Back and forth. In and out. Spit rolled down my chin, my throat making cute, wet little noises for them in place of my moans.

I was full, and then I was empty. Full, empty. Full, empty. Full—

The pressure exploded through my pussy, and I lifted my head enough to get smacked with Rush's balls as he thrust back into me. Pleasure rushed through my body in waves, my legs beginning to tremble.

Arch slowed his pace, just like he usually did right before he was about to come, but instead of coming deep inside me, he pulled out of my pussy and walked over to my head, switching places with Rush.

After shoving himself into me, he forced me to taste him on his huge, throbbing cock. Rush placed my legs over his shoulders, grabbed my hips, and slammed into my tight pussy. I cried out in pleasure again, almost coming immediately.

Arch stilled inside my throat, burying himself as deep as he could go, his hand around the front of my neck, stroking his huge cock inside it. I choked, and I gagged, but the more I tried to push him away, the faster he moved his hand against me.

Rush flicked his thumb across my clit, building me up again, this time much faster than the last. I curled my toes, my entire body feeling like it was about to explode. Suddenly, Arch came down my throat, and my body jerked up instinctively into the air. Rush gripped my hips tightly so I couldn't go anywhere and buried himself deep inside me, filling me up until I felt his cum dripping down my thighs.

Rush was right. I didn't belong to just one of them anymore. I belonged to all of them.

And I would hear every single one of them tell me that … they loved me too.

CHAPTER SIXTY-SEVEN

ASTRID

WHEN WE STEPPED into the ice cream parlor, the bell above the door jingled. The scent of sugar and fresh waffle cones drifted through my nostrils. This place was pretty empty for it being early spring, just a couple of students crammed into a red-and-white booth near the back. Fluorescent lights buzzed softly, casting a warm glow on the ice cream flavors.

I hummed to myself and walked ahead of Arch and Rush, who had been closer to me than usual on our walk from Redwood to downtown. Honestly, I had been surprised that Rush didn't want to drive. But it was warmer and sunnier than usual today.

Their footsteps were heavy behind me, the tension still thick from earlier.

My lips curled into a small smile as I approached some freshman behind the counter. He readjusted his glasses on his nose and peeked over at me shyly, his cheeks tinting red.

Oh, this shall be fun.

"H-hi, Astrid. What can I get for you?" he said, peering at me, then looking away.

"Hi"—I scanned his uniform for his name tag—"Robbie."

His eyes widened. "Y-you know my name?"

Arch wrapped an arm around my waist and pulled me to him so my front was flush against his hard body. "She's not interested. Tell him what you want, Hellcat, so we can get the fuck out of here."

For not wanting to tell me that he loves me, someone is jealous …

I pushed myself away from Arch and turned back toward the ice cream flavors, smirking.

"Cookie dough or brownie batter?" I asked Arch and Rush.

Again, Arch's arm came around my waist, as if he *still* didn't like the way that cute little Robbie was looking at me, even though Robbie hadn't made eye contact since Arch had pulled me closer the first time.

"Both are trash," Arch muttered beside me.

Rush didn't say anything, but chuckled from my other side. I peered over at him and wrapped my hand around his pinkie, then turned back to the counter. To my surprise, he didn't pull it away, but instead moved closer so I could grab his entire hand more easily.

"What are you picking then?" I asked Arch.

"Vanilla."

I burst out laughing. "You? Vanilla?"

"You have a fucking problem with that?"

After biting back my laughs, I shook my head. "No, not at all, Vanilla Boy."

Once Arch mumbled a few not-nice words, Rush cleared his throat. "I'll also do vanilla."

"Good choice," I said to him, squeezing his hand.

"Oh, so *I* get shit for it, but he doesn't?" Arch exclaimed.

"Yes," I murmured. "Just because."

"A-and for you?" Robbie said, still not looking at me.

"Cookies and cream."

After a few choice words from Arch, Rush paid for the order, and Robbie handed us our ice cream. We exited the parlor and sat on the curb, just outside, the neon glow from the shop spilling onto the pavement.

I sat between them, licking my ice cream, amused by just how much Arch wasn't over what had happened earlier. I didn't know if it was what he had almost admitted, Rush barging in on our time alone, or what Rush had said to him.

But Arch was still pissed.

"How long have you hated Rush?" I giggled.

"Since he became an annoying little shit this afternoon," Arch said.

My lips curled into a smile. "Oh, yeah? Hear that, Rush?"

When I looked over at him, he was already staring at me, but not like he usually did with that intense, smoldering stare. With a softer, hazier one, his gaze focused on my lips. Warmth gathered inside my core.

"Mmhmm," Rush hummed, though he didn't look at Arch once.

Arch growled and took a bite of his ice cream. Yes, a bite. Then he clenched his jaw, his gaze distancing, as if he was thinking about something else entirely. I nudged him with my shoulder.

"You contemplating murder?" I asked.

"I don't like sharing."

"Yeah, well," Rush said, stretching his legs out in front of himself, "neither does Frasier or Calix or Cairo or even me. But you're gonna have to get used to it, Arch. Because none of us are going anywhere."

CHAPTER SIXTY-EIGHT

CAIRO

ASTRID SAT across from me at my desk, her notebook open and her pencil twirling lazily between her fingers. She had come over so I could help her catch up on the work she'd missed, but instead, she was watching me with those intense eyes.

I cleared my throat and shifted in my seat, becoming warm.

While I usually kept my cool pretty well at home, especially when I was alone with her, I couldn't help but feel squirmy under her gaze today. I hadn't mentioned anything to her about what I had heard.

More specifically about Calix and Frasier telling her that they loved her.

And honestly, when I had found her in front of the ice cream parlor this afternoon with Arch and Rush, I'd felt like they had also said it to her. But I wasn't sure. Arch had sure looked like he loved her—for a long time now.

"Do you need help?" I offered as calmly as I could.

But jealousy nipped at my stomach. I couldn't think straight anymore.

She hummed, "No. Do you?"

My dick hardened inside my jeans, and I tapped my pencil against the desk, trying to stay in control. She couldn't help me on any of my work, but we both knew she wasn't talking about that.

"I already know all this," I said.

"I wasn't talking about your homework. I'm talking about … you know …"

"I know?" I asked, amused. "About what?"

Usually, she was so confident around the others, but with me, she was different. And I didn't know how to feel about that anymore. If she loved them and she treated them differently than she treated me, what'd she think about me?

She moved closer to the desk, pressing her cleavage against it. "Come on …"

"You will tell me," I said.

Her cheeks flushed the way they always did when she slipped into my car every morning, and she pressed her thighs together, gently chewing on the inside of her cheek. Strands of hair fell into her face. "Cairo …" she whispered shyly.

"Either tell me or get back to work."

After swallowing, her face still pink, she turned back to her homework.

Fuck, that hurts.

Did she not want to see me like that anymore now that she had exchanged *I love you*s with Frasier and Calix? Maybe Arch and Rush too? Was she playing hard to get? Not interested?

"So, do you think they meant it?" she asked, writing.

"Who meant what?"

"Don't play stupid. I know that you know about Frasier and Calix."

I tightened my grip on my pencil and stared down at the paper, trying to stay as calm as humanly possible because why was she asking me about this? Why now? Why was she forcing me to acknowledge this whole thing when I had intentionally been ignoring it?

"Do you think they meant it when they told me that they love me?" she continued.

Almost as if she were *pushing*.

"Do *you* think they meant it?"

She didn't answer, but kept her gaze on her paper, not writing anymore.

"Did *you* mean it?" I asked.

"Yes."

No hesitation. None. Not a fucking lick.

I was screwed.

She released a breath, glancing down at her notebook. "It's just … a lot. All at once."

"All at once? Did Arch and Rush …" I dragged out, hoping to get any insight.

"No, they didn't say anything." She slouched in her chair and shrugged her shoulders.

"But you wanted them to?"

"I don't know." Which really meant yes.

After setting down my pencil, I cleared my throat again because the awkwardness was building between us.

Here I am, turning into the boy best friend when all I want is to be her boyfriend. Life is shit sometimes, huh?

"You're not used to being loved," I said. "Especially not by so many people at once."

She clenched her jaw for a millisecond before looking up, wiping away her pain and replacing her frown with a smirk. "What, are you about to tell me that you love me too?" she asked, giggling to herself.

Fuck. If she's making jokes like this, she's really not interested.

"Not a chance," I said, laughing it off. "You wish."

She fake pouted, but the expression didn't meet her eyes.

I stood up and walked to the door to take a breather away from her because tonight was not turning out the way that I wanted it to. "Take a break. I'm going to grab something for us to eat."

"But—"

"I'll be back in a few."

"Cairo—"

Before she could finish her sentence, I was out the bedroom suite door and heading down a hallway that Astrid had never been down before so she wouldn't take the chance to follow me.

I needed a goddamn drink after that—or a couple—to wash away these feelings.

CHAPTER SIXTY-NINE

ASTRID

WHEN THE DOOR clicked shut behind Cairo, I sat on the seat, completely confused. All this time, I had thought that Cairo sorta had a thing for me outside of our early mornings at Dunkin'. But I guessed … he didn't?

I didn't want to seem too hurt, but damn.

My gaze fell to the blankets underneath my textbook on the bed, and I bit down on my lip to stop myself from crying. I couldn't cry in his bedroom over him, especially if I didn't know when he'd be back. How'd I explain that to him?

Oh, sorry, I thought you liked me.

After picking up my pencil, I tapped it on the table and shook my head. Of course Cairo didn't like me. Why would he? He was the cute, nerdy type who probably didn't like to share. And here I was, whoring myself out to all of The Crew.

Though it wasn't really whoring. Maybe at first. Now? I had feelings.

For all of them.

I shifted in the chair, thighs bouncing, and released a shaky breath.

I shouldn't have been this worked up. Not after Cairo. But I was because, as cliché as it sounded, he wasn't like the others. Calix was fire, Frasier charm, Arch rough, and Rush … well, Rush was something else entirely.

But Cairo?

The way he studied me, how quiet he was in public but dominant alone …

A low groan left my mouth. Here I was, wrapped up in one guy's scent, sitting in another guy's house, thinking about a third. And I couldn't forget about the fourth and fifth ones too. Maybe Arch was right. Maybe I had to choose one of them.

Or else … things were going to get messy.

Once I pushed myself backward, I stood up and began pacing around Cairo's huge freaking room—no, *suite*—and ended up by the window, staring down at the spring garden starting to bloom even though it was still a bit chilly outside.

When Cairo returned, I'd drop all talk about the other guys, the *jokes* about him liking me, everything. We'd return to normal, and our relationship would be solely intimate. Why? Because I couldn't lose him.

Part of me really, really liked him, and I—

The door opened behind me, and I froze, my breath hitching and my eyes widening.

After a moment, the door snapped shut, and I swallowed hard. The way the air shifted, the quiet dominance that radiated from his body. I didn't need to turn around to know that it wasn't one of his maids, but him.

"Did you find what you were looking for?" I whispered.

No answer.

Instead … footsteps.

Heat coursed through my entire body, my nipples hardening. Once he finally made his way to me, he brushed his fingers across my shoulder, the touch so gentle that I could barely feel it. Fluttering almost.

At least, that was what my pussy was doing.

"Cairo," I whispered, desperate for it to happen again.

No response.

He moved his fingers up the column of my neck and grasped my throat, burying his face into the crook of my neck. "You might've told them that you loved them, but when you're with me, *you're mine.*"

I clenched and cast my gaze downward, slipping into submission. Easily.

"Do you understand me?" he asked.

"Yes, sir."

"I don't play games to win them." He pulled me closer to him until his body was flush against my backside, his lips on my ear, his warm breath fanning my neck. "I play them to dominate, *to own.*"

"Cairo …" I whispered.

I squeezed my eyes closed as the pleasure began to build up, but he hadn't even touched me where I wanted him to yet. He was so close, yet not close enough. Never close enough.

"When you're here, you're mine. Say it."

"When I'm here, I'm yours."

"Again."

"When I'm here, I'm yours."

"Again."

"When I'm here, I'm yours."

I expected him to ask me again, but instead, he fastened something around my neck. A cold metal ring lay on the center of my chest, and my eyes widened. Was this … what I thought it was? Was this a collar?

Cairo turned me around, looped a finger around the ring, and tugged me closer. "You're mine tonight."

CHAPTER SEVENTY

ASTRID

"YES, SIR," I whispered, my nipples hard.

Cairo opened up his bedside drawer, pulled out a blindfold, and wrapped it around my eyes so I couldn't see. Heat coursed through my body from the thought of him using me however he wanted me.

Once it was secure, he slowly stripped off my clothes until I stood completely naked inside his suite, and then he led me to the bed. I crawled up onto it and sat down on my knees on the soft mattress, slowly settling my pussy against the blankets.

He stepped away, and I listened to his footsteps patter around the room, moving away from me. Then he opened a closet door. Then his footsteps returned toward me, so agonizingly slow until I could feel his breath on my ear.

He slipped something underneath me, right against my clit, and suddenly started the vibrator. I jerked up enough, my tits bouncing slightly and the collar jingling on my chest. I gasped, the vibrations quicker than my vibrator at home.

Warmth exploded through my body.

The bed dipped beside me, and I could feel Cairo so, so close.

His warm breath fanned my neck, his scent wrapping all around me. I breathed him in and shifted on the bed, trying to displace this pleasure as the toy vibrated against my clit.

"I haven't touched you yet, Astrid," Cairo murmured into my ear, his hands suddenly groping my tits, fingers squeezing my nipples. He tugged hard on them, drawing his nose up the column of my neck. "And you're already making a mess of yourself on my bed."

A whimper left my mouth, and I tried to press my thighs together, but he didn't let me.

Cairo tugged on one of my nipples. Pressure built higher and higher inside me. I curled my toes and squeezed my eyes shut, even though I was already blindfolded.

God, I loved this side of the nerdy kid from Physics.

"More," I whimpered. "Please, harder."

Cairo tugged on my nipple harder. "You're mine."

My core tightened, and another whimper left my throat. "Yes, I'm yours, sir."

"Do you know what that means?" he asked.

"Mmhmm."

He wrapped a hand around my throat. "Words, Astrid. I need words from you."

"Yes, I know what that means."

"Tell me then," he murmured. "What does that mean to you?"

"It means you own me," I said in a breath, the pressure building up inside me. "It means that I belong to you. That nobody else can touch me when I'm with you, when I'm in your bed, when I'm yours."

His lips fluttered against my skin. "Good girl."

The vibrator continued to buzz between my thighs, and my pussy began dripping onto the sheets. I whimpered and gently dropped my head to the side to give him better access. He gently bit down on my shoulder.

"Do you know what else that means, my pretty girl?"

My pussy clenched, and I shook my head. "N-no, sir."

"It means that I can use you however I want."

He tugged on my nipples, bringing me so close to the edge that I could almost feel the pleasure exploding through my entire body. I cried out in pleasure, desperate for him to push me over the edge.

Then he stopped.

I dropped my head back and whimpered, "Please, don't stop."

The bed dipped, as if he was leaning over to grab something from the drawer. When he returned, he began tying what felt like rope around my wrists and up my arms, binding them together behind my back.

Next, he moved to my ankles, tying them up. Then my knees, fastening something metal between them so I couldn't move my legs together even if I tried. And I tried. The closer I got to my orgasm, the more and more I tried.

The more desperate I became.

"I own you," he said into my ear. "I can use you however I want."

"Y-yes, sir."

"I'm glad we understand that."

I whimpered, "Please, can I come?"

"Do you want to come?"

"Yes, please, sir."

He moved around me, and suddenly, the vibrator stopped.

"No! No. No. No. No. No. No. No! Please!"

No response. Only shuffling across the floor.

"Please, Cairo," I cried desperately. "Please!"

Again, no response. No sound. Nothing.

But he was still in the room, still watching, *waiting*, as if he wanted me to cry and plead for him all night. And if that was what he wanted me to do, then that was what I would do. Anything to please him.

CHAPTER SEVENTY-ONE

CAIRO

"PLEASE," Astrid whimpered, desperately grinding her hips against the vibrator. I hadn't turned it on, but she continued and continued to rub against it, begging—no, *pleading*—with me to let her come. "Please, I need it."

I leaned back against the seat and watched that pretty body move.

If I couldn't have her emotionally, I'd have her like this, and I'd take my time with her.

The others in The Crew could use her as they wanted, but she would always come crawling back to me because nobody could give her the experience that I could. Nobody could make her cry and plead and beg for them like this.

She struggled against her binds, moving her arms back and forth in a weak attempt to escape, her tits bouncing for me. I pressed my hand against my bulge and grunted to myself, wanting nothing more than to be inside her.

Her patience wasn't the only thing tested tonight.

"Cairo," she cried, "please."

After undoing my button and zipper, I slipped my hand into my pants, grabbed my throbbing cock, and pulled it out. My thumb glided over the pre-cum coating my head, and I imagined her drawing her tongue around it.

"Cairo, I know you're still in the room with me," she said. "Please …"

I wrapped my hand around the base of my cock and slowly started to jerk it up and down, up and down. She quieted down, her nipples becoming harder and her breath catching in her throat.

"Fuck, that sounds so hot," she whispered, brows drawn together. "Don't stop."

While I continued pleasuring myself to her perfect fucking body, I took out my phone and hit record. If they wanted to have Astrid, I'd let them. But they'd know that only *I* could have her like this.

"Please, Cairo, more," she whimpered, grinding her hips faster against the vibrator, which was still off between her legs. Her tits bounced, her lips full and pouty. She leaned her head back slightly, her hair falling behind her shoulders. "God, please … keep going."

A groan left my mouth, and I stroked my cock faster.

"Are you going to come for me?" she asked.

My dick throbbed as I tried to control myself.

"Tell me you're going to come for me."

Another grunt left my mouth, and I couldn't handle it any longer. I had waited all fucking day to be inside her, and I wasn't going to pass up the chance to dump my load deep into her desperate little cunt.

Once I kicked off my pants while stalking toward her, I crawled onto the bed and set the phone down on the mattress. Sure, it was recording, but I didn't care what angle I got anymore. I needed to be inside her. I was desperate for those screams, aching for that pussy to be wrapped around my cock.

"Oh, baby," I grunted into her ear, tugging her hips back and leaning her forward. When she rested onto her shoulder on the mattress and arched her back, I turned the vibrator back on. "The only place I'm coming is inside you."

She cried out in pleasure, settling down against the vibrator, lips parted. "P-please!"

I pressed the head of my cock against her entrance and shoved myself deep into her cunt. She threw her head back, her small whimpers turning into loud moans, her tits pressed against the mattress.

"Fuck," I grunted under my breath.

"Oh my God!" she cried. "Oh my God! Don't stop!"

I pounded deep into her, leaning over her body and sucking on her neck, getting deeper with every single thrust. She pushed her hips back into mine every time, and I grabbed the camera, turning it toward us so she could see herself, and then I yanked off her blindfold.

It took a moment before she adjusted to the light. Her eyes squeezed closed in pleasure before slowly opening and watching us through the camera. Her cunt clamped down around my cock, and I stilled deep in her pussy.

Because—*fuck*—she was going to make me come just like this.

"Tell them who you belong to," I growled into her ear, taking the vibrator and pressing it hard against her clit. I drew my lips up the column of her neck and gently bit down on her earlobe. "Tell them you're mine."

With her brows drawn together and her eyes rolling into the back of her head, she screamed out in ecstasy. "I'm yours! I'm yours! God, I'm yours, wherever, whenever, however you want me, Cairo. Oh my God!"

Her tight little hole pulsed around the base of my cock repeatedly, and I groaned as I came deep into her pussy. The vibrator was building her up again—I could feel it by just the way her body was all tense—and she continued to milk the cum out of my balls.

"F-f-fuck," she groaned, legs convulsing. "I'm yours."

Once every last drop of my cum was inside her pussy, I slowly pulled out of her, shifting the camera from her pouty face to her cunt drooling with my cum so they'd all see it. After tonight, they'd know that she was mine, whether she told me she loved me or not.

CHAPTER SEVENTY-TWO

ASTRID

WAVE AFTER WAVE of pleasure rushed through my body. My chest was pressed against the mattress, my back was arched, and my ass was in the air. All for Cairo. He gently tugged off the binds, one by one, undoing me completely until I collapsed onto the bed.

The feeling of him *owning* me ...

God, I'd happily do that every night.

Cairo lay down beside me, one arm tucked under his head, the other gently tracing patterns on my bare hip. While his touch might've been absent-minded, there was a certain ... possessiveness to it.

Even though he was deep in pleasure himself, *I* was still *his.*

I released a breath, stretched out my legs, then turned to curl into his body. "That was ..."

A small smirk crawled onto his face. "You don't need to say it."

"Don't want me to praise you?" I giggled.

"Only you need to be praised," he murmured. "I know how fucking amazing it was."

"How amazing it was or how amazing you did?"

His smirk widened, and he peeked over at me. "Both."

I playfully rolled my eyes. "Oh, I don't need another ego-heavy man on my hands."

"Hey, you were the one who brought it up," he said, his gaze still locked on to mine, those devilish brown eyes making me feel all sorts of things. "Besides, I'm sure their egos will be hurt a bit after they see how much of a mess I made of you."

"What do you—"

Before I could finish my sentence, Cairo lifted his phone to show me the group chat that he had with the guys. Not one that I was in, but one with just them, and he'd sent a video of me, tied up, blindfolded, naked.

My eyes widened because when he had taken it, I'd thought …

I honestly couldn't remember what I'd thought at the time.

When I started to see the messages flood in from the other guys, I yanked the phone away from Cairo and hit play on the screen to watch the video he had made of me. He was sitting across from me, watching me on the bed, begging, pleading.

Warmth exploded through my body, my nipples hardening.

Oh my God, this is so hot.

Once the video was over, I exited out of the full screen and read his message with it.

Cairo: Look at my pretty girl beg.

Holy fucking—

The phone was buzzing in my hand repeatedly from the nonstop messages that all the others kept sending in the group chat, but I couldn't get myself to read any of them. Because Cairo … he'd called me his *pretty girl.*

My skin suddenly felt like it was on fire, even though the hum of the AC filled the space. Cairo grasped my hips and pulled me on top of him, his lips against my ear. I shivered in delight, though my body was on fire.

How is Cairo so quiet yet so … dominant at the same time?!

Arch's contact filled the screen, and Cairo tapped on the Answer button.

"If you don't tell your fucking maids to let us inside in the next ten seconds, I'm breaking and entering," Arch growled, and I listened to the other guys in the background agreeing. He banged on the door. "Let us the fuck in."

Cairo turned toward me. "You did this."

"*You* sent it to them." I giggled.

"Are either of you listening to me right now?!" Arch shouted.

My lips curled into a smirk because an angry Arch was a sexy Arch. I scooped the phone away from Cairo and hit End before either of us could answer him. Arch and the rest of them could break and enter and try to find us in his big house.

A nice little game of hide-and-seek and fuck Astrid. Who wouldn't want that?

CHAPTER SEVENTY-THREE

ASTRID

THE FRONT DOOR SLAMMED OPEN, and I froze halfway down the hallway. My heart pounded inside my chest, the hairs on my arms sticking up. The sound echoed through the mansion—loud, commanding, and impossible to ignore.

"Astrid!" Arch shouted.

One set of footsteps followed, then another, then two more.

Shit!

How had they broken in so quickly?! Or maybe Cairo had let them in. Maybe he wanted me to run so they could chase me. Maybe he wanted us all to play this little game because his ass was kinkier than all of them combined.

I glanced to my left and out the window. How big was his property?

Once their footsteps became louder, I bolted down the hallway. The hardwood floor was cold underneath my bare feet, turning into sleek marble when I entered another section of the mansion.

Hide ... I need to hide.

While I had no idea where I was going, I had to find a good

place. And quick. Cairo must know this place like the back of his hand, and the guys had to have been here more than just a few times.

If I wasn't careful, they'd find me soon.

"Astrid!" Frasier murmured. "We can hear you running."

My heart leaped into my throat, and a thrill rushed through me. I veered down a curved staircase, nearly tripping on the last step and catching myself on the banister. The lights were dim here, the walls lined with shelves, stacked with books upon books.

God, this library was every book girl's dream!

I found a side room filled with dark wooden cabinets and slipped into one. Yes, into one of the cabinets, holding my breath to fit all the way in. I pressed myself against the back of it, hoping that I didn't leave any trace behind me.

When I pressed my ear to the door, I heard footsteps.

"She went down here," Calix said.

"Arch, check the kitchen," Cairo said.

"I swear to God, if Frasier finds her first," Arch growled.

"It's not like she can hide forever," Rush said.

Warmth spread throughout my body, and I pressed my thighs together. This wasn't just a game of hide-and-seek. No, this was a game where it was them against me. And they all wanted to find me first.

I waited. Thirty seconds. Then a full two minutes.

Nothing. Complete silence.

And then … someone stepped into the library.

I slapped a hand over my mouth, eyes going wide as I curled tighter into the cabinet space. The guy walked in, his footsteps rough. I'd recognize him anywhere—Arch, my bastard step-brother.

What happened to him searching in the kitchen?!

"Astrid," Arch taunted. "Come out, come out, wherever you are."

I held my breath for what felt like five minutes, my shoulders tense.

Another moment passed, and I listened to his footsteps leave the room. I released a heavy breath and dropped my head lightly. *Whew, that was close.* Another moment, and he would've found me.

If I wasn't careful—

More footsteps.

"Astrid," Cairo murmured, walking through the library, "I know you're in here."

My eyes widened as the footsteps became louder until they stopped right in front of me.

Shit!

"If you're going to hide, there's an underground passageway that leads out into the garden out back," Cairo said, his voice so close, as if he was squatting down right in front of the cabinet that I was hidden inside of. "You have five minutes before I tell them where you are."

He was bluffing. There was no way he knew I was in here.

Another moment of silence passed, and then he walked away. "Time starts now."

When I heard the door close, I slammed the cabinet door open and hurried out of the library. I didn't know *where* this underground passageway was, but I had to find a different place to hide.

Somewhere. Anywhere.

I slipped into a dark hallway, opposite of where Arch and Cairo had come from, letting the door click shut behind me. The air here was dustier, much different from the sleek interior in the rest of the house.

My breath caught in my throat. To my left, I stared out of the massive floor-to-ceiling windows that overlooked the gardens. I had to be close to the underground passageway, right? Adrenaline rushed through me, and I turned another corner.

I wasn't sure how long I'd be able to—

Before I could think, I slammed into someone's hard chest.

Strong hands wrapped around my waist, pulling me against them.

"I caught you, Hellcat," Rush murmured into my ear. "Looks like you're all mine."

CHAPTER SEVENTY-FOUR

ASTRID

WARMTH EXPLODED through my body at Rush's touch.

I hadn't heard him coming—but of course I hadn't—because Rush didn't make noise. No, he silently watched, stalked, and pounced whenever he felt it was the most convenient for him. And finding me alone? It was the perfect scenario for him to take me.

Any way that he wanted.

With his hands around my waist, he tugged me into a dark room that I hadn't noticed before. I gasped softly, my heart pounding from the chase *and* from being caught, not just by anyone, but by him.

He drew his hands slowly around my body, up my chest, around my neck, and to my lips, letting his fingers drag across them. My nipples were taut and aching against the front of my top, and I pressed my thighs together.

"You're mine, Hellcat," he murmured into my ear, sliding his hand up my inner thigh and forcing me to spread my legs. He cupped my pussy and slipped two fingers between my lips, finding my clit. "All mine."

"Yes," I said in a breathy whisper.

God, he barely has to touch me, and I am already a puddle!

"You like being chased?" he asked, drawing his fingers agonizingly slow across my clit. Back and forth. And back and forth. Making my pussy clench, desperate, aching for him. "Like being *hunted?*"

"I love it."

After releasing a breathless chuckle, he continued to tease my clit with his fingers. I spread my trembling legs, desperate for more. I needed him to touch me, to fill me. I knew that he only did it on his terms, but God, I couldn't handle much more.

"Please," I whimpered.

"Please what?"

"Please … tell me what you're going to do with me now that you've caught me. I … I—"

Before I could finish my sentence, he turned me around and pushed me against the stone wall behind me. He placed his hands on either side of my head, trapping me between the wall and his huge body, his eyes dark and his lips … suddenly on mine.

It wasn't soft. It wasn't careful.

Nothing about him ever was.

He gripped my thighs, lifted me into the air, and pressed me harder against the wall. I wrapped my legs around his waist and ground myself against his throbbing bulge. God, the things I'd do for him to be inside me already.

When he felt me grind against him, he pressed against me in a thrusting motion even though his jeans were in the way. Back and forth and back and forth. Again torturing my precious little clit.

"Please, fill me up," I cried into his mouth. "Please, before the others find us."

Something about them hunting me, finding me, and fucking me …

It did desperate things to every part of my body.

He kissed down my throat and sucked on the crook of my neck, one hand fumbling with his jeans between us. When he finally got them undone and pressed the head of his cock against my entrance, a door creaked open.

My eyes widened, and we both looked toward the door of this room, which was still closed. I listened to footsteps approaching, my heart pounding inside my chest and my pussy drooling on his huge cock.

"Astrid …" Arch taunted outside in the hallway.

Rush placed a hand over my mouth and slammed into me. My eyes shot open even wider, the pleasure exploding through my body. I clenched around him and moaned softly into his hand, his eyes daring me to make a sound.

The footsteps became louder, as if he was right outside the door, but Rush continued to thrust into me, over and over. I dug my fingernails into his shoulders and clutched down on his fat cock, the pressure rising quickly inside me.

Oh, if he didn't stop this soon … or if Arch didn't leave … I'd …

"You're a fucking whore," Rush growled into my ear.

Usually, he was the quieter one out of him and Arch, but *fuck!!!* My pussy exploded around him, and I arched my back against the wall, coming harder than I ever had. My eyes rolled back inside my head, my legs trembled uncontrollably. And Rush? He slammed deep into my pussy and didn't pull out.

Not until his cum was dripping down my thighs.

Arch growled under his breath outside the door, as if he was pissed, and his footsteps retreated down the hall. When the door slammed closed, Rush set me down and leaned against the wall himself, breathing more heavily than usual.

I took this as an opportunity to sprint toward the door and get out of here. One of them had caught me, but I still had four more to take care of, and I wasn't going to let Rush's cum be the only thing dripping down my thighs tonight.

CHAPTER SEVENTY-FIVE

ASTRID

CAIRO'S cold marble floor sent shivers up my body as my bare feet smacked against it over and over. I kept my breath low, though my heart was pounding so hard that I could hear it in my ears. The mansion had turned into a maze of hallways that I couldn't keep straight.

Rush hadn't followed me out of the room, but the others were still searching for me.

His cum ran down my thighs. I kept running through the hallways and turned a sharp corner, narrowly missing a statue. After placing my hand over my heart, I pressed myself up against the wall and listened to the voices in the next room.

Calix and Frasier.

Adrenaline surged through me, my pussy clenching.

I nestled my body into the small corner and crouched down behind a side table, their footsteps approaching quickly. They were fighting—or more specifically, Frasier was saying something smart and sarcastic to Calix, and Calix was getting pissed.

When their footsteps became louder, heading straight for me, I pressed a hand over my mouth and sucked in a low breath, hoping that they would pass quickly. Yet my heart was pounding in my throat, my legs trembling from the awkward position.

"It sounded like she went this way," Calix said.

"You sure about that?" Frasier asked.

As they stepped into the room, warmth spread through my body. I couldn't wait to be found by both of them, and at the same time?! They pissed each other off often but loved me. The thrill of the back-and-forth, the enemies and friends …

I shifted slightly, trying to keep quiet.

My chest rose and fell quickly, my thighs quivering.

Fuck!

"You hear that?" Frasier asked.

"You're hearing things," Calix growled. "Shut up and listen."

"Why don't you shut up and listen?" Frasier said. "She's here."

I pressed my hands against my thighs in an attempt to still them. If they didn't get out of here soon, I was totally going to give myself away! But I loved this thrill, this excitement. Who would've thought that this would happen after three weeks ago?

At that party …

My nipples hardened, and I bit back a whimper from the memory.

"There she is," Frasier said.

When the words left his mouth, I was sprinting out the door that I had come from. I pumped my legs fast as Calix and Frasier sprinted after me. I rounded corners too sharply, scraping my thigh against some glass, and continued.

I didn't have time to waste.

No, I needed to get out of here. Now.

My lungs burned, but I found a door and ran out into the darkness, heading straight for the garden. The cool nighttime air hit my skin, the grass tickling my feet. They were approaching quicker than I'd expected.

Fuck, I need to go faster! I need to get out of—

Before I could reach the garden, someone wrapped their arms

around my waist, turned me toward them, and tackled me onto the ground. "Got you."

We hit the ground with a thud, Calix's hand on the back of my head so I didn't slam it on the dirt. His eyes darkened from above me, lips twitching into a smirk. Then more footsteps approached, and Frasier was crouching beside us.

"Didn't think Calix would catch me first," I murmured to Frasier, knowing it'd piss him off.

Calix sat back between my thighs, grabbing my waist, as if claiming me. "She can't be both of ours tonight."

Frasier wrapped his hand around the front of my throat, pinning me to the ground. "Why not?" he murmured, his lips grazing over mine, his fingers strumming across the column of my neck and making me warm in all those sinful places.

Their touches were so different.

Calix—all soft and possessive. Frasier—rough and willing to share.

"She's ours," Frasier mumbled against my lips. "Both of ours."

CHAPTER SEVENTY-SIX

ASTRID

CALIX CRASHED his lips onto mine, hungry and possessive. For someone who didn't want to share with Frasier, he sure didn't mind Frasier pushing him out of the way to kiss me next, his tongue slipping into my mouth.

I moaned against his lips as Calix gripped my waist, his thumbs digging into my skin. He positioned himself against my entrance, my cunt already sopping wet from Rush's cum. But they didn't need to know that.

"You knew we'd catch you, Hellcat," Frasier murmured against my mouth, reaching down with one hand to rub my clit.

When I spread my legs wider for both of them, Calix took it as an opportunity to shove his fat cock inside me. A feral grunt left his mouth, and I clenched hard around him from the mere sound, my pussy wet and aching.

"Fuck, you're tight," Calix growled, stilling all the way inside me.

Frasier continued to rub my clit in torturous little circles. "You like being used, huh?"

I whimpered against his mouth and nodded. "Yes."

"Yes, you do," he said, smacking my clit.

My knees jerked up, and I tightened around Calix again, making him grunt once more. Frasier peered over at him, then smacked my clit again. Another clench, another groan. And suddenly, my pussy was even wetter.

Seeing Frasier use me to make Calix feel good?

They didn't swing that way at all, but—*fuck!*—it was so fucking sexy.

"Do it again," I cried, wanting Calix to groan again.

Frasier smacked my clit, I tightened, and Calix grunted. Over and over. Until Calix finally rested my legs on his shoulders, wrapped his arms around my thighs, and began thrusting into me hard and fast.

"I-i-it feels so g-g-g-good!" I cried into Frasier's mouth.

Calix pounded into me, each time releasing a soft grunt, while Frasier moved his hand from my clit to my breast, capturing my nipple and gently tugging. My eyes rolled back, a wave of heat rushing through me.

"Fuck," I groaned. "Oh my God!"

After sliding one of his arms down my thigh, Calix placed his thumb against my clit, where Frasier's fingers once had been, and massaged the sensitive bud back and forth. My legs began trembling uncontrollably, the pressure rising higher inside my core.

"Please, don't—"

Before I could finish my sentence, an orgasm ripped through my body. My back arched, and I kissed Frasier hard on the mouth, toes curled, head in the fucking clouds. Wave after wave washed over me.

Calix stilled inside me, waited a moment, then shoved himself even deeper. Once he finished filling me with his cum, Frasier shoved him out of the way and took his place, undoing his jeans and lining himself up at my entrance.

He moved the head of his cock back and forth, coating it with Calix's and Rush's cum. I stared up at him and spread my trembling legs even further apart, desperate for him to fill me all the way up too.

"What do you want?" Frasier asked.

"For you to fill me up," I cried. "Please!"

"Good girl," he said, pushing himself into me.

Calix was at my side, one hand stretched out across my stomach, fingers crawling toward my clit. I lifted my hips, helping move it closer because he was teasing me. They both were, and I couldn't handle it anymore.

"Please," I whimpered. "Please. Please. Please!"

When his fingers finally touched my clit and Frasier was pumping in and out of me, feet from the garden, I moaned out in pleasure.

Calix's lips brushed against my neck. "That's it, Hellcat. Let him hear you."

Frasier grunted, and Calix continued rubbing my clit.

"You're a fucking mess," Frasier grunted, looking down at my cunt. "A fucking mess."

"All this for us?" Calix murmured against my mouth.

Pressure built higher inside my core, and I curled my toes and nodded. "Yes. Yes, all for you!" I cried, the pleasure exploding through my body for a second time in just minutes. I nodded through the orgasm as Frasier stilled inside me. "For both of you!"

CHAPTER SEVENTY-SEVEN

ASTRID

THE GRASS WAS cool underneath my legs, the moonlight sprawling across Cairo's backyard. I released a soft hum and rested my head on Calix's shoulder, Frasier's fingers gently gliding against mine.

"Really made us work for that one, huh, Hellcat?" Frasier murmured with a slight laugh.

I turned my head to look at him, my heart still racing. "That's the best part."

"The chase?" Calix asked. "I think the best part is having you."

Warmth spread throughout my chest, and a small giggle left my mouth. Who would've thought that I'd be lying between two boys who'd admitted that they both loved me? *And* they loved me so much that they didn't mind sharing me.

They put their differences aside to have me. Every inch.

When I was lost in thought, I didn't realize that Frasier had sat up until it was too late. He had one hand posted on the grass behind him, his head turned toward the window, and loud-ass words left his pretty mouth.

"Arch!" he shouted. "Hey, Arch! She's out here for you!"

My eyes widened, and Calix didn't have time to grab me before I was on my feet, sprinting across the lawn and throwing two middle fingers behind me at those idiotic—*but loving*—boys.

There I had been, thinking they were on my side all this time …

"Y'all are traitors!" I shouted, sprinting as quickly as I could to get back into the house, where I could hide from Arch, who was *definitely* going to use me in any way that he could. That was … if he found me.

The back doors were still open, and I dived through them, my bare feet slapping against the wood. I tore through the first hallway I saw, nearly knocking over another statue and listening to Arch's footsteps barreling in behind me.

He was somewhere. Close.

While I wanted to be quiet, I knew that it was more important for me to *get away* than stay silent. So, I took corners fast, skidded along the marble floor of another kitchen, gripped walls to stay upright.

Anything to separate myself from him.

Because once he caught me? He wasn't going to let me go willingly.

No, he'd use me until I clawed my way out.

"Astrid!" he shouted as I ascended a sweeping staircase.

My legs took me toward another unfamiliar wing. *Goddamn, why is Cairo's house so big and so confusing for no reason whatsoever?! And where are his parents?! I've only barely dodged a few of the maids.*

"Come out, come out, wherever you are," Arch called. Closer this time.

Lungs burning, I continued. My heart raced. My thoughts were somehow even faster. I turned another corner and screamed when he caught my wrist and whipped me back toward him, mid-sprint.

I bumped into his chest, then stumbled back against the wall. He pressed his hand flat beside my head, tilting his head down slightly at me, caging me in, just like Rush had. My chest heaved up and down, and his face was inches from mine.

"I told you not to run," he growled, grabbing my throat.

My psychotic ass smirked up at him. "I had something to run from."

"Oh, no. You didn't have anything to run from before, but now I'm going to fucking give you something," he said between his clenched teeth, roughly shoving his thumb across my lower lip. "Everyone has been inside you tonight, except me. And, Hellcat? You're going to fucking pay for that."

CHAPTER
SEVENTY-EIGHT

ASTRID

ARCH SHOVED one leg between my thigh and ground his knee against my cunt. I bit back a whimper and glared up at him as if I were mad. But honestly? I just fucking loved the tension between Arch and me.

The fighting. The hate sex.

I'd continue to eat that shit up as long as he gave it to me.

"You won't. You're too—"

Before I could finish my sentence, he smacked me hard on the mouth. I sucked in a sharp breath, my nipples aching. Heat exploded inside my core, and he drove his knee up further, moving it back and forth against my clit.

"You're mine," he said, smacking me on the mouth again. "And I'm so fucking done with watching you act like you're not." He lifted one of my legs and undid his jeans with his free hand, positioning himself at my entrance. "Fucking bitch."

In one thrust, he slammed himself inside me, shoving Cairo's, Rush's, Calix's, and Frasier's cum deeper into my cunt. I had expected him to shove me to my knees and stick his huge cock down my throat.

But …

This was just as fun.

Arch pulled out of me just as quickly as he shoved himself into me, then pushed me down to my knees. He gripped his cock at the base and slapped it against my lips. "Open your mouth like the dirty little whore you are."

I glared up at him through my lashes, lips pressed together.

There it was … I just didn't know why he hadn't started with this.

Instead of demanding again, Arch rubbed his wet dick all across my face, not caring where he was spreading their thick cum. More heat rushed through me at the thought of him decorating my face with his friends' cum.

When he glided the head over my lips, I instinctually opened my mouth to lick up the mess. And he took it as an opportunity to shove himself deep into my throat. I gagged on it, but sucked as much as I could, my eyes filling with tears.

"For once in your fucking life, you look pretty," he growled, smacking me on the cheek again. "With all The Crew's cum covering your face, my dick down your throat, your eyes filled with tears," he grunted, grabbed my head, and began pounding into me. "Fuck, *Hellcat*."

Tears rolled down my cheeks, and spit rolled down my chin. I gagged over and over, the pressure everywhere becoming almost unbearable. I found myself wrapping one hand around my throat to feel his dick as the other sank between my legs to touch my pussy.

"There she fucking is," he growled. "Show me how much of a desperate whore you are."

I stroked his cock in my throat, spitting and gagging and hoping he'd pull back soon.

"Fucking bitch," he growled, smacking me on the cheek. "Say it."

"I'm a fucking bitch," I said, words muffled and incoherent, as I rubbed my pussy faster.

He stilled deep down my throat. "What was that?"

"I'm a fucking bitch."

"A what?"

Stars danced in my vision, and suddenly, an orgasm ripped through my body. My legs shook uncontrollably, my back arching, my mouth widening to cry out in pleasure. Arch took his chance to pound into me, making my cries turn into the hottest fucking gags I had ever heard.

"Fucking bitch," he growled, finally pulling himself out of me, seizing my neck in his hands, and tugging me to my feet. "That's all you are. A bitch who gets off on gagging on my cock, huh?"

"Yes," I whispered, the pleasure still rushing through me. "Yes, please. Give me more."

Arch picked me up and slammed his dick back into my pussy. My eyes rolled back inside my head, and I grasped onto him with weak fingers. All this pleasure … all the pressure … *oh my fucking God!*

"Yes, more! More. More. More. More. More. More. More. More. More!"

Arch gripped my hips and slammed into me over and over, again and again, setting a brutal pace. I sank my nails into his back and dragged them down the muscle, hard enough to break skin. But that did nothing to stop him.

No, he thrust even faster.

"This what you wanted? This what you've been begging for? Running for?"

"Yes. Yes, God, don't stop," I screamed, another orgasm ripping through me.

He growled and stilled deep inside my body. "That's right. I'm your fucking god. Don't forget it."

CHAPTER SEVENTY-NINE

ASTRID

BY THE TIME WE FINISHED, my trembling legs completely gave out. I gripped on to Arch's biceps just to keep myself upright, pressed my thighs together from being used over and over tonight, and whimpered into his shoulder.

To my surprise, Arch scooped me up in his arms. No teasing. No scolding. No smug smirk. Just me in his arms as he headed through the mansion as if he knew exactly where we were, his footsteps slow.

I curled up into his chest and rested my head on his shoulder, enjoying the moment before he turned all cold again. Arch couldn't be nice for long. At least not with me, not in the several years I had known him.

But something had been changing with him lately.

And honestly? I kinda liked it.

When the sound of The Crew's voices drifted down the hallway from what I remembered as the movie room, Arch continued past it and didn't even look inside. No, we kept walking until things turned familiar, and then he stepped into Cairo's suite.

Cairo poked his head out of the bathroom and offered me a soft smile. "There you are."

Once Arch stepped into the room, a wall of steam hit us. The lights were dim, tiny candles flickering around the tub's marble edge. The Jacuzzi tub was filled with bubbles. The scent of lavender and roses drifted through my nose.

"You ran a bath for me?" I asked, peering at Cairo.

"It was Arch's idea," Cairo said.

My eyes widened even more, and my chest filled with warmth. Arch clenched his jaw and set me down gently in the bathtub. Before he could let go of me completely, I grasped his forearm, brows drawn together.

"Did you really?" I whispered.

His jaw twitched, and he looked away. "Don't get used to it."

When he went to pull away, I tightened my grip on him to keep him here. "Thank you."

I didn't even get a gruff groan before he ripped his arm from mine and headed to the bathroom door. The water melted away all my stress, and while I'd have preferred that Arch stayed, I knew he couldn't be that soft for that long.

He wasn't ready yet.

"Do you need anything?" Cairo asked once the bedroom door closed.

My body sank deeper into the water, and I closed my eyes, feeling them swell. Arch had been so brutal, so rough, so hard on me, and then … he brought me to Cairo's room. He'd told him to run a bath for me *before* he caught me, making me feel … all these *feelings*.

"Take a bath with me, please," I murmured. "Arch …"

"Doesn't know what aftercare is," Cairo said, tugging off his clothes and slipping in the bathtub. He pulled me toward him, letting me lay against his chest. "He'll come around eventually. He's just confused."

"Yeah, confused …" I repeated.

His hand came up, and he cupped the back of my neck, his fingers massaging softly, slowly, in a way that made it easier to breathe somehow. I let my shoulders roll forward and a tear slip down my cheek.

I didn't know why I was crying. I had just had the night of my life.

But still … I wished Arch had stayed with me for a bit more time.

"You're not," I whispered. "Are you?"

"I'm not what?" Cairo asked.

I sucked in a sharp breath, unsure if he was really into me like that or if this was all just fun and games for him. But here he was, taking a bath with me after his friends fucked me because he wanted to make sure I was okay.

A guy who didn't care wouldn't do that, right?

"You're not confused about …" I started, heart racing. "About us?"

He tensed for the slightest moment, his fingers stilling. "No."

I turned around in the tub, some water sloshing over the edge, and then I wrapped my arms around his shoulders, staring at his torn expression, though … it was softening by the moment. I glanced down at his lips.

"You're not confused about my relationship with your friends? You don't mind that I like being with them too? That I love them?" I asked, really wanting to know how this affected him. Because while he hadn't admitted his feelings, I had feelings for him too.

And I wanted him to be okay with it.

"No, I'm not confused about any of that," he said.

"But …"

"No buts. I'm not confused. I get it."

"You do?" I asked, searching his eyes for anything. "Why?"

He pushed some hair off my forehead. "Because I … I love you."

Warmth exploded through my chest, and my lips quivered. "You love me?"

"Yes," he said, looking away. "And you don't have to say it back. You don't have to—"

Before he could finish his sentence, I crashed my lips onto his. "I love you too."

CHAPTER EIGHTY

ASTRID

THE FIRST THING I noticed when I stepped into Redwood Academy was that ... it was one of those days where something immediately felt off. And I didn't mean like there had been a big party last night and everyone was tired.

No, something was going to explode today.

Everyone was too quiet, and that meant someone was bound to stir up some drama.

I stuffed some books into my locker and scanned the hallway. No sign of Rush. Arch was scowling at his locker after refusing to talk to me all last night. Cairo was holding his computer, brow furrowed at the screen. Frasier was leaning against the wall, flipping a pen between his fingers and watching me.

And Calix? He had his hands in his pockets as he headed toward me.

But he wasn't alone.

Mira, that stupid little ho, was right behind him, dressed in a skintight dress and loud, clanky heels. Heat rose in my chest, and I tightened my fists. She jogged to catch up with him, and when she wrapped a hand around his arm, his smile immediately dropped.

Frasier stepped in front of me, blocking my view. "Breathe."

"I am breathing, but she's not going to be in a second."

"I don't want to share you with him, but you should know by now that Calix isn't into dollar-store knockoffs," Frasier said, wrapping his arm around my shoulders and finally stepping out of the way to show me that Calix was heading back toward us. "See?"

I furrowed my brow as Calix approached. "Where's Mira?"

Calix sidestepped and nodded toward Mira, who was glaring at us with hot tears pouring down her cheeks, along with her runny mascara. My eyes widened, but a giddy feeling bubbled in my stomach. I didn't want anyone to get hurt, but she deserved it.

"What'd you say to her?" I asked.

Calix smirked. "You don't wanna know."

Frasier smirked and threw an arm over his shoulders. "Oh, yes, the fuck we do."

My phone buzzed in my hand, and I glanced down at the caller ID—*Diya*.

I left the boys to be the drama queens they were and walked to the window, phone to my ear. "Hey. Is everything okay? I didn't see your car in the lot this morning. I thought you were staying home today again."

"Can you come over tonight? I need to talk to you."

"Of course," I said, chest tightening. I had left her all yesterday to fuck around with The Crew, and I couldn't let them corrupt me anymore. Diya came first, and plus … I couldn't let her get too suspicious. "Is everything okay?"

"For now."

I scrunched my brows. "Is it about … *you know*?"

"I don't wanna talk about it right now," she said with a sigh. "I'll see you after school."

Before I could get another word in, she hung up. I stared at my phone for a long moment and blew out a low breath. She was going through so much, and I didn't know how to help her. And honestly? I had been a shitty friend.

If she found out about Calix, it'd only make this all worse.

The bell rang throughout the halls, and people headed toward their first period class.

Frasier grabbed my hand and steered me through the crowd. "Something's going to happen today."

"You feel it too, huh?" I asked, intertwining my fingers with his.

"Rush isn't here. You think that's a coincidence?"

"Doesn't he miss, like, half of the school year usually?" I asked.

Frasier chuckled. "He'd be pissed if he knew you didn't notice him that much. He's usually here every day, more than Goody Two-shoes over there on his computer," Frasier said, nodding to Cairo.

My lips curled into a smirk. "Well, don't tell him."

"Oh, I'm going to."

I gently shoved his shoulder and let out a soft giggle. "Stop it."

"There's another race tonight."

"Tonight? Why am I just finding out about this now? I told Diya I'd go over to her place later to talk," I said, my lips curling into a frown. "But I want to see Rush race again. It was fun last time."

"No, you don't," Frasier said. "Remember the guy who tried to start that fight last time? He'll be there. And Rush isn't going to play nice this time. He'll want you to stay out of the way so he doesn't have to worry about you."

"But—"

I didn't even have time to finish another word before the sound of shouting rang out near the gym. A crowd started forming, kids running to the edge of the hallway to get a look. Two teachers broke into a sprint. Then I saw him …

A student was being pulled out of class. Handcuffed. Escorted by two officers.

"What the hell ..." I started.

"They're here about the races," Cairo said behind me, suddenly appearing with his phone still in hand. "They're looking for someone."

A second student was dragged out next. Another kid we'd seen hanging around the last race. I felt the blood drain from my face.

"Where's Rush?" I asked, heart hammering.

No one answered.

Then my phone buzzed.

Rush: Don't go to the race tonight.

I stared at the message until the screen dimmed.

And the dread in my chest exploded into something heavier. Something worse.

Something that told me, this wasn't just about cars anymore.

CHAPTER
EIGHTY-ONE

ASTRID

"YOU'RE BOTH HERE?" I asked with my brow arched as I stared at Calix and Frasier at Calix's front door. I glanced at them to see if I could figure out their motives because they had been hating each other's guts lately. "How'd you make it here before me?"

Frasier moved out of the way to let me in. "We left school early."

I stepped inside and kicked off my shoes, my backpack slung over my shoulder. Diya's car was parked in the driveway, but she hadn't answered the door herself, like she usually did when I came over, which meant … something was off.

My stomach twisted. I could only imagine how much hate she was getting right now.

Calix shut the door behind me. "Principal gave us a pass."

I side-eyed him. "We both know you didn't ask the principal for a pass."

"You know us, babe," Frasier hummed. "We're good boys."

Lips curled into a smirk, I headed straight for the fridge because I was hungry. "Yeah, sure. *Good boys*. That's what we'll call you." When I didn't find anything appetizing in the fridge, I looked at Calix. "Where's Diya?"

"In her room."

"All right, well"—I started toward her room—"I'll see you boys tonight."

Frasier captured my wrist. "We need to talk about the race."

"Is that why you're both here and not fighting for once?" I asked. "Let me guess. You're both going to tell me not to go."

"Because you *shouldn't*," Calix said, his voice firm. "Rush texted you, didn't he?"

Frasier leaned on the counter. "The cops are going to be there, Astrid. It's not just a few kids racing for fun anymore. There's money involved. Reputation. And after what happened last time? It's going to get ugly."

I crossed my arms. "And you're both still going."

"That's different," Calix said.

"Why?"

"We just ..." Calix looked over his shoulder to make sure Diya hadn't popped out into the hallway, and then he grabbed my hand. "We want you to stay here tonight. With Diya. She needs you. And we don't want you getting hurt."

His hand tightened around mine, and I stared up into his desperate eyes. I had never seen him so serious before, and I hated that he wasn't wrong. I should stay here, away from the drama, so I didn't get hurt. Because that guy seemed crazy.

Before I could answer, I heard footsteps down the hall, and I yanked my hand out of Calix's. Diya appeared at her bedroom door in leggings and an oversize hoodie, hair pulled back into a messy bun.

Her smile didn't meet her eyes. "You're here."

Fuck, she looks terrible.

"Yeah," I said, walking away from the guys and toward her. "Just got here. You know, you don't have anything in your fridge. Those assholes ate up your entire grocery run already, and it's really pissing me off."

I tried to keep it light, keep it casual, usual, so she wouldn't suspect a thing. Though I could feel their gazes burning into me from behind, as if telling me again not to show up tonight. But I'd see how I was feeling after my talk with Diya.

If she needed me, then I had to stay. But if her little *fling* was coming home soon, then I'd probably be forced to leave. I didn't want any part in watching them suck face or do something worse to each other.

Diya closed the door behind me, and I flopped onto the bed, sighing through my nose. After grabbing a pillow to hold it over her belly, she sat beside me and leaned against the headboard.

"Sorry for being weird earlier. I'm just really tired," she said.

"It's okay," I said. "You've got every right to be."

She offered me a weak smile. "Thanks for coming."

"You didn't say much on the phone."

Diya looked down at the pillow. "There wasn't much to say. I just ..."

I brushed my fingers across her knee. "You know I'm here for you."

We sat in silence for a few moments, but it wasn't the comforting kind. No, Diya definitely had something she needed to tell me, but she was waiting. For some reason.

Downstairs, I heard the front door open, then close, the boys gone.

"What's wrong?" I asked.

Diya didn't meet my gaze. "How'd you do it?"

"How'd I do what?"

She finally lifted her head and looked me right in my eyes. "How'd you go behind my back and fuck my brother without any guilt?"

CHAPTER EIGHTY-TWO

ASTRID

"WHAT?" I asked, opening and closing my mouth a handful of times in an attempt to form words, but … how … was she … who told her? How'd she find out? I sat up on the bed and swallowed hard. "What do you mean?"

She didn't flinch. "I know you're fucking my brother."

"I don't know—"

"Stop it!" she shouted. "Stop with the lying!"

My eyes widened slightly, and I stood up slowly. "Diya … I …"

"Don't try to smooth this all over. You're supposed to be my best friend, and you're fucking my goddamn brother when I'm dealing with all this shit with the baby, the rumors, people fucking hating me. And *you're* fucking my brother."

Mouth drying, I shook my head at her. "It's … I … how'd you find out?"

I didn't know why that was the question that had come out of my mouth when I could've apologized, but she was putting all this blame on me. I hadn't told her to go out and get pregnant, to have to deal with the rumors, to fuck *her* stepdad.

"Are you fucking kidding me right now?" she snarled. "No apology? Nothing?"

"No," I said, crossing my arms. "I'm not going to apologize."

"You're fucking my brother when I'm dealing with all this shit!"

"Well, it's not my fault that you had to suck off your stepdad whenever you had the chance! It's not my fault that you're pregnant and dealing with all this shit! Why the fuck are you blaming that on me?!"

Tears formed in her eyes, and I immediately wanted to take it all back.

I hadn't meant to make her feel bad. It wasn't her fault that people were dickheads. But still … that didn't give her a reason to blame me for it. I had been supporting her this entire time and even taken the heat of it so she wouldn't worry too much.

"I'm sorry," I whispered because I loved her. "I shouldn't have said that."

"You're sorry for that and not for sleeping with my brother?"

"I wasn't—" I took a deep breath. "I didn't mean for it to happen, and I was going to tell you, but it never felt like the right time. I didn't want you to stress out over it. I didn't want you to think I was using you for him. Not when you're pregnant."

The warmth of her room vanished, and suddenly, it felt like I was suffocating.

"I've been here for you through all of this. I've kept your secrets. I've protected you—"

"Bullshit!" she hissed, nostrils flared. She stood up and shook her head. "You're protecting yourself. You think screwing around with my brother and lying to my face makes you a good friend?"

"I didn't lie—"

"You hid this from me for, what, months now?!"

I took a shaky step toward her. "Diya, this isn't fair—"

"No," she said, shoving me back. "What's not fair is that I needed you, and you were off playing house with the same guys who look at every other girl like a game. What's not fair is that I'm in the middle of a nightmare, and you don't care."

"If I didn't care, I wouldn't be here."

She crossed her arms and looked away, a tear falling down her cheek. "You came because you felt guilty, because you were covering your ass for sneaking away with my brother and the rest of those assholes."

Another tear fell down her cheek, and my chest tightened.

"Go," she growled. "Now."

I opened my mouth to argue, but she whipped the door open and pointed toward the hallway. Tears welled in my eyes, and I grabbed my belongings and walked out the door. She slammed it behind me.

The tears finally started falling as I headed down the hallway and toward the front door. The air outside hit like a fucking train, the sun low, casting long shadows over the pavement. My eyes were burning, my throat tight.

While I so desperately wanted to see the guys, to tell them what had happened, to even support Rush tonight, I knew they didn't want me there. Diya didn't want me here. Which left me with only a few options.

When I reached my car, I leaned my elbows against the top of it and rested my head in my hands, sobbing. After everything that I had done for Diya, why couldn't she understand that I … that I loved her brother? I wasn't just fucking him to fuck him.

Why would I do that to her? She was my best fucking friend.

My best friend!

"Hey!" someone called from behind me. "You Astrid?"

I wiped some of my tears from my cheeks and turned to face the unfamiliar man. "Who's asking?"

Before I could react, he lunged at me and slapped a hand over my mouth. I threw my elbow back in an attempt to get out of his strong hold, but he dragged me across the street and toward a black car.

The next thing I knew, he was hurling me into the back of his car and slamming the trunk on my head. Hard enough that stars danced in my vision.

CHAPTER EIGHTY-THREE

RUSH

BURNED rubber and gasoline filled my lungs. I leaned against the hood of my car, crossed my arms, and watched the crowd gather near the abandoned lot where the races were about to start. Astrid had better not show up.

After scanning the crowd once more for her and not seeing anyone who remotely looked like her, my gaze landed on that *fucker*, surrounded by a bunch of other assholes. Their laughter was too loud, their gazes too pointed.

Something felt off. It had all day.

Too many of the wrong people were here tonight, and for the first time in my life, I thought that maybe I should pull out of this race. I didn't care about getting my ego stroked for winning. I didn't care about the supposed popularity winning gave me.

But really? I wanted to see that asshole lose. *Again*.

Still though, something felt off in the pit of my stomach.

Across the lot, Calix talked with Cairo and Arch, their heads low. Frasier stood off to the side, spinning his keys on his finger, eyes flicking to every unfamiliar car that pulled up. I didn't know how to fucking explain it, but I couldn't shake this feeling.

If Astrid showed up, I'd be fucking pissed.

My fists clenched by my sides. I'd told her not to come, begged her in my own way. She had no idea how bad tonight would get based on all the shit that fucker and his friends had caused last night and into this morning.

They weren't playing fair, and they wouldn't.

Because they couldn't win any other way.

Phone buzzing in my pocket, I slipped it out, only to see a couple of social media notifications that I hadn't turned off. Astrid hadn't said a word to me or in the group chat for hours now, and I didn't know if that was a good or bad sign.

Hopefully, she was still at Diya's house. She was safe there.

"You good?" Frasier called across the lot.

I nodded once and responded with, "Just ready to get this over with," but I doubted he could hear me over the revving engines. I shoved my phone back into my pocket and pushed myself off the car.

That asshole pulled up beside me with custom and illegal car mods, his friends gathered near him, laughing, lighting cigarettes, passing a joint and alcohol between them. I grimaced and sank into my driver's seat.

Perfect. He's distracted.

He got out of his car and sauntered over to mine. "Ready to lose, princess?"

I looked up at him, expression unchanged because I wasn't going to give him what he wanted. I wasn't going to react. He knew that he had lost last time against me and that he'd lose today. I wasn't going to play into his little games.

Frasier flipped him off behind my back, and I almost smiled. *Almost.*

When he finally returned to his car, our engines roared to life at the starting line. The crowd gathered around from all sides, hungry to watch this feud unfold. I revved my engine and glanced over at that asshole, who was smirking.

As if he had already won.

One second passed, then another, and then the flag dropped in front of us, and I hit the gas.

Tires screamed against the asphalt. The world blurred around me. We flew down the empty streets, going well over one hundred fifty miles per hour. But I didn't stop, barely even slowed around the corners.

I peered into my rearview mirror to see that dickhead way behind, not even close, like he usually was. I hit the gas harder, wanting to go faster, loving the fucking rush of it, and zoomed through the finish line.

Once I spun the car around at the end of the strip, I headed back to the starting line, where The Crew was waiting for me. That dickhead pulled up a few seconds later, with that same shit-eating grin.

Frasier clapped his hands together. "And you thought you'd win."

"Winning?" he said, jumping out of his car. "Who said anything about winning?"

Calix tensed beside me, and the asshole grinned wider.

"I said he'd lose." He nodded at me, slow and deliberate. "And he did."

Frasier stepped forward. "Maybe you need to clean your eyes out because you were miles behind him."

He tilted his head. "Funny that you all think I was talking about the race."

My stomach twisted.

"What the fuck are you talking about?" Arch growled.

After slipping back into his car, he started it up, rolled down the window, and tossed something out of it. A lock of hair, tied with a black ribbon, landed at my feet, and the world suddenly stilled.

"Tell your girl thanks for playing. We'll be in touch real soon." Then he was off.

I stared at the lock of hair—*Astrid's hair*. Everything suddenly clicked into place, and then I was hopping in my car to follow that fucker. Only one thing was certain … I'd kill him for touching our Hellcat.

CHAPTER EIGHTY-FOUR

CALIX

MY CAR ZOOMED AHEAD on the freeway toward Astrid's last known location—my house. I pressed my foot to the floor and whizzed past cars in the right lane, heart pounding against my rib cage.

Did they really take her?

Frasier sat next to me in the passenger seat, phone in hand, barking updates to Cairo through the group call. Arch followed behind us, his headlights cutting through the darkness. One of us should've stayed with her.

Why the fuck didn't I think of that?! My hand tightened around the wheel, and I took the exit, nearly flipping the car on the turnaround. *If Mira had something to do with this, I swear to fucking God, I'll kill her myself.*

With one hand on the steering wheel, I fumbled with my phone and called Diya *again*. But she wasn't answering. Why wasn't she answering?! Had they taken her too? Astrid was supposed to be with Diya all night.

She hadn't told me that she'd be anywhere else. She hadn't told me that she'd be leaving, hadn't said anything had happened between them. So, why the fuck wasn't she answering now, out of all fucking times?!

After speeding through Redwood like a fucking maniac, I finally pulled into my driveway. Astrid's car was parked out front, but her phone was in the middle of the road. I slammed on the brakes and headed straight for the front door while Frasier jogged to her car with Arch.

Diya was sitting in the kitchen, eyes red and puffy.

"Where's Astrid?" I asked, taking two stairs at a time to make it to the kitchen.

She glared at me, her eyes filled with tears, and didn't say a word.

"Diya?! Where's Astrid?!"

Nothing.

"Are you fucking kidding me right now?! What's wrong with you?!"

She slammed her hands onto the table and stood. "I don't know, and I don't care!"

"Her car's out front. Where is she?!"

"Did you not hear a word that I just fucking said, you stupid asshole?!" Her cheeks reddened, and she scrunched her brows even more, her eyes widening. "Besides, shouldn't you know?! You've been fucking her behind my back for months now!"

I clenched my jaw. "You didn't."

"I didn't what?" she snapped.

"Please, don't tell me that you had her kidnapped because you were pissed."

She shook her head. "Are you kidding me? Do you think I'd do that?"

I stared at her for a couple of moments. "I don't fucking know. But she's missing."

Pain, hurt, anguish, and confusion rushed through her, and then she finally crossed her arms over her chest. Then she went to the front window to look outside. "Is she really gone? Did someone … really take her?"

"She's not here, and someone had a lock of her hair at the race."

"What?" she asked, eyes snapping up to mine. "They did?"

"When did she leave?"

"A couple of hours ago," she said. "I told her to leave."

I ran a hand through my hair. "Oh my fucking God. She's dead. She's fucking dead."

"She's not dead," Diya said.

But I was already down the steps and heading out the front door because talking to her wasn't going to help us find Astrid. She had asked Astrid to leave because she was pissed at us for hooking up behind her back, and now ... Astrid's gone?!

"She's fucking dead," I repeated, my strides long and quick toward her car.

Frasier ran a hand through his hair, pacing in front of Astrid's car. Arch hurled a fist at his car, a string of curse words leaving his mouth barely a moment later. I jogged up to him with Diya close behind.

"Did you find anything?" I asked Frasier.

"No."

"Did Cairo?"

"He's looking at the cameras, got access through Kai from Poison. It'll take a minute."

"And Rush?"

"I haven't heard from him yet," Frasier said. "He's not answering his phone."

"Fuck," I murmured, my stomach in knots. "Fuck!"

"I think—" Frasier started, then looked down at his buzzing phone and answered it, putting it on speaker. "Did you find anything?"

"The same car that picked Astrid up was at the Overlook fifteen minutes ago, dumping something," Kai—not Cairo—said.

Kai was the tech geek of Poison, Redwood's most notorious student-led gang, and he could find anything. I could hear cries in the background, ones that sounded like Cairo.

"It looks like a body."

Everything suddenly stopped, and my entire body felt like it was giving out.

"What?" I whispered. "It hasn't even been two hours since ..."

Arch was squealing out of the driveway and speeding toward the Overlook. Frasier dropped the phone. And I was shaking. I couldn't stop. My fingers wouldn't be still, my mind was racing, and my heart? It felt like it would burst out of my chest.

"What?" I said again. "Wh-what'd he say?"

"No," Diya said to my left. "No, they said ... they said they wouldn't hurt her."

I slowly turned to face her. "What did you just say?"

Diya stared at me for a couple of moments and shook her head. "I ... I'm sorry, Calix. I messed up."

CHAPTER EIGHTY-FIVE

ARCH

THE SALTY AIR burned my lungs, like fucking acid. I paced the edge of the rocks at the Overlook, gaze shooting between the ocean waves slamming against the shore and the gravel underneath my feet.

Why the fuck didn't I check Astrid's location tonight? I should've seen her phone location in the middle of the street and immediately left the race. She was more important, and I would fucking kill myself if she was dead.

My hands balled into fists as I looked over at Calix fighting with Diya.

That bitch … I should kill her.

Everyone around me was yelling: Calix and Diya, Frasier at the rescue team, Poison *and* Cairo at the police. Who the hell knew where Rush was? He wasn't answering his phone, but he surely had to have caught up to that fucker he had been chasing.

The rescue team lingered by the rocks, flashlights beaming into the ocean.

"It's too dangerous," one of the men said.

I gritted my teeth and tugged off my shirt. "I'm going down there."

Calix snapped his head toward me. "What?"

"She could still be alive," I said, jumping onto the first rock, the water already soaking my socks. I took them off, too, and tossed them aside. After wiggling out of my jeans, I hopped onto the next rock, almost slipping and landing on my ass.

I wasn't going to wait for these fuckers to make up their mind whether they were going to try to find her or not. I would.

Frasier grabbed my elbow. "You're going to break your neck."

"Then I'll break my fucking neck," I said, ripping my arm out of his hold. "Don't touch me."

While I expected Cairo to come running over and attempt to stop me, too, he stayed quiet near the police. Everyone watched me take another step. They knew that they couldn't do anything to stop me, not when it came to her.

Another rock, and I was mid-thigh deep in the water, the waves pushing and pulling me violently. A couple of trained members of the rescue team followed after me, telling me that it was too dangerous, that they'd handle it.

But they had already made their choice.

I'd handle it. Like I always did.

"Where'd they dump the body?" I shouted over the crashing waves.

"More to your left," Cairo said. "But the body could be anywhere by now."

It could be fifty miles out at sea, but I would still fucking find her. Those assholes didn't have the balls to kill anyone, but it didn't matter if it was her body or not; I needed to see for myself. I wanted proof.

"Arch," Cairo said, "you should—"

"Give me a flashlight," I shouted, trying to stabilize myself on the rock.

Waves continued to crash against me, rocking me backward. Frasier threw down a flashlight, and I snatched it before it landed in the water. The rescue team searched to the right, where the waves were pulling us toward, telling me that was where she would've gone.

After turning on the flashlight, I turned it toward the left, spotting a patch of hair—the same color as Astrid's—two rocks over. I moved to the next rock, and the waves slammed into me so hard that I lost my footing and slipped into the freezing cold water.

The current pulled me to the right, but I held the flashlight in my teeth and swam toward the body. My heart pounded inside my chest, so loud that it was all I could hear over the crashing waves.

Thud after thud after thud.

That couldn't be Astrid. It couldn't. I wouldn't let it.

The faster I swam against the ocean, the harder it became. I was just treading water, not making it anywhere. If anything, I was heading backward, toward the rescue team. A low, frustrated growl left my mouth, and suddenly, someone grabbed my arm.

Frasier.

He tugged me back toward the rock, and I grasped it with all my might, completely out of breath. I used my grip on the rocks to move myself to the left, desperate to get to the body, to prove to myself that it wasn't her.

It couldn't be her.

And then, just as I reached the body, she reached out and grabbed my wrist.

CHAPTER EIGHTY-SIX

ARCH

WITHOUT HESITATION, I pulled her halfway onto the rock I stood on to get her to safety. My breath caught in my throat, and a million fucking thoughts were rushing through my head. That was, until the hair fell from her face, and my stomach dropped.

Mira.

Soaking wet. Shivering. Mascara smeared down her mutilated face.

And blood. Tons of fucking blood.

I released her hand and stepped backward. She wasn't Astrid. Where was Astrid? I had come to the Overlook to find Astrid, not for Mira. Why was she here? Why had she died her hair to look like Astrid? Who had done this to her? Where the fuck was my girl?

Mira coughed and reached for my wrist again. "Please, help …" she sputtered from the wound straight down her lips to her chin, separated almost completely so that I could see all her bottom teeth and jaw.

My blood boiled at the sound of her desperate, hoarse voice.

"Please, help me. They left me here. I … I—"

"Where's Astrid?"

"I don't know," she said, shaking her head.

I lifted my head and stared out into the ocean as the rescue team climbed out of the water to get supplies for Mira. This was all … it was all a fucking setup. They'd used Mira to throw us off. Astrid could be anywhere.

"Where is she?" I asked again, voice deathly calm.

"I don't know." She grabbed my ankle and tried to hold herself upright. "I really don't."

After shrugging her hand off me, I stepped on it so hard that I could hear the bones snap. A scream left her lips, blood spewing everywhere. But I didn't care. Astrid had cried over this bitch. She had fucking cried over this bitch!

"Arch, please. I'm telling the truth. I don't—"

Before she could finish her sentence, I kicked her back into the ocean. The current grabbed her instantly, her screams being drowned out by the crashing waves. She flailed, trying to find a grip on the slippery rocks.

"Arch!" Diya screamed, scrambling down the rocky slope behind me. "What the fuck?!"

I turned toward the group. "It wasn't Astrid."

"I know that, asshole!" Diya said. "You think Astrid would want this?"

"Yes," I growled, snapping my hand around her throat. "You don't even know your best fucking friend. You have no idea who she is or what she'd want. Because all *you* care about is yourself." I pulled her even closer so we were face-to-face. "You're lucky that you're Calix's sister, or I'd throw *you* in right after her."

The rescue team ran past me, sliding down the rocky ledge and back into the water, trying to rescue her. One threw a rope into the waves, as if that'd do shit. Two more jumped back into the ocean.

Mira slipped underneath the current. Once. Then twice. Then she was gone.

Officers at the top of the Overlook pointed their guns at me.

"Put the girl down. Step away from her. Hands where we can see them!"

I kept Diya in front of me and shoved her up the rocks toward the street, using her as a shield. Honestly? I didn't care about her getting hurt because what the fuck had she done with Astrid? Who had she called? What had she wanted to happen to her best friend?

When we reached the street, one of the officers reached for her cuffs. "Turn around."

But I didn't move because if I did, I'd probably throw them in the ocean too.

Kai from Poison stepped forward and raised his gun at the officers. "Put it down."

"Are you threatening an officer—"

Cairo stepped forward. "How much to make this entire scene disappear?"

The female officer shook her head. "Disappear? Are you trying to—"

A male officer placed a hand on her shoulder and looked at Kai. "You know how much we need."

Kai whispered something to Cairo, and Cairo nodded, heading to his car.

"Meet me at the abandoned church on Granite, thirty minutes. I'll have what you need for this to have never happened."

A moment passed, and then the cuffs were returned to the female's belt. Once the officers returned to their cars and left the scene, along with the rescue team, I tossed Diya aside and headed to my car. I didn't know where the fuck to look next.

Where could they have taken Astrid?

"Arch, hold up!" Frasier called, looking down at his phone. "Rush just texted the chat."

I grabbed the phone from him.

Rush: 184 Bridge Way. Come alone.

CHAPTER EIGHTY-SEVEN

RUSH

I DIDN'T REMEMBER THROWING the first punch or the second or the third.

But that fucker was sitting in a puddle of his own blood in the middle of an abandoned building on the outskirts of Redwood. The thick crack of his jaw breaking on the first collision replayed through my head, the way blood had flown out of his mouth in strands, how his body had hit the ground.

My hands were balled into tight fists, and I tried hard not to hit him again.

Because if I hit him again, I'd kill him.

But—*fuck*—I wanted to murder this fucker right here and right now.

He had sped all around the fucking state with me on his ass the entire time, thinking that I wouldn't *or couldn't* catch him, only to drive his ass back to Redwood. Wrong move on his part because I rammed him into a tree in the backwoods, dragged him out of his shitty car, and drove him here.

Hands trembling uncontrollably, I paced the room in front of his almost-unconscious body. He was tied to a rusted pipe, the roof half collapsed around him. This place reeked of piss, mold, and a rotting, disgusting fucking human.

One that I *would* kill once we found Astrid.

He sat there, using his last few breaths, laughing. Fucking laughing.

"You think dropping pieces of her is funny?" I snarled.

Another laugh left his mouth, and I grabbed him by the neck and slammed him against the wall, his skull cracking. His nose was already broken, blood pouring from his mouth onto his scrawny body and onto the ground.

"I'm going to have my fucking fun killing you," I snarled. "Where is she?"

"As if I'd tell you."

After slamming my fist into his face again, I dropped him. He landed on the ground with a thud, and the door behind me creaked open. Several sets of footsteps followed, and then Calix's voice filled the room.

"Rush …"

I turned slowly to see Calix, Arch, Frasier, and João and Landon from Poison standing in the doorway. My entire body shook with rage, and João stepped into the room, a smirk on his face. I just turned back to the bastard in front of me.

"If I hit him one more time, I'm going to fucking kill him."

Frasier grabbed my shoulder. "We need him alive to—"

Before he could finish his sentence, Arch slammed his fist into that fucker's face.

Calix grabbed Arch and tried to hold him back. "Arch, we need him to talk."

João crouched by the guy and pulled a knife from his boot. "He's got about thirty seconds before I find another way to make him speak." He drew his knife down his throat. "You want to see your sister again, don't you?"

His laughter stopped completely. "Fuck you."

"We have eyes on her right now. She's finishing up her hot yoga class, isn't she?"

The guy twitched, blinked, and clenched his jaw. "You fucking wouldn't."

"She's about to go pick your youngest sister up from dance too," João said. "They both can make a little bit of a detour here, don't you think? That wouldn't disrupt their night too much." João looked up at Landon. "How do you think it'd feel for him to be forced to kill them both?"

"Don't fucking touch them," he growled, his voice cracking. "Please, don't touch them."

"Then tell me where she is."

"Shipping yard. Pier 8. One of the old containers."

João peered up at me. "See if it's true. We'll wait with him."

"Fuck no," I snarled. "As soon as they fucking find her, I'm killing him."

I wasn't leaving this in anyone else's hands. As soon as she was safe, I was ripping this fucker limb by fucking limb. He didn't deserve to be alive for a second longer than he had to. Nobody was going to kidnap our girl and get away with it.

"We'll go," Calix said, heading to the door with Frasier by his side. "We'll find her."

CHAPTER EIGHTY-EIGHT

FRASIER

I RACED through the town at over a hundred miles an hour on a back road. Calix had just gotten off the phone with Cairo and Kai, who had paid off the cops and were heading toward the shipping yard.

"Arch should've come with us," Calix said, running a hand through his hair. "She's definitely not alone. This is probably a setup, and they have guys waiting at the shipping yard for us. She's not going to be there."

"Relax," I growled. "She'll be there."

But honestly? I was just as worried. Astrid might not be there. She might not even be in Redwood, or the state, or the country at this point. I didn't know what the fuck they were planning to do with her, but she wouldn't be left alone if it was anything big.

"How the fuck am I supposed to relax?!" Calix snarled, hitting the dashboard with his fist. "Between my sister and Astrid, I ..." He stopped mid-sentence, his voice cracking. "What she did to her ... I ... I don't ..."

Slowing down just enough, I placed a hand on his shoulder, peered over at him, and squeezed. "I know. I know. But we're going to find Astrid alive. She's going to be here, and she's going to be safe. Landon is right behind us."

Calix ran a hand over his face and nodded. "I fucking hope so."

I did too.

Once we hit the shipping yard, I turned off my lights and parked toward the front. Several cars were parked sporadically around the lot, all empty—at least the ones that I could see into. Calix and I exited the car, meeting Landon behind us. Cairo and Kai pulled in next.

"She's here?" Cairo asked quietly.

"Sure fucking hope so," Calix said.

"Yes," I said, not knowing if it was a lie or not.

Who knew if Astrid was here? Who knew if we'd all get out alive? All I could do was be strong, not only for her, but for Calix too. Knowing that his own sister had ratted Astrid out to these fuckers … was taking a toll on him.

Kai opened the trunk of Cairo's car and tossed Landon a machine gun. My eyes widened when he threw one my way too. After peering at Calix for a second, Kai handed the last one to Cairo, which was probably a smarter idea than giving Calix, in his state, a loaded weapon.

"I don't know how to use this," Cairo whispered.

"Aim and shoot," Kai said. "You'll learn quick."

Just as Cairo was about to respond, Landon started toward Pier 8, Kai following after him. I clapped Cairo, then Calix on the shoulder, and headed in their direction. This was our chance to get Astrid back.

Safely.

The wind whipped across the pavement. Kai and Cairo went one way, Landon another, and Calix and I a third, surrounding the container almost at all sides. It was oddly quiet, and while there were cars in the lot, it didn't seem like anyone else was here.

Was that a good or bad thing? I wasn't sure.

Landon or Kai didn't seem concerned.

Suddenly, a man approached the container's entrance with a loaded gun in his hand, his gaze traveling around the yard. Before I could react, Calix was running toward him, grabbing him by the head, and slamming him down onto the pavement.

My eyes widened, and I ran toward them. But Calix was already on top of him, slamming his head into the ground repeatedly until his screams vanished and Calix's hands were covered in blood.

Holy shit, I didn't think Calix had it in him.

Landon tugged a key out of the man's pocket and nodded to the container. "Take it. We'll watch for others."

Calix snatched the key from him and headed toward the container, a different guy than the one who had been almost hyperventilating in my car. Or maybe it was the same emotional one, but this time angry.

After shoving the key into the lock, Calix yanked the chains off the container doors. It creaked open, and in the center of the metal container, Astrid was there, tied to a chair, duct tape across her ankles and wrists, hair matted to her forehead.

And not breathing.

CHAPTER EIGHTY-NINE

ARCH

"WHAT THE FUCK is taking them so long?" I growled.

Rush glared at the fucker, sitting in a puddle of his own blood. His head was hung low, his lip was busted open in several places now, and both of his eyes were swollen shut. Neither of them had moved an inch in the past ten minutes.

I paced in front of them and ran a hand through my hair, wanting to tear it the fuck out. Astrid had better be there. She'd better fucking be there. If she wasn't … I didn't know what I was going to do. My hands were aching to kill this fucker right here and right now.

When Rush's phone rang, he lifted it from his pocket and put it on speaker.

"She's not breathing," Cairo said, voice cracking, echoing through the phone. Frasier was flipping out in the background, and I could barely hear Calix. "We're heading to the hospital with her."

Cairo didn't even finish his sentence before I was barreling toward the man, hands balled into fists. I slammed one into his beaten face, feeling satisfaction in the sound that his head made against the concrete wall before hitting him with another one.

He groaned, "She … she was alive when I left her. I didn't … I didn't touch her like that."

Wrong answer.

My fist shot through the air and slammed into his throat. He choked on his own breath, gasping and coughing up blood. Rush stepped toward us, quieter than he usually was, his lips set in an eerie line. The fucker tried to scream again, but nothing but muffled panic left his mouth.

"You broke something that belonged to us," Rush said, pulling a knife out of his pocket.

I didn't know where he had gotten it from because the only weapons that Rush usually carried around were his fists, but it was sharp and pointed straight at the fucker's face. My gaze flickered to João, who was smirking at the situation, and then I turned back toward them.

"Now it's our turn to break you," I growled.

"If you didn't do this to her, then who did?" Rush crouched down in front of him and pressed the blade against his forehead, cutting into his skin until blood covered his face. "Start talking, or we'll cut parts off that don't grow back."

"She's … not the only one," he said. "There are others. It's a ring, trafficking."

João walked over. "Trafficking? Sex trafficking?"

"Only the women," he said. "They take children and men too. For labor."

"Who's they—" Rush began.

But I couldn't stop myself from snatching the knife from his hand and slamming it into the center of his chest. Trafficking? They were going to fucking use *our girl* for trafficking?! I stabbed him again and again and again, my sight filled with red.

From rage and from blood.

João wrapped his arms around me and hurled me to the other side of the room. "We could've used that fucker."

"I don't give a fuck," I said, dusting myself off and heading to the door. "He's dead now."

All that mattered to me now was making sure Astrid was alive.

CHAPTER NINETY

ASTRID

A SLOW, steady beeping drifted through my ears. I slowly blinked my eyes open, adjusting to the low light in the room. My lips were cracked, my muscles aching, like I had been hit by several cars in a row.

Above me, the ceiling was a soft, pale beige. I tilted my head slightly to the side, wondering where I was and why it was so quiet. When I turned, I saw *him* sitting right by my bed—hood up, legs spread, and arms crossed.

Arch.

His head was tilted slightly, but his heavy eyes were focused on me.

"Arch," I whimpered, my voice coming out broken. "Where am I?"

After stiffening for a moment, he stood up. "The hospital."

"Why?"

"You almost died," he said, heading to the door. I didn't know why I'd expected any softness from him, especially after he told me that I almost died, but I'd expected *something* other than that. "I'll go get the others."

Before I could say another word, he was out the door. I stared at his retreating figure through the small window and furrowed my brow. No hug, no relief, no biting insult that meant that he cared.

Just a, "I'll go get the others."

A couple of moments later, Cairo threw the door open and hurried into the room. He scanned the machines before approaching, then fell into the same chair that Arch had been in and grabbed my hand.

"You're awake," he said gently.

I gave him a soft nod. "Do you have any water?"

He grabbed a cup from the side table and lifted it to my lips. I drank some down, my gaze lingering on the door to see if the others were here too. Don't get me wrong; I loved Cairo, but I wanted to see the others.

The last thing I remembered was leaving Diya's house.

"Diya? Is she here?" I asked.

Cairo set down the cup on the table, tense. "Why don't you ask Calix about her? How are you doing? Do you need me to get a nurse? You're breathing now, which is a good thing, right? Feel any different?"

"I'm fine," I said. "What happened?"

"A lot." He drew the pad of his thumb across my knuckles. "You almost died."

"That's what Arch said too."

"When we found you in that storage container, you weren't breathing."

My eyes widened. "Storage container?"

He furrowed his brow. "You don't remember? You were kidnapped."

Faint memories drifted through my mind, and I closed my eyes. I didn't remember—or at least couldn't remember fully. Diya and I had gotten into a fight, and then I left, and someone had come up to me on the street and …

Tears filled my eyes. I didn't even *want* to remember.

"Where are the others?"

"Calix and Rush are in the lobby, sleeping, and Frasier got kicked out for shouting at a nurse about your IV," he said, glancing at the door. "Arch has been by your bedside all night. He hasn't stepped out since he got here."

"Arch? As in my stepbrother Arch?"

A low chuckle left his mouth. "Yes. He didn't want anyone else in the room with you, said he'd kill them first. So, we all camped out in the lobby once we found out that you were breathing again."

My lips twitched into a small smile. Arch had so much emotion that he didn't know what to do with it, and I thought it was actually … kinda cute. He hid behind his coldness, but I was beginning to see through it.

Little by little.

"Rush and Arch killed the guy who had taken you," Cairo said.

I sucked in a breath and nodded. I didn't want details.

"Oh yeah, and Mira's dead too."

Eyes widening, I sat up. "She is?"

"Arch," he said, as if that answered my question.

"He … killed her? Why? How?"

"For an hour or so, we thought that they had dumped your body off at the Overlook. Arch went in the water to try and find you, but—"

"Wait, wait, wait. Arch went into the water at the Overlook? Is he crazy?!"

"I know, but we found Mira instead, so he kinda … sorta …" He shrugged and made a kicking motion. "You know?"

While death *definitely* wasn't something to laugh over, I found myself giggling. Yes, giggling for some sick reason. As much as Arch didn't want to admit it, that asshole had feelings for me. I'd even go as far as to say that the fucker loved me.

And honestly? I loved him too.

CHAPTER NINETY-ONE

ASTRID

SUNLIGHT FLOODED into the hospital room through the blinds, and I sat up in bed. My entire body ached in places I hadn't even known *could* ache. God, I was getting so old, and I was still in high school.

I grabbed the water that Cairo had in his hand and sipped it. He had fallen asleep in the chair next to me sometime in the past hour, his soft snoring filling the room. My head throbbed, and my throat was burning.

While Cairo had told me *some* of what had happened in the past forty-eight hours, I was still trying to piece it all together. Who had taken me? What had Diya had to do with any of this? And most importantly, where were my other guys?

The door creaked open, and Calix stepped in quietly, probably still thinking that I was sleeping. Messy hair, wrinkled shirt, clenched jaw, he looked rough. His eyes met mine, and he blew out a sigh of relief.

"Thank fuck," he murmured, hurrying over to me and kissing me on the forehead. "Arch said you were awake."

"How are you doing?" I whispered, wrapping my fingers around his.

"How are *you* doing?"

"I'm fine," I said. "But I was asking about you."

He ran a hand through his hair. "That's not for you to worry about right now. You need to rest and heal."

"Diya ..." I started, but paused for a moment when he stiffened. "Is she okay?"

"Diya is ... *fine.*"

"Cairo said I should ask you about her."

"I don't want to talk about her, and I don't think you wanna know what happened until you're better. Let's just say that she will not be in contact with you, no matter how many times she tries to come here."

My stomach twisted. "I want to see her. I know we got into a fight because you and I are dating, but I want to make things right."

"She tried to get you killed," he said, and then his eyes widened as if he hadn't meant to say that aloud.

My eyes widened too. "She what?"

"Apparently, she was the reason that they kidnapped you."

"No. You're lying." I shook my head. "She wouldn't do that."

"She's a hormonal pregnant teenager who just got knocked up by my stepfather. She does whatever she wants, like she always has, Astrid." He drew his thumb across my knuckles. "I'm sorry, but it's true."

"Did she tell you that herself?"

"Sorta."

"Sorta? Well, sorta doesn't cut it for me. I want to see her. When can I—"

Before I could finish my sentence, the door opened again, but this time, it was Rush and Frasier. For being the player out of the bunch, Frasier had three bags of chips and a pack of Gatorade in his arms, looking more like a soccer mom by the day.

"Where'd you get all of that?" I asked, stifling back a giggle.

"Probably raided my kitchen," Cairo murmured, still half asleep beside me.

"Don't you dare fucking scare us like that again," Frasier said, placing the chips and Gatorade on the table beside me. "No more being kidnapped for you."

"Deal," I said, glancing over at Rush.

He stared at me intently, his gaze never once leaving mine. I swallowed, never seeing that look in his eyes before, and then the door opened again.

"Sweetheart," Dad said, rushing over.

Arch's mom was right by his side, and Arch was at the door, lingering again.

Dad pulled me into a hug, his voice cracking. "I thought I'd lost you."

The guys stepped out of the room to give us some space, and I squeezed Dad tighter because while we never really were that close, I missed hanging out with him. It seemed like life was constantly getting in the way.

"I'm still here," I said when he finally pulled away, glancing over at Arch. "But can I … maybe have a minute alone with Arch?"

After they kissed me once more on the forehead, they left the room. The door clicked shut behind them. Arch still had on his dark hoodie, his hands stuffed into his pockets.

"What do you want?" he growled.

I smiled over at him. "You stayed."

He narrowed his eyes. "Cairo told you?"

"Yes."

"You should rest."

I moved over on the bed and tapped the space beside me for him to sit. He eyed it for a couple of seconds, then actually came over to sit beside me. The bed dipped, and my body slid closer to his.

"What?" he asked.

"Why did you stay?" I whispered.

He opened his mouth, as if he was going to say some typical Arch shit, but then closed it. I wrapped my arm around his and cuddled closer to him, my head on his shoulder.

"Arch ... please ..."

"Because I couldn't leave you. Not again."

"Why not?" I asked. "Why couldn't you leave me?"

A hundred emotions drifted through his eyes, and then finally, they softened. "Because I love you, Astrid. I fucking love you."

CHAPTER NINETY-TWO

ASTRID

I LOVE YOU.

The words replayed in my head over and over, and for a moment—even though I had nudged Arch to say it to me—I thought that … that I had been hearing things. Arch loved me? And he'd said it aloud too?

A moment passed without me saying anything, and Arch tore his gaze away.

"Forget it. I was just—"

Before he could finish his sentence, I grabbed his face and kissed him right on his mouth, savoring all those words that I knew he wanted to say to me, but hadn't. He had been holding this back for so long—I could just feel it.

"Astrid," he murmured, pulling away, "I didn't mean—"

"Don't you dare say that you didn't mean it," I whispered against his lips.

He stayed silent for a while, his body tensing. "Then why didn't you say it back?"

My lips curled into a smirk. "I fucking love you, Arch. I was just … surprised that you'd actually said it. I didn't think you'd ever tell me that you loved me. And maybe ... I'm a little scared about how long I've loved you."

I didn't realize how long I had had a crush on him until now.

Since our parents had married, I'd always thought that he was my annoying stepbrother, but he had been protecting me from the first day that I met him. He had been that guy in kindergarten class—when our parents didn't even know each other—who shoved a kid off the slide for cutting in front of me when it was my turn.

Definitely *not* saying that should be the standard, but ... why couldn't it?

He didn't speak, just relaxed slightly beside me.

"My life is a mess," I whispered. "I don't know what happened. Diya is ... I don't ..."

"Yeah, well, nothing like that will happen again to you," he said. "I'll make sure of it."

"Oh, yeah?" I asked, finally pulling away. "And how're you gonna do that?"

Arch stood up, his expression still unreadable, but his eyes telling an entirely different story. They were softer and more alive than they ever had been. "You'll see."

And then he stepped out of the hospital room, leaving me alone.

And honestly? I hadn't expected anything else from him.

That was enough to last lifetimes.

A couple of moments later, a nurse stepped into the room with a clipboard, followed by Rush. She eyed him cautiously even though he didn't say a word, then walked over to me with a soft smile. "You ready to go home?"

"Yes."

Once she discharged me and left, Rush handed me some clothes, still not speaking a word. While he had always kept to himself, he was watching me more intensely than usual today, and I knew why.

All the guys had been overprotective, and if Rush really had killed someone for me …

"How are you doing?" I asked him, buttoning my jeans.

"How are *you* doing?"

"Oh, you know, hanging in there," I said. "But I asked you first."

"Fine." He swung his keys around his finger. "We're going for a ride."

I arched a brow. "Do I have a say in this?"

His lips curled into an unusual smile. "No."

CHAPTER NINETY-THREE

RUSH

I GRIPPED the steering wheel and drove around Redwood's coastline, glancing over at Astrid. Waves crashed against the jagged rocks at the Overlook, midnight beachgoers jogged across the road toward the dunes, and people exited the popular bars.

She was quiet. *Too* quiet.

Astrid was always running her mouth. Teasing and challenging and stirring up shit.

But now she sat in the passenger seat with her legs bouncing, swimming in my oversize sweatshirt. She stared out the window like she wasn't really here, and I didn't blame her.

Moonlight bounced off the streets, the night swallowing everything else around us. The hum of the engine drifted through my ears. I told myself that this was all to clear my head, but I couldn't be around the others right now.

We had almost lost her, and while I wanted to blame them, this was all my fault.

If I hadn't done those stupid fucking races, then Astrid would've never been harmed.

"I'm sorry," I whispered.

She looked over at me, surprised. "For what?"

"This is all my fault."

"What?"

"Them kidnapping you, them almost"—I gripped the wheel even tighter—"killing you." Tears welled up in my eyes, though I didn't let her see them. "I almost lost you. I almost fucking lost you, Astrid."

I kept my eyes on the road, shoving away my feelings. If I looked over at her, I'd break.

She stayed quiet for a moment, then placed her hand on my forearm. "Rush, it's not your fault."

Fuck.

"Rush, please, pull over," she murmured.

I wanted to keep driving, to speed up, but I didn't plan on wrapping her around a pole. I could do that on my own time, risk my own life. So, I pulled over on a side road across from the beach.

"It's not your fault," she repeated.

My heart pounded hard inside my chest, and I stared ahead through the windshield, not daring to look over. My eyes were burning.

"Look at me," she pleaded, hand on my chin. "Please."

When I didn't, she took off her seat belt and crawled into my lap, so I was forced to meet her stare, to look at the girl I almost had gotten killed.

"It's not your fault, okay?" she whispered, her hands on my jaw.

"It is."

"No, it's not."

"The guys who took you only took you because they were pissed at me. I should've quit street racing. I should've—"

"Stop it, Rush," she murmured, swiping tears from my cheeks with her thumbs. "Stop it. You didn't cause this. I don't blame you."

I gripped her waist tightly. "You should."

"No, I shouldn't, and I won't. You protected me. You killed someone. *For me.*"

"I'd do it again," I said. "I'd do worse. I'd burn the world down for you."

Her fingers brushed against my cheeks again. So warm, so small. Yet she didn't say anything.

"Killing him wasn't enough for me. I want them all to pay for what they did to you. I want them to hurt. To cry. To plead. To beg for their lives. Then I want to take away what matters most to them."

"Rush, I don't want you to hurt anyone for me," she whispered. "But I appreciate what you've done."

"You don't get it," I murmured, brushing some hair off her face. "All these fucking years, I've felt so dead inside. I haven't felt as alive as I have after I met you. And I can't lose that. I can't lose you. I fucking love you, Astrid."

CHAPTER NINETY-FOUR

RUSH

MY ENTIRE BODY TENSED, and I gripped on to Astrid's waist as hard as I could without hurting her. I hadn't wanted to admit it aloud to her, even though everyone else already had, but I couldn't keep it in much longer.

After what had happened to her, I needed her to know that I loved her.

Astrid stared at me through wide, teary eyes, her breath caught in her throat. After opening and closing her mouth a handful of times with no words coming out, she finally wrapped her arms around my shoulders and hugged me. Hard.

"I'm so fucking glad you're safe, but I wish ... God, I fucking wish I could've found you before they touched you. I wish I hadn't told you not to come to the race."

"It's okay," she murmured into my neck. "I know you were trying to protect me."

Somehow, I tensed even more. "I fucking lost you, Astrid."

The silence stretched on again, filled with the crashing of waves on the shores a block over. Wind tousled my hair through the cracked window. Astrid pulled away just enough to grasp my face in her small hands.

"You didn't lose me," she said, her forehead on mine. "I'm right here."

"I almost did."

"I don't blame you for any of this," she said.

"You promise?"

"I promise." She pulled away a couple of inches and stared down at me. "I fucking promise, Rush. I … I love you too. So much."

My pulse raced the way it did when my car was flying over a hundred miles per hour down the back roads, the blood rushing through my body.

I brushed my thumb across her cheek. "Say it again."

A small giggle left her mouth, her lips curling into a smile. "I love you, Rush." She leaned into my hand. "I fucking love you."

Without thinking, I leaned in and kissed her on the mouth. Soft.

Nothing like the first time.

When I was with her, I used to be *restrained*, but now? Now I wanted to devour her. Every inch of her body, her mouth, her mind. My lips moved against hers slowly at first as she dragged her fingertips gently down my arms. I adjusted the seat back just enough, my hands settling on her hips again.

She undid the button on my jeans and reached inside to grab my throbbing cock. With her lips still pressed against mine, she wiggled out of her pants and settled down on me, slowly, letting me slide into her, inch by inch by fucking inch.

Those hours without her when she had been gone had felt like days, weeks, even years. And now? I finally had her back, and I would savor every second with her.

CHAPTER NINETY-FIVE

ASTRID

THE SECOND I stepped into Calix's house, the heavy tension hit me like a wall. My arm was wrapped around Rush's, and I tucked some hair behind my ear.

"Why's everyone stressed?" I asked, slowly letting go of Rush.

Cairo sat on the couch, knee bouncing. Frasier had his lips pressed together without one of his usual comments. Calix leaned against the doorframe, running a hand through his hair. And Arch sat, pissed the fuck off, like usual.

"We were waiting for you," Cairo said, standing.

"All this stress for me?" I asked as a joke.

"Yes," they said, almost in complete unison.

My lips parted slightly, and while I remembered very little about what had happened the past couple of days, it seemed like they might have a bit of PTSD from it. They all looked stressed beyond belief, and I had been with Rush this entire time.

Calix looked especially nervous when the wind knocked a branch into the window outside the house, his eyes flickering to it, then toward the door, as if he was waiting for someone to arrive.

"Diya?" I asked.

"Don't say her name," Arch hissed.

"Can someone please explain more about what happened?" I asked. "Where is she?"

"She *helped* them. She lied to us. She cried and played the fucking victim while you almost died in a fucking warehouse," he continued. "That's what happened."

My stomach twisted. "That doesn't sound like her."

"Well, it is," Frasier said.

"She was pissed, but she wouldn't do that," I said. "I've known her for years. She has never betrayed me."

"She's hormonal because that fucker knocked her up," Calix said. "She's not thinking straight. And …" He paused for a moment and looked down, shaking his head. "And she said it herself."

"She said what?"

"That she didn't think they would take it this far," Cairo said. "She had to have told the guys who took you that you were here. That's why she wanted you to come over when nobody else was home."

My stomach twisted, and my eyes started to burn. I didn't believe it. I couldn't. This wasn't the Diya I knew, no matter how many times they told me what she had done.

Suddenly, the front door slammed open, and Calix's stepfather stood there, out of breath, his cheeks flushed. "Have any of you seen Diya? I've looked everywhere. Her room. The guesthouse. The beach path. Her phone's on her nightstand, her car abandoned at the school."

Calix stiffened. "What are you talking about?"

"*Diya,*" he said. "She's gone. She's not anywhere."

"When was the last time you saw her?" Calix asked.

"This evening. She made tea, said she was going to lie down. I went to check on her thirty minutes ago, before you all got here, and she was gone."

"She wouldn't just leave," I said, turning toward the guys. "We have to find her."

"We should let her rot," Arch growled, arms crossed over his chest.

I smacked him upside the head and headed for the door. "You can, but I won't."

And if I knew anything about these assholes, they would follow and help me find Diya too.

CHAPTER NINETY-SIX

ASTRID

WIND WHIPPED across the rocks at the Overlook, tangling my hair into knots. I left the guys in the car and walked toward Diya, who sat at the edge, where the ocean met the land. Nobody would've found her here, even if they had looked. It was far too dark, and she was hidden away behind a couple of larger rocks anyway.

When it was low tide, we used to walk all the way down the rocks to the sand, but tonight, it was high, and the water was extremely rough. *Too rough.*

My stomach twisted into tight knots as Diya's shoulders trembled.

I wasn't sure she'd heard our car approach or my footsteps.

"Diya," I murmured softly.

She didn't move.

After walking slowly so I wouldn't scare her, I found myself at the rock that she was sitting on, her shoulders still bucking forward and back, tears pouring down her cheeks.

"I knew you'd be here," I said to lighten the mood.

"You shouldn't be here," she said between sobs.

"Everyone is worried about you."

"No, they're not. And I deserve it."

I wrapped my arm around her shoulders. "You don't deserve it."

"Yes, I do." She stiffened, the tears wavering in her eyes. "I thought about jumping."

My chest tightened, and I pulled her even closer, hugging her to me as much as I could. Hearing her say those words … I … I couldn't fathom it. I didn't believe that she'd really wanted to hurt me. I thought that … that maybe she had been framed in a way that she shouldn't be.

But Diya wanted to kill herself.

Kill herself.

Bile rose in my throat at my best friend, who was hurting so badly that she wanted to end it, and I swallowed it down. How? How could she feel that way? What was going on with her?

"Your brother has been looking for you," I said.

She laughed emptily. "Calix hasn't looked at me the same since that night."

"You didn't help them, Diya."

"You don't know that," she said, finally looking at me. "You don't know what I did."

I grabbed her hands, brow furrowed. "Then tell me."

She hiccuped and glanced at the cars behind us. "If I tell you … they're gonna kill me, aren't they?"

"No," I said, shaking my head for emphasis. "They're not going to touch you, no matter what you did. I know you're angry about me and your brother, and you're feeling sick because of the baby. I don't blame you. Just tell me … what happened?"

A long silence stretched between us, until she finally pulled her hands away from mine and wrapped her arms around herself, looking down at her knees pulled to her chest. "Mira told me in the morning that you and Calix were fucking. I didn't want to believe her because she's a bitch, but she showed me pictures, videos. And it hurt so fucking badly."

"I'm sorry," I whispered. "I should've told you."

"Don't apologize," she said. "Mira told me that I should talk to you in the afternoon, and I listened. I thought … I *stupidly* thought that she wanted to help me through it. We used to be best fucking friends, so I thought she still had a heart. But she didn't."

A hot tear slid down my cheek, and I pushed it away.

"So, after you left, I texted her and told her that you were gone. I told her that she could come over because I needed someone to talk to. I didn't know she was working with them. I … if I had known …" A loud sob escaped her mouth, and suddenly, she was wailing in agony. "I'm sorry! I'm so sorry! You almost died because of me."

Again, I wrapped my arms around her shoulders and pulled her closer to me, lacing my fingers into her hair and gently stroking her head. I couldn't imagine the pain she was going through right now.

She blamed herself for this, and the guys blamed her too.

"I don't blame you," I whispered into her ear. "I promise that I don't blame you, Diya. You're my best friend, and I understand why you did what you did."

"That doesn't make it right."

"But you didn't know."

"I should've."

"Well, you didn't," I said, the wind howling around us. Waves slammed against the rocks, soaking her feet. "Now, please, come home with us. Everyone is worried about you and your baby."

"Don't lie."

"I am," I said. "Calix is. Your stepdad is. Come home."

Diya looked at me, then back at the car, her head down. She stayed silent for a long time, then finally nodded. "Okay, okay, I'll come home. But I … I don't expect you to forgive me. I don't expect them to trust me, okay?"

While I did forgive her, I nodded along because I knew she wouldn't give it up until I agreed. I stood to my feet and held my hand out until she took it. We might not ever get back to the friendship we'd once had, but at least ... things had been cleared up for me.

At least, we were good.

CHAPTER NINETY-SEVEN

ASTRID

A SHEER WHITE top hugged my braless body, my nipples poking through the thin material and my tits on *full* display for the entire Redwood student body who was at A'dré's party. Music thumped through my ears, bodies ground together in the living room, and guys turned to peer over at me with lustful gazes.

I ignored them and continued through the crowd with Ruby.

Astrid the good little virgin would've had a major problem with how I was dressed, but I wasn't that innocent girl anymore.

Not even a bit.

After straightening my shoulders, I grabbed Ruby's hand so we wouldn't get separated. Diya had texted me that she might swing by after I asked her earlier, but we hadn't talked much since everything had gone down.

"You look so hot!" Ruby shouted over the music. "First the sheer top, and now … no panties?!"

My cheeks reddened, and I glanced back at her to see her wiggling her brows. "How do you know that?"

"Your skirt's too short," she said with a smirk. "Everyone can see everything."

"Good," I hummed, making it to the kitchen. I grabbed two beers, one for her and one for me, and headed toward the back room. "Let them gawk. I kinda like it."

"You like their stares, or you like the thought of what The Crew will do to anyone who touches you?"

I sipped the beer and giggled. "You know me too well."

My gaze locked on to Calix, who lounged on the leather couch, his legs spread like he owned the fucking world. He was sipping on a beer, too, his dark gaze on me. Arch sat beside him, his jaw twitching when he saw me, and then he stood.

"What the fuck are you wearing?" he snarled.

Frasier smirked in my direction and shoved him back down on the couch as he walked toward me. "Look at you. You look so fucking sexy, Hellcat." He curled his arm around my waist, dragging me away from Ruby, who started flirting with someone else.

Cairo lingered behind the couch, his hungry gaze on me. Later, I knew he'd punish me for this. His eyes told me everything that he'd happily do to put me in my place.

Warmth exploded through my core, and I looked over at Rush, who had that *expression* on his face again. But what used to be unreadable to me was now clear as day. He *loved* what I was wearing and would probably sneak me out to his car later.

"You didn't have to wear such slutty clothes to get our attention," Arch growled, though his gaze was locked on to mine now. "You already know that we own you."

I walked away from Frasier and took a seat between Calix and Arch on the couch, between all my guys. "Is that so?"

"Yes," Rush said behind me, his voice gruff.

"You're ours," Cairo said.

Calix trailed his nose up the column of my neck. "All fucking ours."

"Say it, Hellcat," Frasier said.

My lips curled into a smile. "I'm yours."

Yes, I was really theirs. After all, they were the ones who had turned me into the good virgin gone bad.

. . .

To continue reading the epilogue of Good Virgin Gone Bad, click here.

ALSO BY EMILIA ROSE

Stepbrother

Poison

The Bad Boy

Detention

My Brother's Best Friend

Science Project

Excite Me

Mafia Boss

Mafia Toy

Mafia Betrayal

Sex Education

Bound By My Father's Best Friend

Pornstar

Submitting to the Alpha

Come Here, Kitten

My Werewolf Professor

The Twins

Four Masked Wolves

Monster Lover

My Bad Boy Alpha

Alpha Maddox

Summoning Sex Demons

The Breeding Cave

Next Door Incubus

ABOUT THE AUTHOR

Emilia Rose is a USA Today bestselling author of steamy romance. She loves writing about dirty-talking bad boys who are obsessed with innocent, and sometimes insecure, virgin heroines. She currently lives in a small town in Connecticut USA with her husband and three playful cats.

Join Emilia's newsletter for exclusive giveaways, early chapter releases, and more!

www.ingramcontent.com/pod-product-compliance
Lightning Source LLC
LaVergne TN
LVHW040038080526
838202LV00045B/3396